Hungry Hearts

13 TALES
OF FOOD & LOVE

Hungry Hearts

EDITED BY

ELSIE CHAPMAN

AND

CAROLINE
TUNG RICHMOND

SIMON PULSE

NEW YORK   LONDON   TORONTO   SYDNEY   NEW DELHI

SIMON PULSE

An imprint of Simon & Schuster Children's Publishing Division

1230 Avenue of the Americas, New York, New York 10020

First Simon Pulse hardcover edition June 2019

Compilation copyright © 2019 by Elsie Chapman and Caroline Tung Richmond; "Rain" copyright © 2019 by Sangu Mandanna; "Kings and Queens" copyright © 2019 by Elsie Chapman; "The Grand Ishq Adventure" copyright © 2019 by Sandhya Kutty Falls; "Sugar and Spite" copyright © 2019 by Rin Chupeco; "Moments to Return" copyright © 2019 by Adi Alsaid; "The Slender One" copyright © 2019 by Caroline Tung Richmond; "Gimme Some Sugar" copyright © 2019 by Jay Coles; "The Missing Ingredient" copyright © 2019 by Rebecca Roanhorse; "Hearts à la Carte" copyright © 2019 by Karuna Riazi; "Bloom" copyright © 2019 by Phoebe North; "A Bountiful Film" copyright © 2019 by S. K. Ali; "Side Work" copyright © 2019 by Sara Farizan; "Panadería ~ Pastelería" copyright © 2019 by Anna-Marie McLemore

Jacket illustration copyright © 2019 by Jess Cruickshank

For information about special discounts for bulk purchases, please contact Simon & Schuster Special Sales at 1-866-506-1949 or business@simonandschuster.com.

The Simon & Schuster Speakers Bureau can bring authors to your live event. For more information or to book an event, contact the Simon & Schuster Speakers Bureau at 1-866-248-3049 or visit our website at www.simonspeakers.com.

Jacket designed by Heather Palisi

Interior designed by Tom Daly

The text of this book was set in Venetian 301 BT Std.

Manufactured in the United States of America

2 4 6 8 10 9 7 5 3 1

Library of Congress Cataloging-in-Publication Data

Names: Chapman, Elsie, editor. | Richmond, Caroline Tung, editor. |

Title: Hungry hearts : 13 tales of food & love / edited by Elsie Chapman and Caroline Tung Richmond. | Description: First Simon Pulse hardcover edition. |

New York : Simon Pulse, 2019. | Identifiers: LCCN 2018041522 |

ISBN 9781534421851 (hardcover) | ISBN 9781534421875 (eBook) |

Subjects: LCSH: Short stories, American. | Romance fiction. |

CYAC: Short stories, American. | Food—Fiction. | Love—Fiction. |

Classification: LCC PZ5 .H87 2019 | DDC [Fic]—dc23

LC record available at https://lccn.loc.gov/2018041522

For all of us with appetites. Let's always keep feeding our souls, nourishing our hearts, and inviting others to the table.

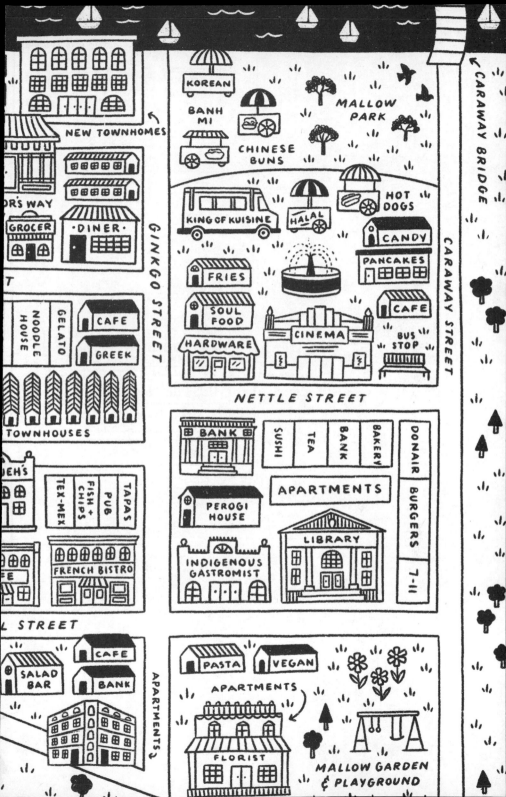

CONTENTS

Rain

BY SANGU MANDANNA

It had rained the day Anna's mother died, but that was hardly unusual because it rained most days in England. Anna remembered it, though. It was a few months ago now, but she remembered the way raindrops had sparkled on the glasses of the police officer who had come to tell them there had been a car crash on the A47, and she remembered that he had said it was the rain that had caused the poor visibility that must have made her mother crash.

It had rained the day Aunt Mynah called to invite them to visit her in Rowbury, thousands of miles away across the Atlantic, and it had rained the day Dad decided to say yes.

And now it had started to rain as they got out of the cab outside Aunt Mynah's home. Anna stepped onto the pavement (sidewalk? Wasn't that what they called them here?)

and looked up at the new town houses in front of them. It was late, almost seven, but summer light kept the streets busy with chatter and noise. There were shrieks from children in the park across the street, protesting having to go home, and Anna could smell sushi, baked bread, and frying hot dogs. She could even catch the faint tang of Indian spices—not the kinds of spices she was used to, of course, the very specific kind in pandhi curry or masala crab, but then she had never come across those flavors outside the small, beautiful corner of India that her mother had once called home.

That said, this place did smell yummy. There was food everywhere she looked: street vendors, bakeries, cafés, take-out places, you name it. Hungry Heart Row, that's what this neighborhood was called, and it seemed its residents had taken that very seriously.

Anna followed her father upstairs to Mynah's flat (apartment?), and she huddled inside her jacket as they waited for Mynah to answer the door. Her father looked tired. He caught her eye and gave her a smile, and she tried to return it, but hers felt wooden, crooked, a smile pulled into place by a puppeteer.

"Long trip," he said.

"It was," she said.

The door clattered open. Anna sucked in a breath. She would never get used to how much like her mother Aunt Mynah looked. The thick, wavy dark hair, the turned-up nose, the bright bird eyes, the way they moved like the world was simply too slow for them.

"Anna!" she cried, and squeezed her tight in a hug. "Look at you! You've grown so much!" She pulled back, laughed, hugged her again, and then kissed Anna's father affectionately on the cheek. "And you're just as handsome as ever, Luke. Do you *ever* age?"

She hustled them into the apartment, chattering the whole time. Anna was grateful for it, because it gave her time to blink away the tears, swallow the lump in her throat, hide how much Mynah's resemblance to her mother had shaken her.

"You must be exhausted after that trip," Mynah went on. "Let's do something quick and simple for dinner. Chinese? Emperor's Way does the best Chinese takeout in the neighborhood, I'll call them now."

As Mynah made the call, Anna went to the balcony and looked out at the neighborhood. She could see the park, the river, warehouses, and blocks of tall apartments that were so different from the sedate detached cottages and messy gardens of her own street back home. The sun had started to set on the river, and a golden light settled over Hungry Heart Row, giving the noise and laughter and rooftops a warm, inviting glow that made Anna feel a little less cold and lonely.

Then the moment was gone, and she turned back to her father and aunt, to the cold and the loneliness and the yawning, empty space where her mother should have been.

Mynah hadn't lied; Emperor's Way did make some pretty incredible Chinese food. "It's not *quite* as good as the Chinese food we used to get growing up," Mynah told them, which Anna was in no way surprised to hear, because her mother had never passed up an opportunity to sigh wistfully and tell them about this one restaurant in Bangalore, where she and Mynah had grown up, and about the Hunan chicken and how bloody amazing it was, and— "No matter how hard we tried after moving away," Mynah said, almost filling in the blanks for Anna, "we never could figure out the recipe and make it ourselves. Did you two ever try it when you visited?"

"It was too spicy for me," Anna said, a split second before her father did.

Mynah laughed. Once Anna would have laughed too, and then her mother would have teased her for inheriting her English father's constitution, but now she just felt a sense of loss, like here was yet another way in which she and her mother weren't alike. That hadn't mattered to her once, but it felt like it mattered very much now.

As soon as they were finished eating, she retreated to the room she had been given for the next two weeks and unpacked. On her way back from a quick shower, she caught the tail end of Dad's voice from the kitchen.

"That's not true," he said.

"Are you kidding me, Luke? I was right there. You two barely said two words to each other all night. That's not how I remember either of you."

Anna slipped back into her room before they realized she was there. She hadn't really thought about it, but

Mynah was right; she and her father hadn't said much to
each other all night. In fact, they didn't speak much at all
anymore. Oh, there was plenty of "Dad, don't forget my
tampons when you're doing the shopping tomorrow" and
"What do you fancy for dinner tonight, Anna?" swapped
back and forth around their home, but they didn't *talk*.
Not like they used to when there had been three of them.
And Anna hadn't even noticed.

She closed her eyes and fell asleep to the sound of the
rain.

The first few days in Hungry Heart Row were okay, all
things considered. It was nice to not be home, where every
room and every day was a reminder that there was someone
missing, and Anna spent her time exploring the neighborhood. It was small and vibrant, full of locals and tourists
alike, with flyers all over the place for music gigs, tarot
card readings, and a Hungry Ghost Festival. (What?)

By the fourth day, it felt like she had seen all of the
neighborhood and eaten at every single restaurant, street
cart, and café. The novelty had worn off, and without it,
there was nothing to distract her from the grief they had
come here to escape. Her walks around the city grew listless,
she avoided Dad and Aunt Mynah as much as possible, and
she spent more and more time in her room with her books.
She was a jigsaw girl, fragile and in pieces, slotted clumsily
together. One careless move would break the pieces apart.

Her aunt tried to talk to her about it. "I'm worried

about you, sweetie," she said, catching Anna alone in her room one evening. "You're so *quiet*."

"I'm just tired," Anna said, the default words, the easy words.

"What a crock of shit."

A small smile tugged at the corner of Anna's mouth, but it was brief. Mynah stomped across the room and planted herself in front of the window with her arms crossed over her chest. Waiting.

Anna's heart knotted. "Mum used to do that. Stomp like that when she was tired of my tantrums and grumpfests."

A fond smile warmed Mynah's face. "I think we both got it from our grandmother, that sour old crone. Don't look at me like that—she was! Your mother was always the first to say so. She drove Thayi crazy when we went to visit her as children, climbing trees and bringing frogs into the house and trying to catch cobras. Thayi spent half her life trying to stop your mother from doing something dangerous, and yes, in hindsight I *do* see that the old bat was just being a responsible adult, but at the time Leila and I just thought she was a grumpy crone."

"She kind of was," Anna said. "I only met her once, but she did not strike me as a lady who believed in fun."

"Now that," Mynah said, "is the first genuinely *Anna* thing you've said since you arrived." She kissed the top of Anna's head on her way out of the room and paused at the door. "You're still in there. You'll find your way back out again."

* * *

It rained the day something finally broke.

At least it rained all morning. Then, when it cleared up in the afternoon, Anna went out to the playground near Mynah's town house. Raindrops dripped from the trees, and the ground squelched under her feet. The park was almost completely deserted, and there was a crisp, wet, grassy smell in the air that reminded Anna of *something*, but she couldn't figure out what it was. She sat on one of the swings, watched a bird peck at the ground, and burst into tears.

Just like that. She burst into tears. She cried actual fucking *tears*. And why? Not why was she so desperately unhappy, because of course she knew why, but why now? Why here? There was no real reason why it had to be this moment on this day, yet here she was. *Crying*.

The storm passed, and she closed her eyes. There was that smell again, the wet grass, the rain in the trees, and there, yes, *there*, that was it. It was that smell that had broken her. Why? What memory was it that it pulled at? What almost forgotten part of her heart had it woken up?

"Hi," said a voice behind her.

Anna snapped her head around, startled, and watched a girl approach her. She was smallish, with brown skin, black hair, and a green ribbon for a headband. She moved like a hummingbird, delicate and quick, as if her feet didn't quite touch the ground. There was a box in her hands, and she held it out to Anna.

"Um," said Anna.

"These are for you," said the girl.

"Are you sure you've got the right person?" Anna asked, bewildered. "I don't think we've ever met."

"We haven't," said the girl.

"So those can't be for me. . . ."

"I don't follow your logic," the girl said, raising an eyebrow. "What does one have to do with the other?"

Anna had a feeling she was not about to get rid of this strange, persistent girl, so she took the box. "Um, thanks. That's really nice of you. I think."

The girl smiled, sat on the other swing, and kicked herself into the air.

Anna opened the box. *Wow.* Inside were four beautiful, freshly baked pastries. Anna didn't know what kind they were, but they looked and smelled utterly delicious. Two were in shades of green, the other two in shades of purple, and the warmth of them bled through the box and into her hands and chased some of the cold away.

"They're pan dulce," said the girl. "I knew someone needed them, so I baked them. I knew as soon as I saw you that it was you."

This was extremely odd, but Anna didn't feel it would be polite to say so. "I'm Anna," she said.

"Lila," said the girl. She paused, as if she was waiting for Anna to say something, and then said, "Bad day?"

Anna flushed with embarrassment; Lila had obviously seen her in tears. She thought about pretending nothing had happened but didn't think that would work on this girl. So she told the truth. "My mother died a few months ago."

"I'm sorry."

Anna shrugged, toed the ground with her boot. "Me too."

"You wanna talk about it?"

"No," Anna said, but she wasn't sure that was true. "Yes. I don't know. Maybe. It's like I can feel all these things, things that *hurt*, and I want to take them out of me and put them somewhere else."

Lila nodded. "I know just what you need," she said. She plucked a leaf off the ground and handed it to Anna with a look of complete seriousness on her face. "Here. Spit all the things that are hurting you into the leaf and then blow it away."

"You want me to spit on a leaf? Literally spit?"

Lila stared at Anna. Anna stared back. Then the smallest twitch at the corner of Lila's mouth gave her away, and they both started to laugh.

"Of course I don't want you to spit on a leaf," Lila said, snorting laughter out of her nose, "The look on your face!"

"You just gave me a box of cakes! How was I supposed to know your weirdness had limits?"

Lila laughed harder. When she was done wiping her eyes, she said, "Seriously, though, I'm here if you want to talk about your mom."

Anna was quiet for a minute or two. The laughter had unknotted something inside her, but it was still hard to start. "These pastries are gorgeous colors," she said. "I didn't even know I liked green, but I do. It reminds me of her. I keep thinking of her grandparents' house in India. My mother and aunt grew up in the city, but their grandparents grew coffee on a plantation a few hours away. Have you ever heard of Coorg? It's this region in the south of India where people grow tea and coffee, and they have the most beautiful forests, and we used to go there every year when I was little. My mother would take me out to show me the coffee blossoms and the tigers in the forests. It was always so *green* there, and the air always felt like rain. And now it's raining here and it's all just wet and cold and I'm scared that—" She broke off. "I don't know. Sorry. I'm probably not making much sense."

Lila was quiet for a moment, and then she said, "What are you scared of?"

Anna shook her head. She couldn't shape the words, and she wasn't sure she could say them to someone she had only just met anyway. To distract herself, she took a bite of one of the pan dulce Lila had given her. It almost melted in her mouth, moist and sweet and perfectly crumbly.

"This is *amazing*," she said.

Lila beamed. "I'm glad you like it."

Another bite, another taste. Lila continued to swing gently, back and forth, in an oddly soothing rhythm. The taste of the pan dulce on Anna's tongue felt soft, comforting, like a friend holding her hand. She felt some of her uncertainty crumble away, and she started to shape the words she hadn't dared to before. "You asked me what

I'm scared of," she said. "We were so close, but I'm not very much like her. I look more like my dad, for a start, and I don't know anyone in her family other than my aunt. She was a university lecturer, but I want to be a vet. She liked horror movies, and I run screaming at the first note of the *Jaws* music. I know a lot of that's stupid stuff and it doesn't matter, but it feels like every way I'm different from my mother is another connection lost."

Another connection lost. Another tether gone. And Anna was afraid there would come a day when she would find that there was nothing left of her mother at all.

"What about your dad?" Lila asked. "Can't you talk to him about her? Keep her alive and close that way?"

Anna's voice cracked. "I don't even know how to talk to my dad anymore."

Lila nodded. "I'm sorry."

"Me too. Mostly for rambling at you about all this." They both laughed at that. Anna gestured with the box in her hands. "Thanks for the pastries. They really are awesome. I should probably get back."

Lila jumped nimbly off the swing. "Come by my family's bakery and say good-bye before you go home."

"I will." As they split off in different directions, Anna called after her. "Do you always bake pastries when you want to help someone?"

"Pretty much," Lila called back, and flashed a smile over her shoulder. "What can I say? Welcome to Hungry Heart Row!"

*   *   *

The pan dulce was perfect, and it gave Anna an idea. Talking to Lila about her favorite memories of her mother had shaken loose parts of the past she had either forgotten or overlooked. Like the songs her mother would sing as she cooked the one and only thing she ever cooked; like that time they visited the family coffee estate and Mum shot a rampaging wild boar and then they cooked and ate it later that night; like the smell of rain in the forest; like the fat, sour gooseberries they would pick off the trees; like fresh peppercorns straight off the vine; like countless other jumbled memories and smells and tastes and sounds that had been tucked away in some corner of her mind gathering dust for so long.

Mum's favorite dish, the one and only thing she ever cooked.

I'm going to make it.

Anna had never learned how to make it, because she had always arrogantly assumed her mother would be around forever, but she had eaten it so many times that she was sure she could recreate it by memory and taste alone. *This is it. Her favorite food.* She would have to thank Lila for the inspiration later. This was the connection she had been afraid she would never find. It was a way to hold on to everything she had lost.

"Can I borrow your wallet, Dad?"

Excited for the first time in what felt like months, Anna rushed out to the neighborhood grocery store and picked out the ingredients she hoped would work. Curry leaves, bay leaves, whole black peppercorns, turmeric, ginger, garlic, green chilies, red chilies, limes, honey, and, finally, a fresh shoulder of pork.

The first batch was vaguely nice and vaguely bland and really just *vague* in every way, which was not the effect she had intended.

Okay, more chilies then.

The second batch was so spicy that she gagged and had to down half a can of Coke before she could breathe again.

Fewer chilies. More than the first time, less than this time. That was doable, wasn't it? A happy balance somewhere between *meh* and *murder*.

The third batch tasted great, but—

"It doesn't taste *right*," she said out loud.

Frustration and disappointment made her throat squeeze tight. She'd been at it for hours and had had no luck. She had been so excited, and now even this felt out of her reach.

"What are you doing?"

She glanced back at her father, who stood in the doorway with a puzzled expression on his face.

Anna's shoulders hunched. "It doesn't matter."

He looked into the dish on the stove, and his eyes widened. "You're trying to make your mum's Coorg pandhi curry."

He pronounced the words perfectly, a sharp departure

from his very white, very British accent, but he'd had years to get it right.

His brow furrowed. "Why didn't you tell me?"

"Because," Anna said, "what would have been the point? You do your thing; I do mine. We don't talk unless we have to. That's how it works now."

"Anna, that's not how I meant to—"

"I know, Dad. I know you didn't do it on purpose. I didn't either." She looked away, at a shiny spot of grease on the counter. "It doesn't matter anyway. It doesn't taste like Mum's. I can't get it right."

There was a silence. Then his voice, firmer this time. "Anna, look at me."

She did. His eyes were sadder than they once were, but brighter than they had been the day before.

They crinkled as he smiled. "We'll get it right."

We.

Slowly, tentatively, the corners of Anna's mouth tugged upward. "Okay," she said, and handed him the spoon.

"The flavor just isn't right."

"Do we need more pepper? More honey?"

Dad shook his head, tapping his fingers on the counter strewn with chopped onions. "It's too sweet with the extra honey."

They tried again. "Oooh, that works a little better," Anna said, "I think that batch had extra lime."

"But it's still not right."

"Lime, though, that seems to be the key. Maybe we need even more of it?"

"Maybe it's time to google. . . ."

"*No*. We need to make Mum's version of this, not whatever we find on Google!"

"You're as stubborn as she was."

And still it didn't work. The kitchen was a disaster, the pot on the stove gave off a smell that was closer to death than to deliciousness, and Anna had burned her thumb at least three times.

"Why is this so impossible?" she demanded. "Didn't we watch her make this a million times?"

"I guess we didn't pay attention."

"I never thought I needed to. I thought she'd be around forever."

Dad's jaw tightened. "So did I."

"Dad?"

"Yeah?"

"It's okay if you're crying. You don't have to hide it."

"You're crying too."

"This hug is awkward."

"It didn't used to be. When did we stop hugging?"

"Probably around the time we stopped talking."

"Sorry."

"Me too."

"Anna?"

"Yeah?"

"You're crying into the stew."

"And it *still* doesn't taste right!"

Eventually, they took a break. They went out to eat something that wasn't pork and ended up at Lila's bakery. She wasn't there, but Anna left a note.

Thanks for everything. I was going to bring you some homemade pork curry, but it's not right yet. Maybe next time.

"It's nice here, isn't it?" Dad said. They walked back toward the apartment, his mouth full of a cookie from Lila's bakery.

"It's great. And Mynah's a saint for putting up with our grumpy faces all this time. Maybe we should take her out to eat somewhere nice before we leave?"

"Good idea."

Anna looked down the street at the park, the town houses, the river. It was beautiful here. But it wasn't home.

"Do you think it'll be okay?" she blurted out. "When we go back home?"

"In what way?"

She rushed on before she lost her nerve. "The house felt cold and empty and horrible without her, and I'm afraid it'll feel like that again when we go back."

"Anna, why didn't you tell me you felt that way?"

"I don't know. I just *couldn't*. It felt like every time I opened my mouth to speak, the words dried up, and I just wanted to go away again. Why didn't you tell me how *you* felt? I know you must have been miserable too."

He gave her a small, rueful smile. "I should have told you. I don't know why I didn't. Maybe I didn't want to admit she was gone."

"It wasn't exactly easy to pretend she was still there, Dad."

"I don't know, Anna. I don't know why I didn't talk to you about it. I can only guess. I think I really did want to pretend nothing had changed. Which doesn't make sense, but grief doesn't make sense. *Death* doesn't make sense."

"It's the worst," Anna said, which made her father snort a laugh.

"I'm sorry. I should have done better."

"Me too," she said softly.

Something wet fell on the tip of Anna's nose, then on her forehead. It had started to rain.

When they got back to the apartment, Mynah was home from work. She stood in the kitchen, comically out of place in her crisp skirt, blouse, heels, and suit jacket, and stared at the ingredients strewn around her.

She swiveled slowly to face them, incredulous. "What in actual hell have you two been up to?"

"We've been trying to recreate Mum's Coorg pandhi curry."

"Is that so?" said Mynah. "How was that supposed to work without the kachampuli?"

"The what?"

"Kachampuli," she repeated.

"What is kachampuli supposed to be?" Dad asked, sounding out the syllables carefully.

Mynah let out a shriek of laughter. "Are you telling me you've been trying to make Coorg pandhi curry all this time, and neither of you knows about kachampuli? Which is only the most essential ingredient?"

"But surely the pandhi is the most essential ingredient," Anna protested, gesturing in the direction of the pork rind sitting on the counter. "Otherwise it would be called *kachampuli* curry."

Mynah ignored that and wiped tears of laughter from her eyes. "Kachampuli, my sweet ignorant ones, is what gives the pandhi curry its distinct flavor. It's a little like vinegar, and it's made from a limey sort of fruit they grow in Coorg." She marched to one of the cupboards, rooted around in the back, and retrieved a dusty bottle with a sealed cap. Inside gleamed a thick, dark liquid. "Behold," she said dramatically, "kachampuli."

Anna was amazed. "So if we use this, the stew will taste like Mum's did?"

"I don't see why not." Mynah put the bottle down with a triumphant thunk, and turned on her heel. "I'll leave you to it while I shower." They could hear her laughing all the way into the bathroom. "Pandhi curry without kachampuli," she gurgled, "the very idea . . ."

The mysterious kachampuli wasn't a magic elixir. There were still a few hiccups—a dash too much salt here, an overcooked and chewy chunk of pork there—and it took a few more attempts and a few more days to make it perfect.

It rained the day they got it right. Anna could hear the thrum of it against the glass of the window as she speared a piece of meat on a fork and promptly burst into tears because it tasted just like every time her mother had made it. It tasted like rain on the air and frogs hopping across the grass and coffee beans in a jar and the green, green leaves of the forest rustling in the night and the sound of her mother humming a song. It tasted like a future in which the rain and the coffee beans and her mother weren't out of reach after all.

"You did it," said Dad.

"We did it," Anna replied, and grinned.

"One could argue that *I* did it," Mynah called from the other room, "but sure, you two take all the credit."

It rained the day Anna and her father left Hungry Heart Row, but the sun was out by the time they got home.

Kings and Queens

BY ELSIE CHAPMAN

As I always find her after school, my mother is seated at the small table in the restaurant kitchen, prepping vegetables. Broccoli is piled high in a wide silver bowl, and sliced onion turns the air prickly.

"I hate school," I declare in Chinese. My mother's English holds a fraction of the wealth she finds in her native tongue—I never forget which language is really hers.

"Ming, hush, there are customers."

Barely, though—it's between lunch and dinner, so only two tables out in the dining room are occupied. And the waiter is one of my many cousins, the kitchen staff my father and two uncles—all are used to my complaining.

My mother breaks apart heads of garlic. "Do you have a test?"

"No, just general hate." I drop my backpack to the floor and sit down across from her. "And an essay, but it's not due until Monday."

"Start it now." She crushes cloves with a blade, strips off their skin. "Don't leave it until Sunday. You're going to be busy starting tonight, helping us get all the food ready for tomorrow."

She's talking about Saturday's engagement dinner. The one the restaurant's agreed to host and cater.

Because I'm both sickened and furious whenever I think about it, I take out homework so I don't, scribbling thoughtless answers I'll only have to fix later.

My mother gets up and takes a bowl from a shelf. She ladles something into it from a pot on the stove and sets the bowl down in front of me. "Eat it while you work."

It's macaroni soup. Curls of pasta swim in steaming, fragrant broth, and pieces of boiled chicken are all tangled up with them, the meat nearly fallen off the bones. It's comfort food, the kind my parents brought over the ocean with them twenty-five years ago, and the kind that doesn't fit westernized Chinese restaurant menus. My mother used to make it for us for breakfast, before we got older and told her we had no time to eat in the morning if we wanted to make the school bus. For years now it's been only the occasional snack, a rare treat.

But I still like it best made with sugar, and so does my brother Lei. Only our older sister Yun asks for it this way, savory and salty.

She's upstairs right now, silent and unmoving in her new life. The doctors have made it clear what's no longer possible because of the bullet that smashed into her brain to leave her changed forever. Still, the sight of the noodles makes me ask my mother the pointless question anyway: "Did she like it?"

For a second my mother's expression is pained before going carefully blank. It's hard to look at, and I wish I'd opened my mouth only to eat.

She sits back down, picks up her knife again, and nods. "Her face said so."

Another impossible.

I take a bite. The meat is as creamy as the noodles, soft on my tongue. It is the taste of my mother's desperation, gone dull and dogged; it is the taste of a time that is no longer retrievable.

"It's good," I tell her.

She smashes apart more garlic. "I'll make it with sugar next time. For you and Lei."

The restaurant phone on the front counter rings, and I get up to answer it. Lei and I take turns covering, and today is Friday, which means my brother has robotics club. He won't be home until dinner.

"Emperor's Way Chinese Restaurant," I say into the phone as I grab an order pad. It's half past four—time for dinner orders to start coming in.

"Special combo from the special menu." The voice is

flat, mechanical. I don't know who it is because I'm not meant to, the voice distorted by a phone app anyone can buy. "You understand, yeah?"

I barely keep from rolling my eyes at the question. I've known about "specials" all my life, considering everyone in my entire family are members of the Kings and Queens.

My mother and father had joined as teens, back when they still lived in Hong Kong. Our leader is Wen, and it'd been his ancestors who'd founded the secret society more than a hundred years ago. Wen himself had personally plucked my parents from poverty and given them security of a sort, asking only their unwavering loyalty in return. Then his family had sent Wen and my parents, along with a dozen or so other members (some of them my aunts and uncles), halfway across the world to lay down roots for a new division.

The Kings and Queens still control the streets in Hong Kong. And because Wen's father is still the leader over there, it makes Wen the leader over here.

Membership passes down through generations on this side of the ocean too.

This is how Lei and Yun and I have come to inherit more than blood from our parents.

Until Yun's accident, I never hated being a member of a secret society. It used to mean safety, the comfort of a large extended family. But now that safety's a trap. And not all family means well.

"Special combo, you got it," I say into the phone.
"Which one?"

"The winter melon soup."

Winter melon is symbolic of a wife—a special order of
the soup means someone's is about to be abducted. A special order of egg fried rice? Someone's kid. Fried pot stick-
ers? A husband. Shanghai chow mein with chopped-up
noodles? Someone's doomed to have their life cut short,
the promise of longevity broken.

I scribble down the order. Which rival gang messed up
with Wen this time to require that a message be sent? And
who of the Kings and Queens, on our leader's behalf, is
going to make them pay? "The address for delivery?"

"Fifty-five sixty-six Lionsbridge, apartment seventeen.
Leave it at the entrance. Got it?"

Annoyed at being questioned again, I hang up before he
can say anything else. Sure, a member can be close enough
to Wen to know about the secret menu and to be trusted
to order from it, but it doesn't have to mean they still
aren't half-stupid.

I'm tempted to bail on the delivery—my cousins Kris
and Lulu are about to come on shift as waitresses, and
I bet I can convince one of them to go for me. But my
mother would expect me to do it, and my father's already
coming over to see what dish to make in the name of a
gang whose say over us goes back decades.

"Someone's husband has messed up." I show him the
order slip.

He calls it out to my uncles—"The winter melon soup, special order!"—and then frowns at me. He is not my mother—annoyance tempers his worry instead of the other way around, my glibness is trouble instead of tolerable, and he's accepted that Yun is beyond recovery—but for his weary eyes. "It'll be ready in ten minutes, Ming."

I grab my wallet from inside my backpack. My mother's slicing up shiitake mushrooms, their toughness having soaked all day in order to be cut.

"Do you know who?" I ask her quietly. *The Red Den? The Sun Gods? The Black Seas?*

These are the names of our rivals, the other secret societies that exist in Rowbury. Like us, their members run cover places all over the city too, from delis to banks to florists, so that honest money crosses dirty hands, and it gets hard to say one's not the other. All of us fight over turf, over shares of a business, over how much someone's supposed to fear and respect us.

My mother doesn't look up from her slicing. "Not the Black Seas," she murmurs.

I leave through the kitchen, both disappointed and relieved. The Black Seas is one of the reasons why I miss my sister so badly, but *I* want to be the one who makes them bleed.

Even if I have no clue yet how I'm going to do it.

I place the take-out container of soup into the delivery box of the restaurant scooter and zoom down the street.

* * *

It happened nearly a year ago, at the end of last summer. The shoot-out that day had been between a bunch
of Kings and Queens and some of the Black Seas. Yun
wouldn't have even been there, except that her crush had
been, a guy who's a King.

Cross fire. A bullet. The sister I knew . . . gone.

Brain dead, the doctors said. *We're sorry, but there's nothing
to be done.*

I shouldn't hate the Black Seas any more for it just
because they happened to be the gang who'd been there that
day. It could have been any of the others, just as easily.

But it hadn't been.

And so it'd been Black Sea bullets we'd had to answer
with our own.

And how it happened that it'd been a bullet from one
of *our* guns that took Yun away.

Wen himself had met my stunned parents at the hospital that night, insisting on paying all the medical bills.

Such an honor, our leader coming to see us, my mother had
whispered to Lei and me after returning home, *a sign of true
respect for his members.* But her smile had been a stranger's,
just as Yun had become a stranger to me. And there was a
kind of flat, cold fire in her eyes. It was the first time I'd
ever seen her be anything less than adoring of Wen, the
man at the wheel of the world that had ground Yun into
someone else.

It was months before anything my mother cooked for
us tasted right—her congee was thin, her steamed pork

cake dry, her red-bean soup never sweet enough no matter how much sugar she poured in. Now I taste hints of
her caring in her food again, her mother's love a force. As
though she's imagining Yun there beside her, saying what
she always said when one of us was upset, my sister who'd
been fascinated with the night sky: *Let's go outside and look
for stars. We can imagine other places in the world coming close to
smelling and tasting and feeling as good as Hungry Heart Row, but
know it's not possible. And then we can laugh at how lucky we are.*

Still.

Each bite continues to leave behind an edge of bitterness, the sourness of stubborn denial. Sometimes the tears
my mother cries into her pot come while she's cursing
beneath her breath; sometimes when I eat, it's an image of
our leader that flashes through my mind.

The apartment for the delivery is just outside the food
district, and it takes me less than ten minutes to get there.
I place the take-out bag on top of the mailboxes at the
main door.

I don't bother ringing the buzzer. Whoever's watching
for the delivery has been instructed to not answer, just as
they've been instructed to wait for me to leave before picking up the order. After that, the order might be passed on,
or it might be executed right away—I've never been told
how long and winding the chain, how deep it goes. But
I am the daughter of long-serving Kings and Queens, so
soon I'll know it all, and already I can feel the tightening
of Wen's grip.

Heading back, I'm waiting at a light when a King crosses the street in front of me, take-out coffees in hand. Our members are scattered throughout the city, so he's not anywhere he shouldn't be, but seeing him still leaves me frozen.

Cheng.

The boy whose bullet it'd been. The boy Yun had thought she'd loved, even if he had not loved her back.

Sometimes I think of him—older, as slick as oil, stringing along a teenaged girl he found more amusing than interesting—and I can't breathe for my rage. He's engaged to a Black Sea now, a twentysomething-year-old named Jia. The other gang's leader, Shan, had proposed the match to Wen, and Wen had agreed. News is that the Sun Gods are growing fast enough to soon be bigger than even the Kings and Queens. And numbers, they can tip the balance of power—Wen would know this. So this past winter, when Shan threatened to align his Black Seas with the Sun Gods unless the Kings and Queens had a better offer, the alliance became an opportunity Wen couldn't pass up. With the Black Seas on his side, the city would always be his—the inconvenience of Shan as an equal would, of course, be dealt with later.

What did Wen care that he was asking my parents to work with the same gang who'd destroyed their firstborn? By having the very boy who'd doomed Yun be the one to ensure his own status? Did they not owe him for everything?

Like salt stirred into my coffee, my mother had choked out to my father after they'd been told of the engagement. *Like weevils crawling in my rice. Our leader might as well be spitting in our faces.*

Wen hadn't bothered with a personal visit that time—a phone call to my parents was good enough.

Then it was spring, and Wen ordered that Emperor's Way host the engagement-party dinner. He'd forgotten Yun entirely.

The demand had left my father pale. My mother had made a succession of all his favorites—salty duck eggs, steamed spareribs on rice, the smelly preserved fish so pungent she once used to be embarrassed the neighbors would complain—to melt back his helplessness, return it to bearable. *I cry enough for the two of us,* her dishes had said on her behalf, *so eat, for me.*

The traffic light changes; Cheng disappears around a corner. I keep heading toward the restaurant, pretending instead I'm running into him with my scooter, a bullet driving through bone.

I am the daughter of long-serving Kings and Queens.

And one day I will do more than just imagine a death.

The dining room is crowded now. Emperor's Way isn't the only Chinese restaurant in Hungry Heart Row, but it's the most popular. My mother's at the counter, handling payments and orders; my father and uncles are in the kitchen; my cousins and aunts are waiting on and busing tables.

There are familiar faces in the dining room: Ami Dimatibag with her regular order of dumplings and orange chicken, whose grandmother runs the Filipino carinderia a block over. A new black kid I've seen around a few times, headphones slung around his neck if they aren't already clamped over his ears. And Lila Manzano from school, who I'd once nearly delivered a special order to by mistake.

I'd caught it just in time, turning the corner on the scooter even as Lila was walking up to the apartment building I'd been headed toward. We'd exchanged casual waves as I'd passed, and I drove another block before pulling into the 7-Eleven, covered in cold sweat. I'd stayed there, hissing to my mother on my cell that no way could my sixteen-year-old classmate be involved in any Kings and Queens business.

My mother had been confused. *Maybe a relative of hers is a member of the Sun Gods?*

Mom, her family runs the bakery over on Pepper and Tansy! They sell birthday cakes for little kids and pastries for old ladies! They're not members of any secret society, trust me.

People can be puzzles, Ming. We cater parties for lots of customers. We don't really care if they're druggies or anything, as long as they pay.

Mom! They gave me the wrong address! Can you just check with whichever one of Wen's guys is behind this special order and tell me where I'm delivering?

Lei's home from robotics, seated at the table in the kitchen. He's eating dinner—sweet-and-sour pork, chicken fried rice, a heaping pile of fried rice noodles topped with beef.

My uncles have a soft spot for my thirteen-year-old brother and will cook for him whatever he requests from the menu. My mother says it's his age, his liking restaurant Chinese food more than home Chinese food, food that feeds you but never touches your heart. She once said his tongue was too quickly formed by the West so that the East could never catch up. *You and Yun are steamed chicken feet, while Lei is baked chicken nuggets.*

He's typing into his cell between bites. I bet he's on Served, Rowbury's online restaurant site. Users can rank and review their dining experience, and Hungry Heart Row even has its own section. Only Lei's closest friends— and Yun and I, having caught him once—know that my brother's "Internet famous" when it comes to Served. HungryMan07 is a Gold Plate reviewer, meaning he's got at least a certain number of followers, and his reviews are usually rated the most helpful—the followers because his reviews are scathing and snarky, the helpful rating because he really does know a lot about the restaurants around here. He's so popular the site's creators advertise their other apps on HungryMan07's profile page.

Lei likes to keep Yun updated about Served. About what users are saying about the food district in the forums, about the latest reviews for Emperor's Way and how right or wrong they might be. He talks to her about food because they've always talked about food, and he doesn't know what else to talk about with this new stranger-for-an-older-sister.

He waves me over. "Ming, come check this out!"

"Hey." I peer over his shoulder at his cell and pretend I'm trying to make out what's on the screen. "Homework, right?" It'd once been Yun's job to check.

"Ha-ha, no. But look—" His voice drops to a loud whisper. "Head dudes on Served just approved me for another banner on my profile. I'm going to be making even more money now."

"Cool, Mr. Silicon Valley." I pluck a pineapple chunk from the sweet-and-sour pork on his plate. The sauce seems even redder than usual today. "Just don't forget us little people."

I'm kidding, though. Because while Lei and I are blood, and he's as much a King for life in some form or other as I am a Queen, beyond all the sibling jokes and jabs, he's the thoughtful one. His anger over Yun is for my sake as well as the rest of our family's, while mine is still all about me—*Yun, I still need you; you need to keep being the sister I understand.*

Sometimes I'm awake at dawn, so busy hating Cheng and Jia and everyone else for making this horrible wedding happen that I can't sleep. Lei must wake up to my hate through our shared wall, because he fries me eggs for breakfast without my asking, always able to keep the yolks whole while I break them each and every time.

Lei's always sweet, like smooth red-bean buns, my mother says of this, *while you, Ming, are the meat-filled ones, all chew and salt.*

She never says the rest. That Yun had somehow been able to be both.

I ask Lei, *"Do you have homework?"*

"Later." He forks more noodles into his mouth and goes back to typing.

I go to the small stove reserved for family and heat vegetable oil in a pan. I slice two tomatoes into wedges and toss them in along with a knob of ginger and a fat pinch of sugar. The sound of sizzling is low, muffled by that of my father and uncles' cooking in giant woks nearby.

As soon as the juice from the tomatoes thickens, I take the pan off the heat and pour the contents over a bowl of hot white rice. This tomato-and-rice dish is also another that's not on the menu, a grown-up version of the hunks of rock sugar my mother used to place between our lips whenever we fell and hurt ourselves. *This will make it all better.*

"Want some or are you full?" I ask Lei over the sounds of the kitchen.

"Full."

"So hurry up and do your homework—tonight you're helping prep for the engagement dinner, remember?"

He sighs extra loud as he gets up and begins to clear his dishes. Bright red sweet-and-sour sauce smears his knuckles, like he's gotten into another fight at school.

I head up the back stairs, steaming bowl in hand, forever searching.

* * *

I knock out of habit, and because I don't like that I no longer need to.

Her room is mostly quiet, threaded through with the beeps and hisses from the machines that have become a part of her. The air is stagnant, uninviting.

But the sun's setting late now, and everything inside is warm, painted amber. My mother has replaced the flowers on the desk, fresh peonies for wilted carnations. My father has hung up yet another oil painting of stars—because it's for Yun, because he once promised her plane rides so she could get closer to the sky, because he never got around to it. My brother has left behind on the desk a national magazine, open to an article about Hungry Heart Row. There's a photo of Emperor's Way below the article's headline. I'll need to ask my parents if they've seen it. They would be pleased.

Yun is propped up in bed, staring at nothing.

I place the bowl on the bedside table and sit down beside her. "Hi, Yun."

She blinks.

If not for what the doctors say, I could lie and pretend she's the same. I could pretend she's about to start senior year. That her popularity at school continues. That she will once again be on the student council, the volleyball team, and the drama club. That she'll know better this time than to fall for older guys with sweet faces and cold hearts.

"So I made tomatoes and rice." My voice is too loud

in the room, even against the beeps and hisses. I feed her, pretending also that she can tell it's one of her favorite dishes.

I talk and imagine answers.

"Has anyone told you about Cheng's engagement?"

Yes. I can't believe I ever thought he was hot.

"I'm sorry we have to host the dinner."

What can Mom and Dad do? It's the Kings and Queens. Family's family.

"Wen's not family."

Except he is. You think he's as powerful as he is because he has guns, knows them? All of us do. But we don't all have his blood, his silver tongue that reminds everyone of his love, what the absence of that love means. So he leads as he does, just as Mom and Dad serve as they do. Don't do something stupid just to avenge me, Ming.

"Will you understand if I do? One day, when I think of a plan?"

Her lips tighten slightly against the spoon. The doctors say this, too, is merely reaction. A boat drifts, carried by a current. A kite flies with the wind. Things burn in the face of fire.

The restaurant closes at nine, and my mother sets Lei and me to work. Her mouth smiles because of the staff still finishing up, while her eyes glow bitter because of Yun forever upstairs.

At least there's nothing traditional about an engagement dinner, so we'll be spared having to prepare a twelve-course wedding banquet loaded with meaning. There will be no roasted pig to symbolize purity. No bright red lobster for luck. No shark fin soup for wealth.

But Wen will still expect a menu full of significance. Each dish must bless his power, must symbolize the rising of his Kings and Queens.

My parents must celebrate a betrayal.

I ask, "So what are we serving, then?"

"Beef and broccoli?" Lei looks hopeful. "Egg rolls?"

My mother begins to pull out ingredients from the huge fridge. There is nothing I don't know, everything restaurant staples. Bean sprouts. Snow peas. Blocks of tofu. Fish searching for steam, their mouths agape.

"Yes, Lei, we will cook the delicious food we're known for." My mother hands us knives, but the blades in her eyes stay—they wear labels of tired despair, of useless fury. *We will cook the food that feeds, though it does not touch the heart.* "No more, and no less."

Lei and I start chopping.

"But I wanted to try fancy Peking duck," he whispers to me.

Duck.

For loyalty.

After Lei yawns for the tenth time, I tell him to go to bed.

"We're nearly done, anyway," I say, starting the dishwashers and grabbing fresh rags to wipe down the counters. It's just the two of us in the kitchen, which smells of garlic and raw meat and detergent. My uncles and cousins and aunt have gone home, one by one. My father is doing paperwork upstairs in our apartment, and my mother has retreated to her room, sleeping off a headache. "And set your alarm—we have to start early tomorrow."

Lei's footsteps have just faded away when the restaurant phone rings.

I keep wiping the counter—this late, the answering machine should pick up—but the phone rings and rings, and finally I answer it just to make it stop.

"Emperor's Way Chinese Restaurant, but we're closed. Sorry."

"This is a special order," the distorted voice says on the other end, "from the special menu."

I nearly laugh. Another of Wen's most trusted who's hardly a genius. "It's almost midnight."

"For tomorrow. The special order is for a creature, served whole. A chicken."

My heart pounds; my mouth goes as dry as western brand instant rice.

A whole chicken is a symbol of completion, of completeness. For celebrations it means family, for weddings, unity—as a special order, something else entirely.

The last one had been before I was born, and it had been for our own. Some members of the Kings and Queens had grown crooked, the type of crooked that didn't suit Wen's plans. He'd ordered the entire family destroyed. An entire diseased branch cut back to healthy growth.

Whose family this time? My mind races with thoughts of my mother, my father, the sprawl of my cousins. Is it possible? What can any of them have done—?

"Is it—who—?" My voice stutters.

"Not yours."

But relief is short lived. Killings are a normal part of secret societies, like a currency of dirty cash, like rules never meant to be broken. But I'm only used to killings at a trickle. Floods—they drown people in their path.

I ask, "The address?"

"Emperor's Way Chinese Restaurant."

A hollowness fills me. "What?"

"By order of Wen, you will execute this order during the engagement dinner tomorrow. Kill all those in the wedding party, Kings and Queens and Black Seas both."

Me? *I* would execute this order? My mouth is beyond dry now—even my lips hurt when I move them. I knew I'd kill as a Queen one day, have already trained in all the ways I might have to do it and how to do it well, but— "Why me?"

"Your sister—don't you want revenge for what's happened? You must dream about it, right? I'm doing you a favor, giving you this chance to make it personal. For you to find some kind of peace."

It's like having someone reach into my brain, into the darkest parts of my heart, and pluck out the truth like a song from strings. Of course I want revenge, to be the one to do it.

I try to swallow. "How?"

"Check the delivery scooter."

The line goes dead.

I hang up and run outside, pulse like thunder.

The scooter's exactly where it's supposed to be. Who was the last person to use it tonight? Kris? Lulu? Might they have seen anything?

But it actually doesn't matter. Whoever Wen called in for this special order is whoever he called in, no questions asked and no answers expected. It's been this way for as long as he's been a leader. Since his family's power is also his, so that it draws in others—others like my parents— the way nectar draws in bees. Making them dizzy, keeping them close.

I lift up the lid of the scooter's delivery box.

There's a gun inside.

Eight courses, the most expensive dishes served first. This means seafood, meat, vegetables, rice, noodles, and finally dessert.

In the kitchen, my uncles plate the Kung Pao chicken, and Lei and my cousins bring out the food, platter by platter. My father stands by, helping the transition go smoothly. My mother watches over all, a silent, appraising statue with a face of stone.

The dining room—closed for a private occasion, as per the sign on the front door—is the most crowded I've ever seen it.

Every single one of us is a criminal.

Kings and Queens fill the tables on the left side, Black Seas the right.

And seated around the head table are Cheng and Jia and their parents, the best man, the maid of honor—the wedding party I'm supposed to kill.

I hadn't been sure, at first. I'd wavered, standing there beside the restaurant scooter, gun in hand. My thoughts had raced in all directions.

Just where did my loyalty lie? The Kings and Queens, a part of my life as much as Hungry Heart Row is a part of my life, a fixture as Emperor's Way is a fixture? Wen, who trapped my parents in saving them? My parents, who continue to serve despite being half-broken? My new sister who would also hate this kind of revenge?

In the end, it'd been the stars that helped me decide. A clear night, they'd winked down like lights, guiding me along. And I'd sensed Yun at my side, peering up at the sky the way she once used to, full of the future she thought would be hers. She might never cry for the change of it. But *I* would know. *I* would cry. Each star I ever saw would be one less than she did, when she'd been the one to always remember to look.

Cheng has prawns on his plate. I will him to choke on one, if only to save me a bullet. He laughs at something Jia says, and I'm glad her expression is so smug, because it makes her that much less like Yun.

Wen and Shan are also seated at the head table, their right-hand members at their sides. Wen spins the orange beef on the lazy Susan closer to his plate. He gives away no sign of why he's changed his mind about having the Black Seas join his Kings and Queens. Maybe the Sun Gods rising up turned out to be just a rumor. Maybe the Black Seas are more trouble than they're worth. Maybe Wen again feels the weight of my parents' loyalty. Maybe he's finally heard Yun breathing in his dreams.

As with the rest of my family, I'm also staff today. A waitress. I hold a pitcher of beer in one hand, and the gun's in my pocket.

Now that it's the Kung Pao chicken course, I know it's time. Not because I've gotten any kind of signal from Wen, or any other directive at all from anyone. But because it's chicken, and there's some kind of poetry there, I think. *Completeness.*

Still, my hand trembles as I empty the pitcher and set it down—*So many other guns in this room! Will surprise on my side be enough?*—as I move closer to the head table. Chicken is crammed into mouths, and I reach into my pocket.

I am the daughter of long-serving Kings and Queens. And I no longer need to only imagine a death.

Someone screams before I've even lifted the gun with my hand.

Guests begin to claw at their necks. Their breaths are wheezes; their eyeballs bug out—panic spills from them like water boiling over in a pot.

The Kung Pao chicken—the thought comes slowly, as though my mind is underwater—*actually spicy for once?*

Kings and Queens, Black Seas—all around me they fall face-first into their plates. Cheng. Jia. Shan. And even Wen, the one who ordered me to kill in the first place, has gone still, dead with half-chewed chicken still in his mouth.

A buzz swarms my brain. My cousins and uncles and aunts stumble in among the dead, as shocked as I am. My father has turned Lei away from the ugly scene, trying to make my brother innocent again, whatever innocent means for people like us.

"Poison," my mother whispers into my ear. "The cashews for the chicken. I had to."

I slowly turn to face her. Last night's phone call rings again in my head. "*I* was supposed to—"

"No, you and Lei were never in danger. I made sure to keep you both out of the way." Her expression turns to steel, the Queen in her fully alive. Mother's love is a sharp glint in her eyes. "But Yun—she will never be the same again."

"But last night—"

She grips my arm. My mother and her strong hands that make rice for us, that cook up revenge. "Your father must never know about this. That I went against our own. Yun is his daughter, but Wen was also his family, in a way."

She planned this all herself. Whoever called last night is probably as stunned as I am by what's happened. How the targets are still dead, but I wasn't who killed them. How *Wen's* somehow also dead.

So then who called?

I'll likely never know. Who would I ask? What kinds of questions that wouldn't be a risk to this new secret of my mother's?

"The Black Seas are behind this, do you understand?" She's whispering still, her voice low and steady. "A world of rival secret societies where motives are always messy—it will fit."

And she's right. It will.

Rowbury police—some of them are Kings and Queens too.

"Don't let it get cold."

Our mother slides bowls of steamed rice and Chinese sausage in front of us. She doesn't care that Lei and I have to shuffle papers out of the way—it's Sunday, but we both still have homework—to make room, just as she doesn't care that we're already full. She's been cooking nonstop since the police left late last night, as though her hands are restless from what they've done. Congee, noodles, eggs scrambled with peas—my brother and I are being comforted.

My mother goes back to the stove, prepares a bowl for Yun, and steps out of the kitchen with it. "Eat," she calls out even as she disappears upstairs. The command is for me, for Lei, for her firstborn, each of us equally hers.

The dining room no longer smells of chicken and cashews and death. The restaurant will be in the news for a while, but customers will come back soon enough. People always need to eat. And Emperor's Way serves the best Chinese food in Hungry Heart Row.

My brother has no idea what really happened. Like the police, he's been made to believe the Black Seas are behind it all, our mother just one more innocent bystander. He stuffs rice and red slices of lap cheong into his mouth and types into his cell. "It's all over Served, too," he says to me. "Listen to this: 'Heard the Kung Pao chicken at the place is a real kicker, ha-ha.'"

"You're HungryMan07—any other restaurant, you'd probably be writing up the same thing."

"Still, they got Wen. And I always thought he was untouchable."

The sausage is dotted with fat, and salty sweet, and even though I'm full, I eat another slice. "It's how he lived. He knew the risks, leader or not."

It was how we lived, too. But Wen's death has changed things a bit now. The Kings and Queens need a new leader. My father is being considered, and my mother has decided it doesn't have to be a terrible thing.

Her food has never been so satisfying.

Lei slides me his cell. "Check out what everyone's saying if you want. I need to grab a book from my room."

"See how Mom and Yun are doing while you're up there?"

"Sure."

He heads upstairs.

I don't want to, but I take a cursory glance, because I know Lei will bug me until I do. And it gets old about as fast as I expect. I close the Served app, about to push his cell back, when the app for voice distortion flashes from the screen.

Something tingles along my spine.

I check his recently made calls.

Emperor's Way Chinese Restaurant. The date: just this past Friday. The time: nearly midnight.

Lei, who felt my hate through the wall. Who tried to fill my need for revenge with perfectly cooked eggs, with secret guns left behind in delivery scooters.

My brother, the son of long-serving Kings and Queens.

The Grand Ishq Adventure

BY SANDHYA MENON

Love is both a recurring theme in my life and the greatest pain in my butt.

My name, Neha (pronounced Nay-ha, btw), means love. I'm also the love advice columnist—aka Dr. Ishq—for the library's teen blog here in Rowbury. My pen name, if you haven't already guessed, means "love" in Urdu. And the great love of my life (not that *he* knows it, ahem), Prem? *His* name means "love," too.

I know what you're thinking just based on the fact that our parents cosmically decided to give us names that mean the exact same thing—we're meant to be. Right? That's what I thought too. But I don't anymore.

See, I've been volunteering at the library for two years. Prem's the photographer for the blog, so he's here every day that I am. For almost two whole years, I've been smiling at him. Flirting (totally ineptly—I can dish out the advice, but my secret is that I can't actually *do* it). Asking about him. And what have I got in return? Stiff smiles. Vacant responses. Averted eyes.

Prem's only a year older than me—he graduated high school last year and is doing a gap year now—but his photographs have already won some major awards. He probably thinks I'm just some talentless hack with my advice column that's read by all of 152 teens in Rowbury and a few across the country. And, as if his limitless talent wasn't bad enough, he's also such a kindhearted person.

I still remember the first time I saw him. Two summers ago, I was covering Rowbury's music and food festival, Tunes and Spoons, for the (then brand-new) blog, when I came across a booth for Children of the City, a charity that raises money for underprivileged kids interested in the arts. Anyway, I was immediately drawn in by this Indian boy at the booth who was being completely *mobbed* by a seething crowd of young kids. They were pawing through his collection of pictures (of dogs and cats mid-sneeze), rapid-fire asking him a million questions, and pulling on his shirt to get his attention. Just seeing all that frenzied, kiddie energy made me sweat, but Prem talked to them calmly, smiling and patient. The kids' parents were so charmed that they donated a *lot* of money. I heard later that Prem had raised over eight thousand dollars that weekend, more than Children of the City had ever managed to raise at one event. It's no wonder he's starting as their campaign and brand manager this fall.

Prem never saw me that day, but anytime I see him now, I can't help but remember how he looked sitting there, his sun-dappled skin, his patient smile.

Kill me now. How am I *ever* supposed to get over my crush if he keeps doing stuff like that?

Okay, focus. I need to work on the newest letter that came in today.

Dear Dr. Ishq,

I love your column. I read it every week, and I have since you started. I think what inspires me the most about your advice is that it's usually about more than love. You always try to improve the letter writer's life, too, by helping them step out of their comfort zones. Anyway, all that to say I find myself in sore need of your help now.

See, there's this person I really like. They're perfect for me. We're the same age, we share similar interests, they like to talk to me (I think? I've never been too good at reading those cues. Why isn't there a handbook?). So what's the problem, you ask? It's me, Dr. Ishq.

Whenever I'm around this person, I completely freeze up. Like, it's not cute or funny. I probably come across as an arrogant jerk or like I'm on drugs. Neither of which I'm going for, FYI.

So what do you suggest, Dr. Ishq? How does someone

*like me—a total control freak in most areas of my life—
become such a jelly-filled doormat when it comes to the
object of my affections?*

*You have an amazing ability to shake people out of stasis
and into action, so please, please help me. I don't want to
lose any more time.*

Desperately,

Ansella

I sit back and study the letter again. I've gotten pretty
good at reading between the lines, at seeing what people are
really like by the phrases they use.

Ansella, for instance, describes herself as a "control
freak" and asks to be "shaken" into action. She wants to be
taken out of her comfort zone, to stop being afraid.

To be completely honest, I can relate more than a
little. Control freak afraid to step out of her comfort
zone? Once I refused to set foot into an empty study
room in which Prem was looking at his pictures because
that amount of close contact might have caused me
to spontaneously combust from desire. It might have
been the perfect opportunity to laugh at his jokes and
compliment his pictures and casually-but-calculatedly tell
him a few photography facts I've memorized, but noooo.
That was too scary. So what did I do instead? I worked on
the blog's SEO. S freaking EO. I'm not even kidding. So,
yeah. Control-freak issues: check. Needs someone to shake

her into action? Check. How many times have I wished I
could have my own personal genie appear and somehow
just magic me into taking a teeny, tiny step toward telling
Prem how I feel? It wouldn't be wildly overdramatic to say
I completely, absolutely feel Ansella's letter to my hollow,
Prem-less core.

I flex my fingers and begin typing, using the same for-
mat I use for every response.

Dear Ansella,
Diagnosis: Self-defeating cowardice in the face of the
possibility of great love.
   Prescription: Four acts of bravery over the course of the
next week. A grand ishq adventure, if you will.
   Prognosis: Excellent.
   I believe, Ansella, that you're not a coward at heart. Not
at all. It's clear to me from your letter that you're actually
aching for adventure, for a chance to lasso what your heart
desires and finally be free. I suspect you just need a nudge in
the right direction.
   So here's what I propose: Every day for the next four days,
I want you to eat—alone—at a different restaurant. And
not just any boring old safe restaurant you're already used to.
I want you to visit a restaurant you've never visited before,
to try a cuisine you've never tasted. Bonus points if you're
nervous about it. Oh, and put your devices away. I want
you to be focused on the flavors of the food in front of you, the
world around you, and the feelings inside you.

Here's the thing: As a culture, we're conditioned to
surround ourselves with friends and acquaintances. If we
have to sit by ourselves—say, at a café or in the airport—
we immediately whip out our phones or tablets. We're
afraid to just sit with ourselves. So I think starting by being
brave enough to be by yourself will be a good launching
point.

And why different cuisines? I believe great food and great
self-esteem pave the path to great love. Eating foods you're
unfamiliar with is an instant connection to a culture you
might otherwise not explore or even think about at all. And
who knows? When you're in that restaurant eating a food
you can't pronounce the name of, you may just realize you're
a lot braver than you think. You may just realize that the one
you love is waiting for you to speak up.

So go forth, dear Ansella, and embark on your grand ishq
adventure.

And here's something new—I promise to take up the same
challenge too.

That's right. Dr. Ishq is going to eat at a different ethnic
restaurant every day for the rest of this week, folks. Ansella,
let's begin tomorrow, Wednesday, and end on Saturday.
As evidence that I'm really doing this too, I'll post a daily
blog—complete with pictures—each day of the week, starting
tomorrow.

Why am I doing this, you ask? Because we can all use a
little shaking up, a grand ishq adventure of our own. If you're
reading this and you think you might want to join in too,

*consider this your invitation. Get up out of your chair, pull
up your fave restaurant app, and get going.*
  Let our adventures begin!
xoxo,
Dr. Ishq

I stare at the reply, a little disbelievingly. That's not
right. Where did that come from? Why did I say I was going
to do the same thing as Ansella?

I put my finger on the backspace key—and then hesitate.
The truth is . . . I think my subconscious knows something I
don't. I've felt stuck for so long. And now that I've graduated
high school, I feel like the clock is ticking louder and faster. I
need to tell him. I have to say how I feel one day soon, or we'll
both go our separate ways, and I'll regret it forever.

It was all fine when we were in high school and time felt
infinite and endless. But now . . . now we're both adults. I'm
going to college in the fall, and he's got that job lined up
with Children of the City. How long before he meets some
golden-hearted, beautiful, smart, creative girl there? How
long before he leaves the library for good, and my circle
forever? Just thinking about never seeing Prem again—or
worse, seeing his engagement photo in the paper six or seven
years down the line—makes me sick. That's some deathbed-
level regret in the making. I can feel it.

And deep in my heart, I know we're meant for each other.
So why *shouldn't* I take on the same challenge as Ansella? I
wasn't lying—my life really could use some shaking up. I'm

not as worldly in the ways of love as my readers might believe. In fact, that's so far from the truth I almost want to laugh.

I press publish on my reply and sit back. That's it, then. Starting tomorrow, I'm going to be eating at a different restaurant each day. And after that? Well, after that . . . we'll see what happens.

DAY 1, WEDNESDAY

I'm sitting on a park bench in Mallow Park, checking the blog on my phone. The outpouring of responses after I posted my letter to Ansella yesterday has been tremendous. I always knew the blog was popular with Rowbury teens, but since yesterday, "lurkers" from other parts of the country and even abroad have come out of the shadows to tell me they're taking on my challenge. Apparently there are a lot of people out there looking to become braver.

It makes me feel better that there are all these strangers doing this with me. In spite of my swaggery persona on the blog, I'm pretty nervous. I just keep looking out at the Yarrow River, thinking. How am I supposed to sit at a table by myself in the middle of a crowded restaurant? How am I supposed to not check my phone or bring my laptop? What if people wonder what I'm doing?

And really, how is this going to help me get to Prem?

Maybe I should just nix the whole thing. Say I did it, but not really do it. I mean, it's not like there are police for this kind of thing. No one's going to check the CCTV cameras to find out if I really went where I said I went. Besides, no one other than staff even knows who I am. The blog is anonymous.

But no. I can't be dishonest like that to my readers. It's silly, but I have this bond with them that feels too sacred. Ansella's out there in Rowbury somewhere, doing what I asked her to do. She might even be in the same restaurants I visit this week. If I see another girl sitting by herself, I'll smile and nod, just in case it's her. And if Ansella can do it, then so can Neha.

I'm watching a small family of ducks slice their way across the silken water when someone taps my shoulder. A familiar face smiles at me—brown skin; long, dark hair; brown eyes.

"Lila Manzano," I say, remembering her name just in time.

She's the youngest member of the Manzano family that owns the pastelería here on Pepper Street along Hungry Heart Row. Actually, some people believe the Manzano pastelería serves magical food. I posted on my blog about it once, when I did a rundown of all the supposedly magical restaurants on Pepper Street. Lila's part of the lore too. Apparently she shows up when people are most in need with exactly what they desire. My gaze drops to the basket she holds in her hands.

She smiles. "Hello, Neha," she says in a soft, musical voice. I can't remember ever having told her who I am, but obviously I must have at some point. A long strand of hair blows in her eyes, and she smooths it away with one small

hand. "I have a delivery for you."

I look down at her basket and back into her eyes. Something smells amazing in there.

"But . . . I didn't order anything."

Lila smiles, reaches into the cloth covering whatever goodies are in the basket, and pulls out a concha. The top of the pastry is a swirl of colors—deep purple, inky blue, pink, green, gold. It reminds me of the galaxy, and I stare for a moment, mesmerized, before I take it from her.

My mouth begins to water. "This smells incredible," I say. "What do I owe you?"

"It's on the house," she says, already turning away. "Enjoy."

I want to argue, but the urge to bite into the pastry is nearly irresistible now. I've never had Mexican pastries before. But first . . . I pick up my phone from the bench and take a picture of the gorgeous creation. Then, putting it back down, I take a big bite and close my eyes. My mouth explodes with flavors and sensations—sweet, yeasty, warm. In another three bites, I've eaten the entire four-inch ball of dough and am licking my fingers.

I look up, but the park is empty. Surely Lila couldn't have disappeared so quickly? I stand up, squinting in the sun, and really concentrate. But no—she really is gone.

A light breeze tugs at the hem of my sundress, and, bemused, I sit back down on the bench. I guess that counts as my first day, eating a cuisine I've never eaten before. Mallow Park isn't exactly a restaurant, but it works, I think.

And now that I've already done my first day, it's weird. I don't feel so afraid anymore. In fact, I'm almost eager to go find a restaurant to eat at tomorrow.

Smiling, I reach for my phone again and begin to tap out a blog post.

DAY 2, THURSDAY

I sit at a table inside Manijeh's, the Persian restaurant on Hungry Heart Row. It's lunchtime and surprisingly crowded, with people lined up outside the door. I guess it was lucky I got here early and nabbed one of the last few seats.

The air is redolent with spices and that salty smell of meat that makes my stomach growl. I purposely had a very light breakfast so I could really tuck into the food here. Manijeh's is one of the best kept secrets in Rowbury. People from as far as DC come on the weekend, just hoping to get a taste, although not many people in Rowbury seem to have caught on yet. My hatred of waiting in lines is so intense, I've never even tried to get a table before.

"What can I get you, Neha?" Laleh says, her pen, notepad, and trademark smile at the ready. Laleh's almost nineteen, but we went to the same high school. Her family runs this place.

"That's one of the hardest questions I've gotten today." I make a face and stare at the menu, and she laughs. "Okay, how about . . . a plate of the chicken kebab, the ghormeh sabzi, a plate of tadeeg, and a glass of doogh?"

Laleh scribbles on her notepad and then slides it and

her pen into her apron pocket. "Great choices. You'll be full for days."

"What I'm counting on," I say, patting my stomach.

"So hey, what are you doing with your last summer before you head to college—where are you going, again?" She asks this question with a glimmer of longing in her eyes, and I remember hearing that Laleh had wanted to go off to college when she graduated too. I wonder what happened, but don't know her well enough to ask.

"Rowbury University. And just working at the library," I answer. "Nothing glamorous." It's not a secret that I help out on the library's website, although, of course, exactly what I do there is. We figured people would be more likely to write in if I stayed anonymous.

"My parents have all these plans to take me home to India, but I think we all know it's never gonna happen. They're both too busy with their web-design consultation business." I sigh.

Laleh makes a face. "I get that," she says, looking over her shoulder at the restaurant. "Family businesses. They suck up a lot of time, don't they?"

"Tell me about it."

"Speaking of, I better get back. That line's not getting any shorter or better tempered. Let me know if you need anything else, okay? Your food should be out in about fifteen minutes."

"Sounds good. Thanks, Laleh."

She waves and makes her way to the kitchen in the back.

Fifteen minutes. That's a long time to just sit at a table, isn't it? I look around. I'm tucked away to one side of the restaurant, but even so, I occasionally feel another customer's assessing eye on me. Are they judging me? Wondering where my friends are—or even pitying me for not having any? My hands slide automatically into my bag to get my phone out, and then I remember the rules: no phones. Aaaarrrgh. I have to *do* something. I can't just sit here and stare straight ahead like a weirdo.

Then, with relief, I remember that I have my makeup bag on me. Perfect. I'll touch up my . . . eyebrows. Yes. I've wanted to do that for a while, and I'm right by the window, which means the light's perfect. I pull out my makeup bag, get out my little compact, prop it open so I can see the mirror, and then go to town with my eyebrow pencil.

I feel myself relaxing as I work. No one's even looking at me anymore. All they'll see anyway is a girl doing her makeup—boring. And then, suddenly, I see his reflection behind me. My eyebrow pencil digs into my eyebrow as our eyes meet in the mirror. This is . . . like, a mirage, right? Some trick of light or something?

But then I turn and realize it's no trick. It really is him. Prem.

"Hey," he says, his black hair flopping into his eyes all sexily.

I immediately close my fist around my eyebrow pencil and hope to God my eyebrows don't look patchy or weird.

So sexy. "Oh, um, h-hi?" With my other hand, I sweep my compact quickly into my makeup bag and put it in my purse.

"I *thought* that was you," Prem says. "So you like Manijeh's too?"

"I do," I say immediately. Then I feel my cheeks flush. "Um, actually, I don't know why I said that." Except I do. I was trying to impress him. "I've never been here before, but I've heard good things, so . . ."

Prem grins in that easy, confident way of his, and my heart squeezes. "You're in for a treat. And an unhealthy addiction to the tadeeg."

I laugh, but it sounds more like Bugs Bunny choking.

"Oh, while I'm here," Prem says, sliding into the seat across from me. Aaaaarrrrghh. I've forgotten what to do with my face. And my hands (one of which is still clutching the stupid pencil, the point of which is now beginning to gouge a tiny hole in my palm). And my eyes. "Do you know where the key to the storage room is? You know, back at the library, I mean?"

I can't help but smile to myself. He's asking *me* for the key? This has to be a ploy to talk to me. Everyone knows Henrietta, the head librarian, is the one who knows all the—

"Henrietta left for the day, but I thought you might know where the spare is. Since you've worked there the longest."

Oh. Right. So maybe this isn't a ploy. The smile falls off my face.

"I actually don't know," I say, surreptitiously brushing my face with my closed fist. I'm pretty sure I can feel an eyebrow hair there. It must've dislodged earlier, when I jabbed myself with the pencil. Gross. "Sorry."

"Oh, damn," Prem says, deflating a bit. "I was really hoping to get into storage before the end of my shift. I leave at two."

"What do you need in the storage room?" I ask, eager to keep him talking and in my desperate little love-starved orbit.

He shakes his head and crinkles his nose in that adorable way of his, and I almost die right there on the table. "Just a print of one of my photographs of the Yarrow River. My roommate's always loved it, and I thought . . . Jordan's been going through a tough time lately, so." He shrugs, as if he's embarrassed to have said so much, to have cast himself as a caring friend.

Dead. I am d-e-a-d. Why, Prem, why? Why must you be talented, hot, *and* sensitive? Do you not possess a shred of mercy? Suddenly I want to run back to the library and bust that storage room door down, just to give him everything he wants. "I'm sorry I can't help you," I say instead.

"Ah, no worries." He waves me off. "I'll catch Henrietta later. I guess I'll get my lunch." Then, frowning, he leans in closer. "You have a—" He gestures to my cheek.

I swat at it. "Did I get it?"

"No, you . . . here, let me." He leans forward and, very gently, brushes my cheek with his fingers. I stare into his eyes the entire time, my heart trip-hammering, my brain completely melting into sludge. Prem is touching me. Prem's skin is touching mine. Prem's mouth is close enough to kiss. He leans back and holds out a finger. "See? Eyelash. Make a wish."

I look at his finger. It isn't an eyelash; it's a thick eyebrow hair. But he doesn't need to know that. "Really?" I ask, still not completely able to believe that I hadn't just fallen asleep and stumbled onto this amazing dream.

"Really. It's against the law to not make a wish on a fallen eyelash, you know," he says, raising his eyebrows all mock seriously.

My heart thuds out a rhythm, and the rhythm is: I. Like. You. I. Like. You. "O-okay," I say, and my voice sounds like it's coming from the end of a tunnel. Then, closing my eyes, I make a wish and blow.

When I open my eyes again, Prem's staring at me. I'm staring at him. We're both staring at each other.

This is my chance. This is it; it'll never be this perfect again.

"So, I—" I begin, not sure what to say, but not wanting this to end, either. This is part of being brave, right? Maybe I could tell Prem about my challenge to myself. Maybe I could ask him for restaurant recommendations. Maybe he'll go with me—

"So. I'll, uh, see ya," he says at the same time, his bigger voice swallowing mine. And then he pushes his chair back, stands up, and is gone.

My perfect chance is gone. I've wasted it.

I don't get to marinate in self-pity too much longer before Laleh comes back with my gigantic platter of food.

My stomach grumbles immediately and insistently. "Wow, thanks. This looks delicious!"

She grins. "Best Persian food in this part of the country. Enjoy!"

"Oh, I will—believe me." I take a picture of my plate to post on the blog later and then, without preamble, dig in. I've always found putting food on top of my feelings is a much more pleasant way to deal with any kind of crisis than actually, you know, dealing with the crisis. And in this case, I don't think you can really blame me.

The chicken kebab is moist and fragrant; the chicken chunks fall apart when I bite into them, and the aromas of turmeric and parsley flood my senses. I have to close my eyes to take in all the flavors—spicy, salty, meaty. The doogh is equally delicious; I swear I've never drunk something so creamy, so minty, so refreshing. For the few minutes that I'm eating, I actually forget that whole awkward interaction with Prem. All that exists is the food in my mouth, my ecstatically exploding taste buds, and me.

I sit back when I'm finished eating and sip the last of the doogh, my stomach pleasantly distended under my shirt. But the food endorphins (foodorphins) are fading. My head begins buzzing with discomfort again, and I feel heat creeping back into my cheeks. People are definitely staring at me. No one here is eating alone; this is the kind of place you come with your friends or family. What do they think about me, sitting alone at my table clearly intended for two? I can see the thought bubbles rising up from their heads: Did she get stood up? What's wrong with her? But I force myself to take my time with my drink. This is part of growing up, facing life full in the face. So I messed up with Prem earlier, but that doesn't mean I have to mess this up too. *Finish your meal*, I tell myself. *And don't even think about getting your makeup bag out again. Be comfortable with just being.*

But no matter how comfortable I force myself to be, I can't help but feel exposed, open, raw. This is harder than I thought. I wonder how Ansella is faring.

DAY 3, FRIDAY

For my third date with myself (I refuse to think about how pathetic that sounds) I go to the Indigenous Gastronomist, or the IG, as it's commonly called on Hungry Heart Row.

The IG is this massive, high ceilinged, open restaurant with really cool accents—like that giant painting of a buffalo herd hanging on the wall. The copper pendant lights above the bar and the exposed pale-brick walls all add a kind of modern-rustic, romantic charm that makes it a popular spot for couples on date night.

I was hoping to avoid all the happy people with hearts in their eyes by going on a Tuesday night. I'm sorry to say I misjudged.

In sharp contrast to all the happy couples, though, I catch snippets of a very heated argument between a middle-aged woman and someone who seems to be her daughter. They're off to the side, each of them wearing half aprons, but the daughter's face is flushed and her voice is ringing higher and higher, while her mother darts nervous glances around the restaurant and makes hand motions that clearly mean *Keep your voice down.* Yikes. Prickly.

The waitress, smiling stalwartly in spite of the growing commotion, says, "Follow me, please!" I dutifully do, and she seats me at a small table for two right in the middle of the restaurant. There's a crimson rose in a bud vase, and a candle flickers on the table, setting the mood. I smile and tell her it's a great seat, even though I wanted the one in the back, by the bathrooms, where I won't look like a complete loser.

Still. I look around surreptitiously while holding my menu in front of my face. There are quite a few couples here, but at least all of them seem to be completely focused on each other. No one's even noticed me. I relax a little and begin to peruse the menu. There's so much yummy food here, and all of it is farm-to-table, which—

"Neha? Is that you?"

I jerk my head up to see Eleanor Fields, who was also in the senior class at Rowbury High. I hesitate to say we went to high school together, because I'm sure the Rowbury High Eleanor-the-class-president-and-homecoming-queen knew was quite different from the one Neha-the-writer-nerd knew.

Eleanor is one of those people I want to hate, because everyone thinks she's gorgeous (tall, white, thin, blond— all markers of classic beauty in the US, amirite?), has an easy-to-pronounce name, a family who owns a million malls across the country, *and* she graduated with a 4.0 GPA. She's also one of those people who's impossible to hate, because, in spite of all of that, she's a really nice person. She always made an effort to go out of her way to talk to me.

"Hey," I say, forcing a smile and willing it not to wither as I take in the fact that Eleanor's here with a gorgeous, college-aged guy, and three other equally hot, equally well-dressed couples, all of whom are regarding me and my empty table with a mixture of pity and derision. "How's it going?"

The other three couples take a seat at the table directly across from mine. Oh great. Now I'll have to listen to them laughing and having a good time while I sit here without even my phone to keep me company. Why did I say I'd do this, again?

"Great, great," Eleanor says, walking over on her six-inch heels, her glittery clutch held in front of her. Noooo. Go away, Eleanor. Go take your seat and just pretend I don't exist like any other popular person would do. She tosses a strand of blond hair over one shoulder. "We're just doing a couples' date night, you know, before college starts up." She smiles. "You're going to Rowbury University, right? Full scholarship?"

"Yeah," I say, touched that she remembered. "And you're headed off to . . . Boston University?"

"Harvard," she corrects easily, without any arrogance. "I guess I should get ready for some freezing-cold winters."

She laughs, I laugh, and then there's a slightly awkward

pause. "Well, I should head back to . . ." She points behind her at the table, where her friends are waiting.

"Sure," I say, waving. "See you later."

Eleanor half turns and then looks back at me, hesitating. "Unless . . . You're welcome to join us if you're not waiting for anyone," she says, looking at my single place setting. "My friends would love to get to know you more."

"Oh, no . . . that's okay. Thank you, though." I smile to show I really appreciate her offer. And I do. Eleanor's got class.

"Okay." She waves one last time and walks over to her table.

I order the fragrant bison meatballs in a tart cranberry sauce to start, and then move on to other mouthwatering things—the roasted-vegetable platter sprinkled with just the right amount of herbs and pepper, and the honey-roasted rabbit, which practically falls apart on my tongue. It's all really, really good, but I can't help but think that something feels very slightly off. I can't put my finger on it, but I immediately wonder if the heated fight between the mother and daughter had anything to do with this.

And as I ponder that, eating alone while Eleanor and her friends laugh and chatter and twinkle together, the funniest thing happens—I begin to not care at all.

I don't care when people look pityingly at me, probably wondering if I'm going to cry (the assumption being, of course, that I've been stood up). I don't care when couple after couple is led to their seats, where they sit holding hands or gazing deep into each others' eyes.

I realize this *is* brave, what I'm doing, sitting here, experiencing a cuisine I've never experienced before, by myself. And I realize it *is* doing something positive for my self-confidence. Because what does it say about me, that I'm willing to do this? That I'm willing to face the raised eyebrows? That I'm willing to do what I advised my reader to do?

Only good things. Only brave things. As I pay my bill, I'm smiling to myself.

DAY 4, SATURDAY

Today's Ansella's big day. I had a message from her on the blog this morning.

Dear Dr. Ishq,

It's Saturday. The day I finally take that big step and tell the object of my affections how I really feel. And it's all thanks to you. If you hadn't pushed me to take the grand ishq adventure challenge—which I've enjoyed immensely—I would never have done this. No matter which way this goes, I've changed for the better. And for that, I'm so grateful to you.

I have another favor to ask: Would you consider coming to Mallow Park at one o'clock today before I take this big step? It would mean so much to me. I'll be the one on the bench by the Yarrow River wearing a yellow hat.

Ansella

I talk to Henrietta after I read the e-mail. We have a long chat, during which she keeps saying she thinks it'd be a good idea for me to "foster self-efficacy" by meeting Ansella. Going up to this reader and seeing the good I've done in the world, she says, will "greatly bolster your shaky self-concept."

Henrietta has a PhD in philosophy and a masters in library science (the first black woman at her university to get that distinction), she looks like Halle Berry, and she's married to a judge who looks like Idris Elba. Sometimes I feel like the world's biggest underachiever.

Anyway, I finally say, "Henrietta, I've always been anonymous. I think my readers really need to feel like I'm this nameless, faceless, omniscient person who'll never lead them wrong. I don't want to shatter that illusion for them. What if Rowbury teens everywhere go into an existential crisis because they realize I'm just as human, just as fallible, as them?"

Henrietta looks at me, her mouth twitching a little. "Thank you for that impassioned speech. I can see this means a lot to you. But just think about it, will you?"

I sag in my seat. She isn't taking me seriously. She doesn't get why I don't want to do this. Things with Prem are at a complete standstill. I need to know that this one thing in my life, this thing I'm so good at, will *stay* good. I don't want to meet Ansella and completely ruin everything.

Sighing, I stand. "Okay, fine. I'll think about it."

Henrietta smiles. "Hey, Neha. You already know you helped her. If you meet with her in person, you can really see the effects of what you've done, right?"

"I guess," I mumble as I walk out. Except I don't. I really don't need to see it. But who am I to argue with Henrietta?

After I clock out at the library, I head down to Pepper Street. I've been saving the best for last. Today I'm going to eat at the nameless carinderia run by an eccentric woman people swear is a witch. Apparently, her recipes are all really spells in disguise, able to infuse the eater with great confidence. I'm not sure if I believe that, but I'm willing to try it because her food is said to be so delicious, people talk about it for weeks after eating there.

As I walk past the hardware store, my messenger bag banging on my thigh (regular-size bags always hang really low on me, thanks to the fact that I'm vertically challenged), I think about Prem. Not a surprise, really, because I'm constantly thinking about him. This standstill we're at now . . . what if it's completely artificial? What if it's just because neither of us is being brave enough to take charge?

I mean, I know it's not just me. We *did* have a really . . . electric connection the other day at Manijeh's. I think about Ansella, about to be brave and do something really, really scary, even without me there. She thinks I'm her mentor. But what kind of mentor would I be if I didn't take my own advice? Eating alone has been really good for me, but isn't it time to face my *real* fear? Isn't it time to take matters into my own hands, to tell Prem how I feel before life leads us down divergent paths?

If Ansella can do it, I can too. I don't want to look back

on this and regret it. I'm tired of standstills. I wipe my suddenly damp palms on my jeans and take a deep breath. Yes. I'm gonna do it today. And maybe this food can help me.

In the carinderia, I wait patiently in line, looking at the comments on my phone. So many people have said they're excited for Ansella to take the next step, and I respond to tell them thanks.

I'm not going to tell anyone about my own plan to confess my feelings to Prem. If he says he doesn't feel the same way, I'll need some time to crawl away and lick my wounds. Besides, Dr. Ishq is supposed to have all this stuff figured out. People don't want to hear about my love failures.

Then it's my turn to order, and the old woman who's rumored to be a witch looks at me, her gimlet eyes sparkling, her wild and wavy hair about a foot thick on each side of her head. "Boy trouble?" she asks before I can even say a word.

I blink and slip my phone into my pocket. "How did you—"

"Soup Number Five," she says, nodding. "That is what you need. It is an aphrodisiac, you see." She smiles at me like she's got a secret, and I find myself smiling back.

"Okay then. Soup Number Five it is," I agree, handing over some cash.

I take a seat by the window and wait for my food. It's not awkward, sitting here alone, because a lot of other

customers are also eating by themselves while they read or play on their phones. I people-watch, the hustle and bustle of quick-stepping young folks with dogs on leashes or (slower) retired men and women running errands reminding me of a swarm of busy ants. I wonder what they're thinking about as they walk, whether they're lucky enough to have someone they love waiting for them at home.

"Your soup."

I look up to see a young, familiar Filipina girl setting a bowl on my table. We probably went to high school together. "Thanks," I respond, and she waves to me and disappears back into the kitchen.

Picking up my spoon, I dip it into the broth, making sure to get pieces of the small, fatty meat. I close my eyes and eat my spoonful, marveling at the rich, savory flavors. It's like beef broth, only heartier, and the meat has this really interesting texture. Before I know it, I've devoured half the bowl.

"You like Soup Number Five?"

I look up to see Lola Simeona, the old woman from earlier, standing by my table, watching me. "Oh, yes," I say, patting my mouth with a napkin. "It's delicious! What is this meat? It's like nothing I've ever tasted. And I feel more . . . energetic already, sort of like I can take on anything." Like Prem.

She smiles knowingly. "Yes, yes, Soup Number Five is magical." After a pause, during which her smile morphs into what can only be described as a mischievous grin, she says, "The meat is bull testes."

I stare at her for a long moment as her words filter into my brain. I set my spoon down carefully and take a sip of water. "Bull . . . testes?" I ask in the most neutral way I can.

"Yes! It's an aphrodisiac!" She pats my shoulder and walks off to another table. I think I can hear her cackling.

I look down into my bowl. I just ate a bunch of chopped-up bull balls. For a moment I wonder, in a very detached way (is this what being in medical shock feels like?), if I'm going to throw up. But then the moment passes, and I realize they're really delicious. And Soup No. 5 *works*. I can feel the potent mixture wending its way through my system, infusing my blood with confidence and desire. I eat another big spoonful.

And that's when I look out the window and see them.

I blink several times, because I'm not sure I'm seeing what I'm seeing. Maybe it's some weird hallucination caused by whatever's in bull testicles. Maybe I'm under-caffeinated. The bull testes lodge in my throat like a block of stone.

It's Prem and a girl with chocolate-brown hair and pale skin. They're over at the falafal stand across the street, both of them laughing at something. Prem's eyes are crinkled in that way I adore, his black hair mussed and falling in his eyes. His arm is around the girl, and she's leaning into him in this incredibly comfortable way, like she knows him really well.

I swallow and look down at my bowl. My blood, on fire just a few minutes ago, now feels like it's been doused with whatever that foamy stuff is in fire extinguishers. Even bull testicles can't help me now.

So we weren't at a standstill after all. Prem just . . . Prem just doesn't feel the same way I do. And obviously I can't do it now. I *can't* tell him how I feel when he clearly . . . he clearly likes someone else. So all that connection I thought I felt? I was wrong. I was stupidly, totally wrong.

My phone dings, and, ignoring the rule of the grand ishq adventure challenge, I pull it out of my pocket. I have another twenty-two messages on my blog, all from people telling me that they've been doing the challenge themselves.

STEMGirlinSF says it's made her more confident than she's ever been. FilmFan2020 says she and her boyfriend have both been doing it separately, and it's boosted their relationship because it's infused their lives with adventure. ComicBoyR says he's found so many great restaurants and cuisines his art feels like it's blossoming as a result. And on and on and on the messages go.

I set my phone down on the table. The grand ishq adventure, I realize fully for the first time, is not just about me or Prem or even Ansella. It's so much bigger than that. It's about daring to do what you're most afraid of doing, knowing that it could very well result in spectacular failure. It's about looking life right in the eyes and deciding to embrace it—all of it, good and bad—because to do anything less would be a waste of its gift. It's about being brave, whatever that means to you, however you define it.

I eat another big spoonful of Soup No. 5 and pat my mouth with my napkin, staring off into the middle distance. Something's shifting. I feel a swell of confidence as a bell of epiphany rings through me. I know what I'm going to do now. I'm going to meet up with Ansella after lunch, to wish her luck. Because she needs me. And because I need to see her shining, hopeful, courageous face. And then I'm going to tell Prem how I feel, even if it means being utterly rejected. Because I am Dr. Ishq. And because my life is too brilliant to waste on cowardice.

I arrive at Mallow Park right at one o'clock. My heart is racing, half in sympathetic fear for Ansella, and half because I'm terrified for myself. I texted Prem and asked him to meet me here in twenty minutes, but he hasn't responded yet. I don't want to think about whether the brown-haired girl has anything to do with his silence.

As I walk farther into the park, I can see the Yarrow River glittering like a big sparkly blue ribbon in the distance. And on its shore, sitting on the same bench I was sitting on when Lila Manzano handed me the concha, is someone in a bright yellow ball cap. Their back is to me, but I head over in that direction, smiling.

"Hi," I say to her back as I approach. "Ansella?"

She turns. But the person's not a *she* at all. Suddenly I find myself face-to-face with . . . Prem.

I stop short as he stands, unfolding himself, his eyes careful. "P-Prem? What, um, what are you . . . doing here?"

I glance at his yellow hat, confused. "Where's Ansella?"

"I have a confession," he says, biting his lip and taking a deep breath. "Um, do you want to come sit?" He gestures to the empty spot on the bench.

I walk over, my legs feeling like rubber, my brain screaming a million things at me, none of which make sense right now. He sits after I sit and turns to me so our knees are almost touching. "What's your confession?" I ask finally, thinking how the glittering reflection of the river sparkles so prettily against his brown skin.

"Neha," he says, and takes another deep breath. I take one too, feeling nervous. He looks directly into my eyes. "There is no Ansella."

I frown. "Yes, there is," I say, beginning to pull out my phone. "I had a message from her today."

"No, I mean . . ." Prem exhales and runs a hand through his hair. "Um, I'm Ansella. It's a play on Ansel Adams's first name."

My hands still, my phone forgotten. "You . . . you wrote to me on the blog?" Prem, as library staff, knew who Dr. Ishq was, of course.

"Yeah. I didn't want you to know it was me, though."

"Why not?"

Prem glances down at his feet for a long moment. Then, looking back up, he says quietly, "Because I've liked you for almost a year now. In private, in secret, without knowing how I was ever going to tell you how I felt. You're . . . you're a little intimidating, you know."

"*I* intimidate *you*?" I ask, trying not to laugh. My heart's singing a merry little melody that goes something like *Prem likes you! He's liked you for the better part of a year! La la la la la!*

"You're Dr. Ishq," he says, shrugging. "The love expert. The one with all the answers. On the blog, you always know precisely what advice to give, how to fix any love problem. And no matter how hard I tried, I couldn't tell how you felt about me."

"But . . ." I clear my throat. "I saw you, just a little while ago at the falafal stand. You were with a girl. . . ."

"Jordan?" he asks, frowning.

"Jordan? As in, your roommate?"

He nods. "I was eating the last meal in the grand ishq adventure challenge, and she stopped by to thank me for the print. I finally got Henrietta to help me access the storage room and left it for her at our place." Then, reading the expression on my face, he smiles gently. "She's, ah, like a sister to me. Very annoying, but someone I care for in a very fraternal way. Her dad fell ill recently, and I just wanted to do something nice for her."

I see the truth in his eyes and relax. Feeling suddenly shy, I look down at my hands. "So . . . you like me?"

He leans in just a touch closer. "I like you," he agrees. "A lot."

I look up at him, smiling a little. "I like you, too."

He stares at me like he can't believe what he's hearing. "Really?"

"I've liked you for a long time. Actually, I was going

to . . . to tell you how I felt today. Even though I was sure you were going to shoot me down, because I thought you and Jordan were an item."

"Why?" he asks, shaking his head. "Why would you tell me if you thought I liked someone else?"

"Because . . . because I want to live bravely. I want to wear my heart on my sleeve, even if it means I'm going to get hurt. I want to be the girl the Dr. Ishq readers think I am."

Prem grins. "Oh, you are," he says, putting his hand on mine. "You already are."

And then we're both leaning in at the same time, and this time there's no mistaking it—the electricity is undeniable. We're about to embark on our very own grand ishq adventure.

Sugar and Spite

BY RIN CHUPECO

Fifteen is an appropriate age to test for seasoning. It is not a complicated ritual, but it is an unusual rite of passage and not for the fastidious. It's a prick of a finger. It's five drops of blood. It's drizzling the blood onto sinigang—a heady soup of tamarind broth, with a savory sourness enhanced by spinach and okra, tomatoes and corms, green peppers for zest. Lola Simeona prefers stewed pork, and so that was chopped into the broth, a perfect medley of lean meat and fat.

The old women leaned close to breathe in the aroma while you nursed your wound, squeezing your fingertip. From your perspective they resembled Macbeth's witches— witches of Old Manila rather than of Scotland. Lola Simeona would undoubtedly take offense, despite knowing neither Macbeth nor Shakespeare. "Can they predict futures greater than me, hija?" she would have challenged you, in her sharp accent. "Are their curses better, aphrodisiacs stronger?"

They passed out bowls and ladled your blood-spiced soup into generous portions. You're not the first teenager they've supped on, though supply has been waning over the years. Very few children carry on old Filipino magic nowadays. Very few parents allow them the burden.

Lola Simeona had the honor of first sip. She rolled your essence in her mouth, lips puckered, tongue tasting. A wide smile spread across her wrinkled face. "Asaprán," she said. Saffron: the most expensive spice, the rarest witch. "You are made of asaprán. Just like me."

Lola Simeona had known you were special for the longest time. The ice cream on your halo-halo that you helped prepare as a child always tasted sweeter on everyone's tongue than when your mother prepared it alone, the puto bumbong chewier if you steamed it in place of your father.

But your lolas took offense at being called witches. That is an Amerikano term, they scoff, and that they live in the boroughs of an American city makes no difference to their biases. Mangkukulam was what they styled themselves as, a title still spoken of with fear in their motherland, with its suggestions of strange healing and old-world sorcery.

Nobody calls their place along Pepper Street Old Manila, either, save for the women and their frequent customers. It was a carinderia, a simple eatery folded into three food stalls; each manned by a mangkukulam, each offering unusual specialties:

Lola Teodora served kare-kare, a healthy medley of eggplant, okra, winged beans, chili peppers, oxtail, and tripe, all simmered in a rich peanut sauce and sprinkled generously with chopped crackling pork rinds. Lola Teodora was made of cumin, and her clients tiptoed into her stall, meek as mice and trembling besides, only to stride out half an hour later bursting at the seams with confidence.

But bagoong—the fermented-shrimp sauce served alongside the dish—was the real secret; for every pound of sardines you packed into the glass jars you added over three times that weight in salt and magic. In six months, the collected brine would turn reddish and pungent, the proper scent for courage. Unlike the other mangkukulam, Lola Teodora's meal had only one regular serving, no specials. No harm in encouraging a little bravery in everyone, she said, and with her careful preparations it would cause little harm, even if clients ate it all day long.

Lola Florabel was made of paprika and sold sisig: garlic, onions, chili peppers, and finely chopped vinegar-marinated pork and chicken liver, all served on a sizzling plate with a fried egg on top and calamansi for garnish. Sisig *regular* was one of the more popular dishes, though a few had blanched upon learning the meat was made from boiled pigs' cheeks and heads.

But customers who were wronged and angry, hungry for vengeance against some perceived slight, ordered the sisig *special* instead. The meal itself was a test; if they could finish the dish despite the growing infernal spiciness of each bite, then, in the mangkukulam's eyes, their revenge was justified. The pact was then sealed, with a lock of their target's hair or a fingernail clipping mixed into a tiny portion of sisig previously set aside, then smeared against a straw doll. Payment was then arranged, and it was a rare instance when her client's enemies didn't succumb to misfortune shortly after.

But if the supplicant wasn't worthy? Well, misfortune fell upon *them* instead, and they still had to pay for the meal besides. Upon learning what was required of them, most were quick to back out of the agreement, suddenly finding new reasons not to risk what happiness they had to ruin someone else's. "Humans," Lola Florabel had said, shrugging like she wasn't one herself. "Always predictable. It is only when they realize they have everything to lose that they decide that they can live without their petty vengeance."

You were quick to point out that she lost customers that way, but none of the witches seemed bothered. "It is not the money," Lola Simeona said. "It is the reputation. Who would eat at a carinderia that would serve scum like them?"

It was Lola Simeona who served their bestseller: Soup No. 5 was a horrifying concoction of bull testes and spices, yet still was the best broth this side of the city, a popular meal for the adventurous and for those who prize umami above all. Occasionally a new customer would stagger out, pale and green all at once, because Lola Simeona was never shy about telling them exactly what they were eating, and in great detail. If it tasted good, she liked to say, then why would knowing this change anything?

Lola sold Soup No. 5 *regular* at nearly all hours, closing at two a.m., only to begin again at nine the next day. Soup No. 5 regular was a picker-upper, a mood brightener. Soup No. 5 regular put people in cheerful temperaments, ready to face the day with optimism—a surprising side effect, given the cantankerous nature of the chef.

Soup No. 5 *special*, on the other hand, required a three-day notice. Soup No. 5 special began after Lola Simeona invited her client to the back of the tiny eatery for a mandatory screening. Finishing the sisig special was Lola Florabel's test; for Soup No. 5, Lola Simeona *herself* was the test.

Lola would circle the customer like a tiger eyeing prey, scrutinizing them closely as if she could glean secrets from that alone. She would fire off questions: Why do you ask for the special and not the regular like most? Who do you intend to court? What is the status of your current relationship? What are your intentions with the person you wish to pursue? She sniffed out lies like an old bloodhound, and as far as you could tell she had never been wrong.

Answer poorly, and she would dismiss you, sometimes even chase you out if your explanations disgusted her, as had happened more often than not—Lola was never shy about asking if they intended to seduce or sexually harass the object of their affections. When their guilt became obvious, she would end the interview, the nonclient kicked out with great prejudice. Lola Simeona had been taught arnis as a young girl by her own father, and while wooden sticks were not immediately available at the carinderia, straw brooms were nonetheless deadly weapons in her hands. Few people were willing to report being chased out by an old Filipina lady, especially one who was skilled at exaggerating her aches and limps on the rare instances a cop came inquiring.

But answer right, and a miracle would happen; she would visibly soften, a rare smile gracing her wrinkled face, and she fussed over her new customer, making sure they were relaxed and comfy as one could be in her small food stall before serving them her prized dish.

Lola had only ever sold Soup No. 5 special sixty or so times in her long lifetime: to husbands and wives desperate to rekindle their romance, to elderly men and women hoping to find love again, to youngsters unable to feel. They called Soup No. 5 special an aphrodisiac, but it was more than just a love philter. Soup No. 5 special didn't turn you into a raging pervert or a philandering horndog or any one of the misconceptions often associated with the word. Soup No. 5 special changed you into the person you would have to be in order to find true love, wherever that might lead.

Lola turned down food documentaries, celebrity chefs, news crews. She despised trends with all her being. Most culinary students who came asking for an apprenticeship were promptly turned down—though Lola made one notable exception by hiring a young dishwasher who came at night and left before the carinderia opened the next day. "The others come chasing glory, their personal fame," Lola said dismissively. "They bring nothing to my food. But this one—he is a good man at heart, and eager to make something of himself. You cannot improve your cooking if you feel very little need to improve yourself. He will go far, this one."

On the other hand, you loved reality cooking shows, baking competitions, *No Reservations* reruns. You wanted to be paid to travel the world and eat culture. You wanted to fall in love with shakshuka on a boat to Tunisia, with Belon oysters atop the Eiffel Tower, with xalwo at a Somali wedding. *What's wrong with wanting to explore everything through flavors?* you asked. *Isn't the point of Old Manila exactly that?*

But Lola would scoff and wave her hand like that explained everything, when it only explained nothing.

The first time you were allowed to observe the rituals of Soup No. 5 was with a man unhappy with his marriage, wanting a second chance with his distant wife. He was well dressed, arriving in an expensive suit and tie after what appeared to be a hard day's work, a Bluetooth device still tucked by his ear. Something was missing in his life, he explained, and try as he might, he did not know what that was. Lola Simeona was satisfied by his sincerity. "This shall take you down a road you may not expect to go," she warned, setting the broth before him. "A sip means there is no going back."

He sipped, and finished the soup in twenty minutes.

It was two weeks later, after the scandal broke of the ImmersiTech CEO who had left his wife for a male accountant, that you remembered him. Lola Simeona had beamed with pride at the news. "He's happier now, Ami. No one else can determine that for him anymore. He will still be a rich man, and with the money he makes for them, they will still allow him to build his little applications—"

"Apps," you corrected her, and she shrugged.

"—but now he will find better peace in his life, even though it will not be with the wife as he had thought. Tara, Ami. He has found his happiness, but we will have to work harder for ours."

You called Florabel and Teodora lola out of respect, but Lola Simeona was your real grandmother. Her son, your father, was a nurse and had no instinct for cooking, the magic apparently skipping a generation. Both your parents worked long night shifts at the hospital, and it was Lola who looked after you while they were away.

Your father was delighted to learn you were spending your days at the carinderia. "Your lola isn't always the nicest lady, but she's kind when she wants to be, and she's an excellent cook," he explained to you once. "I'm glad she wants to teach you. I've never seen her in better spirits."

Lola's life revolved around cooking. She didn't have many friends outside Pepper Street, save perhaps for Mrs. Maymoona Jamal from the recipe club, with the granddaughter who was an award-winning filmmaker, and the sweet old lady at the taqueria, who she liked to trade a bowl of Soup No. 5 with for a beef suadero taco. When she died,

Lola liked to say, she wanted her wake at the carinderia, because she *was* the carinderia, and to honor her is to honor *that*, and while her son and daughter-in-law made enough money, she wanted people to come and play cards and gamble by her coffin like they did in the Philippines when funeral costs needed to be paid.

You were never sure if she was joking. Lola was the type of person you felt was going to live forever.

There was more to the magic than just cooking. The day after you became her apprentice, and a week after your seasoning test, she began teaching you how to read people: tics, hand gestures, signs of discomfort at direct questions. Lola Simeona played mahjong, blackjack, poker. She would have earned more at professional tournaments than at the carinderia if she wanted to.

You were disappointed that there weren't more spells involved, but Lola was a pragmatic woman. "All the magic you need is in here," she told you, wriggling her fingers. "It requires no thinking, only practice. Learning to read people—that will take time to master also. You need to understand human nature, hija—both the good and the bad."

But wasn't this being deceptive, all the same?

She looked offended. "Panloloko? No, no. Every one of my clients who have shown me that they are worthy have always gotten what they came for. My magic is real. It is in our bones, Ami, ever since the old days where datu ruled the islands and there were no white-skinned Kastila come to tell our people they were nothing more than servants. No

Kastila, no Amerikano, no Hapones. We are made of spells. Walang panloloko dyan. No deceit. My conscience is clear." She turned to the simmering pot at the counter. "At the very least, they all get a good meal. Practice, Ami. There is no talent without practice."

And practice you did. You hacked at livers and pig brains for sisig, spent hours over a hot stove for the perfect sourness to sinigang. You dug out intestines and wound them around bamboo sticks for grilled isaw, and monitored egg incubation times to make balut.

Lola didn't frequent clean and well-lit farmers markets. Instead, you accompanied her to a Filipino palengke, a makeshift union of vendors who occasionally set up shop near Mandrake Bridge and fled at the first sight of a police uniform. Popular features of such a palengke included slippery floors slicked with unknown ichor; wet, shabby stalls piled high with entrails and meat underneath flickering light bulbs; and enough health code violations to chase away more gentrification in the area. Your grandmother ruled here like some dark sorceress and was treated by the vendors with the reverence of one.

You learned how to make the crackled pork strips they called crispy pata, the pickled-sour raw kilawin fish, the perfect full-bodied peanuty sauce for the oxtail in your kare-kare. One day, after you have mastered them all, you will decide on a specialty of your own and conduct your own tests for the worthy. Asaprán witches have too much magic in their blood, and not all their meals are suitable for consumption. Like candy and heartbreak, moderation is key.

And after all, recipes are much like spells, aren't they? Instead of eyes of newt and wings of bat they are now a quarter kilo of marrow and a pound of garlic, boiled for hours until the meat melts off their bones. Pots have replaced cauldrons, but the attention to detail remains constant.

There was only one rule to being a mangkukulam, Lola told you. Never make it personal. There can be no hidden vendettas, no taking advantage of the magic to cause mischief or harm to someone else.

Even when they deserved it?

"Would people trust a judge who takes matters into their own hands?" Lola Simeona asked. "Would customers trust a cook who killed someone she calls a criminal, knowing that the cook can look into their own souls and see more potential criminals hiding within?"

Lola Simeona let you prepare Soup No. 5 regular for the first time two years into your apprenticeship at seventeen years old. Your customers praised it, and she beamed. "You are stronger in the spells than even I am, hija," she said.

The first time you brought it to school, Steven de Guzman grabbed your lunch out of your hands and tossed it into the trash. "Testicle Girl," he sneered, and for the greater part of two weeks, before he grew tired and looked elsewhere for new cruelties, that was your name. Testicle Girl. Testicle Girl. Amihan Anna Dimatibag was already a mouthful to say, and when the novelty of Testicle Girl faded, he resumed mocking your actual name, gargling it in his throat like it was gibberish. He and his friends laughed at your dark skin, at your hobbit height, at the accents your family carried around that thirty years living in America couldn't slough off their tongue. In another two weeks, he would find something else to mock you for.

The rest of your classmates watched, said nothing.

Your grandmother found their bullying irrelevant. "Pay them no attention, Ami," she would say, though you knew that was easier said than done. "People who pick on others have a rot inside of them the same way bad fruits bruise faster and poor vegetables wither quicker. They are more susceptible to magic, more inclined to break the longer they live. They will get their karma in due time. Let God deal with them."

People, your grandmother always liked to say, were viands made from only three fundamental ingredients: the salt of their blood, the spice of their bones, and the venom in their veins. The latter was the most important; poison, she added, gave character.

But karma's flight was delayed, apparently indefinitely, so when Steven did it again the next day and several people started laughing along with him, you wound up eating your lunch at the library for the next two weeks. All through that first week, you hid your face behind the largest book you could find, so no one else could see you cry. But by the second week you were angry. Something had hatched inside you, coiled around your chest, with rage in every heartbeat. It wasn't fair. It wasn't *fair*.

Lola Simeona herself was a potent toxin. You were slicing pork strips to make liempo when an elderly Japanese man came tearing out of the shop as fast as his old legs could carry him. Not far behind was your grandmother, eyes bulging with rage, armed with a fistful of knife, just as slow as her prey. "Putangina mong Hapon ka!" she screeched. "Papatayin kita!"

The Japanese man had fought in the imperial army during the Second World War. He was no longer the young soldier Lola had encountered in the forests of Bataan, her beloved province, but she had recognized him and his atrocities all the same.

"He escaped," she snarled later on, a hot cup of salabat tea cradled in her veined hands, her attempts at homicide thwarted by the law and a sympathetic but firm-handed cop. "I killed his men, but he escaped."

Bits of the story trickled out, Lola Florabel and Lola Teodora cobbling them together for you because Lola refused to. Your lola had been a young girl forced to cook for the soldiers who had invaded her village, forced to sample the meals herself to prove their harmlessness. The men died anyway, their bodies twisted in agony like the kabantigi plants in her old garden. Lola Simeona said little else about her time with the invaders, only that she had killed them in the end.

The Japanese were a superstitious lot. Her village had

been left alone after that, in the four months before the war ended.

But later that night, when the noise of the city had died down to sporadic sirens, you heard her crying. For the girl she might have been, for a pain that knew no passage of time.

You did your best to be a good student. You chopped and cooked and measured and served according to her wishes. But sometimes you wondered if the stall could stand to be upgraded with modern comfort food. With pandan ensaymada instead of the increasingly popular but also growingly common ube, the bread fresh from the oven and the cheese still melting, sweetly fragrant from the infusion of those steeped leaves and as simple as a summer morning. Or chopped watermelons in bulalo soup to replace tomatoes, for that extra tang. Or even pork adobo, but with chili and sweet pineapples. You had so many ideas.

Some people at school still gave you a hard time over your choice of meals. Since learning that making bull testicle soup was your main family business, many had been relentless. "How many cows have you sucked off today, ho?" Steven de Guzman would taunt you. Other people joined in too—Gary McLeroy and Mike Bayer loved to dump your lunch on the floor like de Guzman did, and Lani Noda would turn her nose up and announce very loudly that you were stinking up the whole class because you smelled like what you ate—but it was de Guzman who made it a habit, who made it personal, who made it his life's work to make yours miserable.

Most just watched—worse, sometimes they walked away.

It was easier when you brought in ube rolls, fried lumpia spring rolls, pancit noodles. Normal-looking food. Fusion-looking food. Food that didn't have to be made from animal extremities or brains. Food that didn't look like it was cooked from them. Everyone knew and liked adobo, even if Steven de Guzman would never admit to it. Some days, when your lunch looked like it could pass for everyone else's, he would even leave you alone. Things were always easier when your food could be mistaken for food that didn't stand out.

It's not like you ate Filipino food all the time. You loved Emperor's Way takeout, and the friendly Chinese girl there who you were too shy to ask but whose name tag said to call her Ming always gave you extra sauce for your orange chicken. The sweet potato pie from Butter was absolutely to die for, and it made you feel soft and warm the same way Lola's leche flan did. The youngest Manzano once handed you a delicious pastry without prompting or demanding payment before drifting away, seemingly lost in a world of her own. If this was a marketing strategy for their pastelería, it worked.

But you could tell that there were differences in the way they cooked and baked, that they took old and treasured recipes and put in their own unique, *modern* spin to them. Why couldn't you do the same?

And so you made ube ensaymada without your grandmother knowing and lugged containers of it to school the next day. You had baked enough of the brioche for a small army; you ran out in ten minutes, and Lani even apologized to you shortly after.

(But had you added spells to the food without meaning to, and was that why she was sorry—or was the food just that good? You were made of magic, Lola said, but this kind of magic didn't come with instruction manuals.)

Lola Simeona caught you experimenting with adobo casserole the day after; her anger was immediate. American food—*bland food*, she sneered—wasn't potent enough, and your fusion concept watered any spells down. "Why would you add adobo to Kano cuisine?" she snapped at you. "They have no taste buds that they had not stolen from those darker than them first! You dilute our magic, hija!"

She showed you how to make her special adobo recipe—*proper* adobo, with soy sauce and vinegar and spices—and it tasted exquisite, better than any other grandmother would have made. She offered both meals for free to the carinderia's clientele that day, much to their delight. Sampling your casserole brought them no perceptible changes; eating Lola's adobo left them fresh, eager, and thrumming with energy, exhaustion falling away like a discarded cloak.

She let you watch the customers eat, long enough to get her point across, before taking pity on you and announcing that she was adding something new to the menu, and that you had made it.

* * *

The dinuguan was your own recipe, made with no help from your grandmother, and it was the first official viand at the carinderia that was truly yours. It was pork belly cubes and sautéed garlic and onions and banana peppers in a rich savory blood stew. Dinuguan was an alarming dish even by bizarre standards, but the regulars who came to your lola's stall were always ready to try new things, and many wound up asking for seconds with their rice.

You'd introduced a spell for better concentration into the savory stew. With exams coming up, it was a welcome addition to many. Lola Simeona assured you it was one of the best she'd ever had.

There's a quiet sort of pride there, creating things with your hands that people take pleasure in.

She made you bring the rest of the adobo to school the next day—to keep your spirits up, she said—along with some of the leftover dinuguan. You tried to hide the latter, pretending to buy the cafeteria lunch, but Steven saw right through your ruse. He snatched it away, opened the Tupperware, and gagged at the sight of the thick, bloody stew within. "You're literally a bloodsucker, you disgusting monkey," he said, and lobbed the whole container at your face.

"She slipped," he said, and no one bothered to say differently.

It took hours to get the stains out of your dress.

* * *

Never make it personal, Lola had said.

You couldn't make it personal, but you were still dripping in blood by the time you arrived home and up for planning a revenge that was a long time coming. You knew exactly what to do—you'd put the spell in an ube roll, because the last time you brought that to school, he had eaten it instead of throwing it away. People like him were more susceptible to magic, you remembered. It will break them in the long run, Lola had said.

You waited until after dinner, after Lola Simeona had returned to the carinderia. You entered the kitchen and turned on the lights before opening the window, so that the fresh telltale smell of baking bread would drift out and be lost amid the blaring horns of the noisy street below. But in the moments before the sounds of traffic wafted in, she spoke up.

"You are walking on dangerous ground." Lola was dressed in her flannel gown, long white hair pinned to her head with half a dozen rollers. You didn't know if she'd anticipated your move and asked Lola Teodora to cover for her at the stall, or if this was an unfortunate coincidence (though coincidences never seemed to apply when it came to your grandmother). Neither explanation detracted from her quiet fury, at the bunched way her shoulders rolled forward. "How dare you disobey me."

You didn't mean to. You only wanted—

"What you want is your own selfishness!" She stepped forward—she would never hit you, but when she jerked her arm back as if she might, you flinched all the same. "Do you seriously think that there are no responsibilities that come with our kulam? Why do you think I select my customers carefully, though I can make more money cooking for everyone without prejudice?"

This was different. You were maybe only going to give Steven de Guzman acne to last until his sixties. Or an untreatable hernia, maybe take away his sense of taste. He was hurting you. Just like the Japanese soldiers had—

Lola Simeona's face twisted, wrinkled skin and hooded eyes suddenly grotesque under the fluorescent light. "How dare you think it is the same thing." Her voice was quiet, as dead as the hour. "Did the boys do to you what those Hapones did to my village? To the children living there? To my family? You get bullied in school, and you think it is exactly the same?"

She yanked the refrigerator door open and snatched up a plate of sisig special that Lola Florabel had prepared beforehand, and you realized she had anticipated this. A granddaughter was easier to read than customers. "Do you think you are worthy enough to seek your revenge? Then come here, Ami. Show me. Eat."

The sisig was cold, but it built bonfires in your mouth all the same. Barely halfway through and already you were struggling, throat burning for a gasp of water, begging for a second of relief. Two more bites and you surrendered, gulping down the milk Lola had set down on the table, the rest of the meal unfinished.

Lola watched you drain the glass, her dark eyes a mystery. "Clean this up," she said brusquely, gesturing at the mess on the table, and left without another word.

When you came home from school the next day, Lola Simeona was not in the carinderia—only the second time she'd ever missed work, the first being just the night before. "She's gone to your school," Lola Teodora informed you. "She never said why, or when she'd be back."

Despite their busy schedules, it was always your parents who went to your school's PTA meetings, the ones who'd always dealt with teachers and principals and administrators. Your grandmother had never set foot there before, and for good reason. You were certain she would wind up traumatizing some of the students, and wondered how your parents would react if it was bad enough for the principal to call, probably begging for help.

By the time you arrived back at school, Lola was already leaving the principal's office. You could tell she was unhappy, with her lips pursed and her left eye twitching. The principal stood behind her, still murmuring apologetic platitudes until she cut him off with a curt "There is nothing more you can say to me that will change my opinion of you, or of this place."

You didn't know what had happened, but from their reactions it was clear your lola had gained the upper hand somehow. You wanted to apologize. You wanted to thank her. You wanted to know if you'd been expelled. You

already knew nobody else was being punished, but at the
moment it didn't matter. She'd come to help you, and that
was more than anyone else had done.

She showed no surprise upon seeing you, only raised her
head haughtily. "Come on, Ami. We are going home."

Lola closed up shop at six p.m. that day—again, another
first. Six p.m. was one of your busiest hours.

Now the three women sat at the table like they once had
two years ago, but it was not for you to season their soup
with your blood. "I had a talk with your principal," Lola
Simeona began, nose all scrunched up, and you were almost
tempted to ask if she'd scared him enough to ban her from
school. "He asked me to schedule a meeting, to talk to him
at another time, but I said that this will not wait. But in the
end, it was a waste of my time. None of the teachers have
helped you. None of your classmates have helped you. And
your principal says he can do very little."

Some of your classmates tried, but there was only so
much they could do before they became targets themselves.
Your grandmother dismissed the defense with a wave of her
hand. "They were not successful. That was all that matters."

She fell silent, thinking. The carinderia was quiet, an
open grave despite the busy sounds of other nearby shops,
as if an invisible barrier lay between you and them and could
not be breached. "And do you still wish to create your"—
her mouth turned up in a sneer without her realizing it—
"your casseroles? Your ube ensaymadas?"

Yes. You still wanted to make them.

"And do you still want to seek revenge on the boy because you think it is the same as—"

No! No, there was no equivalence there. Not at all. Nothing could compare to what the Japanese had done. But you had the right to not be bullied all the same, to be treated like everyone else. You had the right to defend your-self and the right to feel safe in your own school, and just because it was not as bad as other things didn't mean you had to endure and suffer for it.

You could not be an asaprán witch if all you could show for your troubles was being constantly bullied for the food you worked hard to make. It wasn't fair to have dinuguan, kare-kare, Soup No. 5, or papaitan thrown in your face at least once every two weeks. It wasn't fair that people only approached you when you had free food to give—free food they didn't deem too weird to eat, anyway—but turned their backs when you didn't.

You could not be a mangkukulam if you commanded no respect, if you could not make them see why you should be respected. You could not be a good cook if you relied always on your lola's instructions but were not allowed to experi-ment on your own. It could not be your meals and it could not be your magic if all you did was follow a list you had no creative control over. It could not be your own magic if it could not be your own recipes. Fusion and all, even if they turned out to be watered down.

Lola Simeona, Lola Florabel, and Lola Teodora watched you silently after you had finished your diatribe. And then their mouths lifted in unison, and on the speckled seabed of their faces their smiles shone like pearls.

"I lied," Lola Simeona said, then corrected herself. "No, I only kept part of the truth from you. The rule is that we cannot make this personal, that we cannot bear our own grudges. We cannot abuse the magic. We cannot be cruel.

"But we cannot always mask our spite with sugar. We cannot allow transgressions against us to pass. We are allowed to defend ourselves. I wanted to see how far you would go outside the boundaries we set up, if you would come to the same conclusions yourself. I killed the Hapones, after all, because they had made it personal."

(You should have known all along. The story about your lola and the Japanese—she had broken the same rules she had imposed on you, was waiting all this time for you to piece it together.)

"I asked you once if people would trust a judge who takes matters into their own hands," Lola said, and you realized she was expecting an answer. "If you would trust the chef who sees potential criminals in every soul."

You remembered your customers' tendencies to ignore your lola's strange quirks, the way they turned away when she had chased the Japanese man out long before they knew who he had been to her. You remembered classmates who had looked away from your bullying, but were eager all the same to accept the ensaymada you handed out.

Yes, you decided. Because people were selfish, even if they didn't mean to be. As long as they could have their ube rolls and ensaymada, they'd look away. It was not fair—but neither should you be.

Because sometimes real justice can't wait for karma.

Because, like your lola's with the Japanese, your conscience is clear.

Lola Simeona leaned back, her pride apparent for all to see. *Even when they deserved it?* you remembered asking, all those months ago. Lola never did answer that question. "Now you understand human nature," she said. "Now you understand why civility is not always the best option."

You were going to make mistakes, you knew. Your ideas, your recipes, were an untried concept at the carinderia—not because the magic was weaker, but because they'd never been done this way before, and no one but you knew where exactly to begin. Tradition wasn't bad, but it wasn't a leash; it was a guideline for other things that could be just as delicious.

Lola Simeona had made her thoughts very clear on the matter—turn your recipes into spells that were as good as hers or even better, and she would gladly support your creations at the carinderia. It was only a matter of time—you were certain. Already she had taken a shine to your chili pork adobo, though she wasn't ready to admit it yet.

The next morning, you brought your freshly baked ube rolls to school. And when Steven de Guzman took his first bite, you couldn't help but smile.

Moments to Return

BY ADI ALSAID

The hostess led me toward a two-person table in the middle of the dim-sum restaurant I had hoped would cure me of my fear of death.

I looked at the tables I passed, each dish at the restaurant a love letter to garlic and chili and oil. A shrine to steam and starch and meat. By the time I took a seat, my mouth was watering, even though I still didn't know what the hell dim sum technically was. I knew it had something to do with serving tea, and that it was a centuries-old tradition, which in my desperate mind made its supposed magical properties somewhat more plausible. I avoided research that might tell me otherwise so that I could hang on to my belief.

I couldn't go on the way I had been, couldn't face my brothers again until I'd changed.

The menu at the restaurant was an electronic tablet, about ten pages to flip through. Most items were phonetically translated from Chinese or just listed one or two ingredients with no further explanation as to how the dish was presented. There were a handful of pictures, but I couldn't tell which picture went along with which dish. I looked around at the other tables, noticed the way the light was coming in through the large pane of glass at the front of the restaurant and joining the too-bright bulbs overhead. Not a shadow to the place, all these human faces lit up to their fullest detail. Wrinkles and the lack of them, scars, dominant genetic traits and recessive ones, lives leading up to this moment and unfurling afterward, each toward the same final destination.

I had been in the US for all of two hours and had already felt myself on the verge of oblivion twice. My hostel room was cramped, but elegant in that we're-a-hostel-trying-to-be-cool-but-without-spending-any-money way. I took a seat on the bed and ran a hand over the white linen, smoothing out the wrinkles caused by my weight. All five fingers felt the coolness of the strange sheet, a miracle of a sensation. My brain reminded me that it was a gift I'd eventually have to return. Oblivion number one. I stayed put for nearly an hour, unable to pull myself out of the whirlpool of my thoughts.

When hunger finally untethered me, I begrudgingly plugged in the hostel's Wi-Fi password so I could look up how to get to Hungry Heart Row. It had been nice to not have the use of cell service since landing, to look around at this new country I'd read so much about, consumed so much of, had never had much interest in seeing personally. One by one, my apps sent me complaints that I'd been away. My group chat with friends had 243 messages. There were three from my mom, prying in that passive-aggressive way that was trying not to pry. I decided to call her after I got some food in me.

I reached into my backpack and found the little notebook I used to write things down in at work back in Kotor. When I'd first started giving tours of Old Town, I thought I would fill tons of the pocket-size pads, one a day maybe. I'd envisioned stockades of them overflowing from my little room, spilling out from drawers, full of the wisdom of strangers from across the world. But that same eighty-page notebook had been with me for all three summers since I started working for the cruise companies.

The tourists were boring, sure. They spoke too quickly in languages I only had a slippery grasp of, and half of what they said were the same complaints, the same observations of Old Town's cuteness. "Oh, the mountains, the water." I could say that in a dozen languages at this point. But I'd never filled the notebook for a strange and simple reason: The corner of each page had a little illustration of a tiny dancing skeleton. I hadn't given it much thought when I bought it, and I have no idea why it was even there, I must have bought it sometime around Halloween. It kept me from reaching for the notebook as much as I could have, so tourist observations had gone mostly unrecorded, except for the rare occasion when I felt stronger than the grave.

The main example, of course, were the words that would fix me, or at least unlock a way in which I could be okay with it all, stop thinking those same thoughts and enjoy my fortunate life: Qing Xian Yuan.

The Internet told me that the restaurant was a short enough walk from the hostel, just across the river. After that first fall into oblivion, I pictured myself succumbing again, this time in public. The river's murky depths could do it, or a walk past a funeral home, an advertisement in a pharmacy window; the world was full of its reminders, innocuous to so many but not to me. I downloaded a few podcasts and a fresh music playlist, so as not to give my thoughts too much freedom to take over. But I kept the desire to disappear into my headphones at bay, curious about the voices out in the hall and the reception area of the hostel. I closed the door behind me, and as the voices got more and more distinct, I felt around for a familiar accent. I like talking to people. I like foreignness. That is why I loved my job, despite the boring tourists. Small talk is mostly banal, but the potential to break through the small talk is exciting, and redemptive. I don't really know what I live for, but if I can point at anything it is this. A conversation with a stranger that can turn into a friendship. If not that, then just a memorable conversation. If we all die and our lives are forgotten, it is these conversations that make an impression on the deletable history of the world.

When I identified the soft lilt of a French tongue in the hostel's lobby, the clipped vowels of a German accent, I started thinking about languages. How long they went on for. How long my timeline was compared to theirs. I felt that familiar panic building in my chest and rushed past the two girls sitting at a table and the group of three checking in, their hiking backpacks leaning at their feet. I slipped on my headphones, hit play on the first thing that could keep my mind from churning, pushed open the door to the outside world. Oblivion number two.

Like most people, I don't remember the exact moment when I became aware of my mortality. The knowledge came to me early in childhood, I'm sure, but was relegated to some nebulous future thing I wouldn't have to worry about for a long time. Since the day of the swim, though, it has been hard to forget. Every time I look at my brothers and remember that they were born at a time when bombs were falling, and how fragile the human body is. Every time I remember the swim, and how one prolonged cramp could have pulled me under and ended things. A mere mention of the stars and how they would take millions of lifetimes to reach.

Some days there are panic attacks and the inevitable sink into oblivion, moments when all I can do is picture what it will be like to not exist, what it will be like to give back this life I've been granted. Other days it is just a quiet hum in the back of my mind, a frequency that I can tune out if nothing calls attention to it, and which I can escape with a number of distractions—books, television, conversation.

But the hum has gotten progressively louder, and the panic attacks more frequent. Miljan and Radan had started noticing the way I would get up quietly and go to the bathroom until an episode would pass, noticed me never taking my headphones off. When it started happening at work more and more, I knew that I couldn't keep going this way.

I have had a good life. The one thing that I wanted to change was simply knowledge, the same knowledge everyone else had. The knowledge that others seemed to be able to live with but which had constantly frozen me, which had repeatedly marred my otherwise fortunate life. Death would wipe everything away. I didn't even want to defeat death; I just wanted that knowledge gone.

It was easy to find the Swede's writing in my little notebook. He'd used a red pen, and his neat penmanship stood out starkly against my scrawling thoughts in black-inked Serbian—Qing Xian Yuan. My cure, maybe, the catalyst for this whole trip.

At first I was sure the guy had been drunk or on something stronger. The stuff he was saying. Then curiosity got the best of me, and I googled the city of Rowbury, found that blog post. It was written by a Dr. Ishq, detailing all the rumored magical restaurants in the district. The tone had been lighthearted, but there seemed to be real legends surrounding the place and its food. I'd found a review site called Served and a list of exactly how many places there were in the neighborhood.

That led to a descent into the Internet wormhole: reviews, more blog posts, the most far-fetched corners of the Internet, where conspiracies blossomed. I don't know why the Swede chose to highlight the dim-sum place out of all the others, or why I didn't close out of the all-too-many Internet browser tabs and focus on something productive and rational. I kept at it for over a week, until suddenly a plan formed. I'd use my savings to travel. I'd start in the US, a country I'd previously had no interest in. I'd go to this one place first, and then, perhaps, hopefully, I could see the world and be in the world in a way I had never before.

In the morning, when those thoughts I hated surfaced, the theory of magical restaurants was how I kept them at a background hum instead of a full-fledged attack on my day. When waiting for the tourists to unload from the cruise, as if the boat were puking them up, the theory was how I kept myself from falling into oblivion. Magical food. A cure. The thought that I could simply wish away my fear was too tempting to ignore.

"All food is magical, of course," the Swede had said in his near-perfect English, a slick smile on his face, like he'd used the line before. "This is something else, though."

In Kotor, I would wake up and be surrounded by beauty. In the evenings before I disappeared back into home, I was looking out at beauty. The mountains were there; the water was there. In the summer the tourists were everywhere, and many of them were beautiful too. The cats that walked the city, lapping at milk that everyone left out for them, they were beautiful. My country's history, not so much. There was ugliness there, and there is still ugliness around in the world now. In this country too, where they sweep their past so desperately under the carpet like so much dust.

I was lucky to be in my little pocket of beauty in Kotor, lucky to be in that pocket of the country, that pocket of time, that pocket of my family. All three (country, time, family) had experienced much more ugliness, and probably much less beauty. Yet my thoughts superimposed death over all of it. Everyone else seemed to be able to live without the constant awareness, and I wanted Qing Xian Yuan to wipe it clean. I wanted to be able to embrace my good fortune, the way my brothers had.

I noticed a tendril of steam rising a few tables over, followed it down to a large bowl of soup. A group of three Asian guys about my age, maybe a little older, were using chopsticks to pull things out of the bowl, or alternately dipping some unrecognizable morsel back in, letting the juices drip for a second, then popping it into their mouths.

One of them closed his eyes for a moment as he chewed, his tongue darting out slightly to lick his lips. He shook his head as if he couldn't believe what he was going through, a small golden hoop in his ear dangling with the motion. Was it magic being granted, or just simple joy?

When the waiter came by, I pointed at the soup the guys were eating and said, "I want that."

"You sure, man? It's spicy."

The word made me pause. I looked down at the electronic tablet again and shrugged.

"It's a soup, yeah?"

"No, man. It's not a soup. You don't want some dim sum or something instead?"

He offered no clues as to what dim sum might be. I felt my stomach lurch. "Yes?" I tried to laugh it off. "I'll take the not-soup, and one dim sum."

The waiter chuckled again and motioned for my tablet. "How about some soup dumplings?"

"Yes, okay."

"Pork or shrimp?"

I remembered reading a series of tweets from someone who'd come to Hungry Heart Row and, after eating pork tamales, swore that their wishes kept coming true. "Pork."

The waiter tapped on the screen a few times and then bolted away toward another table in the back. I was left with the din of the restaurant. Music playing softly from somewhere, the clink of chopsticks and spoons. People gathered around the hostess stand, talking, looking at their phones. I could hardly believe where I was in the world, and why. So many people in Kotor never exited a two-hundred-kilometer radius of the world.

Although that was probably true of people in the restaurant, too, true of most human beings. They stayed within their limited lives. Even I had done it for most of my life and was lucky now to be in a different corner of the world, experiencing new and exciting things. My appreciation should not be dependent on magic. It should not be dependent on forgetting death. And yet.

I examined the sauce bottles at the edge of the table and poured some out into the little container in front of me. I stuck my pinky in the dark liquid, gave it a sniff then a lick. It wasn't soy sauce, which was maybe the only legitimately Asian thing I'd ever eaten, so I didn't know what it was at all.

To my right there was a black kid taking out these little pockets of food from one of three bamboo steamers and taking notes as he ate, big, clunky headphones covering his ears. To my left a couple in business attire scrolled through their phones and took distracted sips from tiny ceramic teacups. I poured a different sauce directly onto my pinky finger this time, tasted nothing but heat. I coughed and scrambled for a sip of cold water. The black kid looked up at me, lifting one half of his headphones slightly off his ear. "You okay?"

I was about to simply nod and smile and return to my thoughts, but then I felt the urge for more. I thought: The next few months there'll be none of Miljan and Radan. No parents, no friends to provide the conversations that could get my mind off death. No Swedes or tourists coming off in hordes from their cruises. No constant companionship of the cats in Kotor, which were mostly strays but not quite homeless, since everyone in town treated each cat as their own. Just me and my thoughts. If I let them in, they'd be my only company.

I took a gulp of water, tried to act as American cool as possible. "Yeah. It's just we don't have this level of spice where I'm from."

"Where's that?"

"Montenegro," I said, almost like a question. I had assumptions about Americans hearing about foreigners, prepared for their defensiveness and hostility at once, especially since I sound like a drunken Russian when I speak English. But I wasn't quite sure how that applied to black Americans, who were viewed like foreigners in their own land. Even *I* knew that, though Americans liked to sweep that under the carpet. "Next to Serbia."

The boy smirked. "I know where it is. I took a geography quiz once and got one seventy-five out of one hundred."

"How'd you do in math?"

He laughed, and a knot that had been forming in my stomach the more my thoughts raged now eased. If death couldn't be wished away, this would be my other request: to find conversations like these, strangers who offered at least the prospect of momentary forgetfulness. That was the only thing that worked when the episodes started coming at work, at school, at home. At school, I got in trouble when an episode came during a test and I started talking to the girl sitting next to me. I got a few bad reviews from tourists saying I was "uncomfortably chatty," and my boss had to warn me to stick to facts and rehearsed anecdotes. I tried to talk to the tourists, tried to talk to Miljan and Radan, who were suspicious of the new behavior.

"That was good, man." The kid looked down at his notebook, then a silence fell between us. The restaurant was loud with chatter, but it still felt like silence. Silence always brought back the thoughts. And the moment of his laughter was now gone, returned to the universe.

The kid bit his lip, then grabbed the pen resting by his plate and jotted something down. He kept his headphone slightly off, though, a faint thump of music reaching me.

"What are you doing?" I asked, pointing at the notebook.

He tapped his pen against the edge of the table. "This? No, it's nothing, just a little research." He waved his hand at the notebook as if he could make it disappear, laid his arms over it. "What brings you to town?"

When I'd told my parents I was leaving, my dad smiled and nodded like he knew it was coming. Mom cried a little but kept it together, muttering jokes about how it had been a mistake to let me work for the cruise companies. They were sure that I was never going to come back, and I almost told them that if I discovered the fear of mortality did not follow me, I might stay gone. I'd laid out my plans instead, to give them some details to hang on to.

"America? Why there?" Dad had said. "I thought you were interested in speaking Spanish."

What could I have said? *I'm afraid of death wiping me out, and there's a restaurant that might help with that?* "Cheap flight," I'd said with a shrug. "I won't stay there long." Then I dived into a list of places I wanted to go, distracted them and myself from the reason for this first stop.

My parents and I did not talk about the bombs or the days without food; we did not talk about fears or mortality. The only time I had ever told anyone was when Miljan found me outside the house, just a few weeks before the Swede. I was curled up on the concrete dock by the bay, almost catatonic, unable to shake the oblivion from my mind. He'd had to shake me for five minutes before I came to and admitted what had happened. Since that day he'd looked at me like I was damaged, cracking jokes about death constantly.

I thought of going down the path of distraction again with the kid sitting next to me. It was my one imperfect weapon. To force my brain to focus on something else. It only worked for spurts at a time, which was why I loved the summers in Kotor, being distracted by the tourists. It's why I listened to podcasts and music and dove into the Internet as often as possible. There was always something ready to pull me back toward death, though—a song lyric, an anecdote about a dead grandparent, the mere mention of a disease. I could make up some other answer instead of the truth, since thinking about the cure was in a way thinking about death too.

But then I thought of how the moment would be gone soon, how quickly I'd have to hand it back to the constantly taking universe. The universe which had almost taken away my brothers and my parents, the universe which took day in and day out, which could have taken me during my swim or during a million other instances. And I thought that I'd had enough of keeping death to myself.

The kid slid the headphones completely off, looping them around his neck. I decided to extend the moment as long as possible by opening up. I leaned in and confessed. "I heard this food grants wishes."

The kid smirked. "Word of that got all the way to Montenegro, huh."

"It's true, then?"

At that instant the waiter came by with a bamboo steamer and set it down in front of me. "Pork soup dumplings," he said simply, then walked away. I removed the lid, saw six nearly translucent pockets of white dough sitting in steam.

I looked over at the kid, who offered another smirk and said, "You'll have to tell me."

"Okay, I will." I examined the dumplings. "First, can you tell me how to eat this?"

The boy laughed and then gave me a demonstration with his own dumplings, running me through what each of the sauces was, how you could bite off the top of the dumpling so that the steam would get out and the insides wouldn't be as hot as molten lava.

"And when do I make the wish? It's like birthday candles?"

"I don't know if there's a science to that part."

I grabbed the chopsticks, liking the unfamiliar feel of them in my hand. "I can't believe I'm here," I said, more to myself than to my temporary companion.

*   *   *

"Soul food that'll make you feel whatever the chef wants you to feel," the Swede had said. "A Filipino restaurant that can turn your luck, a Mexican bakery that'll make you love." He'd lit a cigarette then, exhaled slowly. We'd been sitting on a bench by Old Town, a pink sunset lighting up the Bay of Kotor. The mountains majestic as always, the water still as a mirror. The Swede had insisted on buying me a beer, and we sat there talking while the tourists meandered back toward their cruise ship. "There are few places in the world that are truly magical. Trust me—I've been around. That place? The food?" He waved his hand like he was shooing away a fly. "Changed my life."

"Cheers," I said to the kid, then managed to pick up the dumpling with the chopsticks. For the first one I bypassed the sauces, wanting to taste it as is. I didn't want to dilute the magic, if it existed. It wobbled a little in my unsteady hand, but then I plopped it onto the large spoon like the kid had showed me. I stared at the dumpling, an imperfect white blob with a liquid hidden within. What a strange, fanciful journey I was on, chasing a thing human beings had not ever been granted.

Although, fuck, what did I know about what human beings had been granted. I lived in Kotor my whole life, a beautiful little corner of the world, where the Adriatic was a blue mirror, and cats licked cream from any bowl they pleased. The way everyone else went about their lives, complaining about what they did, it often felt like I was the only one persistently thinking about death, while everyone else worried about responsibilities and money and sex. My friends at home, the tourists parading around town in their khaki shorts and tucked-in polos, none of them seemed to worry about this cloud hanging over all our heads. None of them had panic attacks when they squished mosquitoes against their skin, none of them were ever paralyzed by their own thoughts. Or maybe they were and were just as good as I was at hiding it. Maybe the only way I was alone in this was in thinking I was alone.

I tipped the spoon and slipped the dumpling into my mouth whole and closed my eyes.

The first sensation was heat. The steam built up against my palate, and I opened my mouth to let it out, shielding other diners from the sight with my hand. A little disappointing to have a feeling rather than a flavor jump out first. I tried not to hold it against the food, let the steam waft out. Then I chewed, waiting for a telling tingle of magic. I scoured my mind, hoping to already be rid of the knowledge.

The broth inside the dumpling spilled out into my mouth, instantly scalding my tongue. I'd forgotten to bite the top off, and now my taste buds were melting or burning away, or whatever happened to taste buds when they came into contact with a hot liquid. My eyes shot open, and I started mumbling curses in Serbian, causing the broth to dribble down my chin.

I reached for a napkin and looked over at the black kid to see if he or anyone else had noticed that I was making a fool out of myself.

My table neighbor was looking away, but there was a slight smile on his lips that made me think he hadn't missed the spectacle and was just being kind. I made eye contact with my waiter, who was standing by the door to the kitchen and laughing in a way that made me feel without a doubt that it was at me. I felt myself flush with embarrassment and anger, followed immediately by the recognition that I would take this embarrassment and anger any day, any minute, if it overtook my worries about death, if the dumplings had worked.

I paused, waiting to see if my thoughts would start to tumble down in that direction, if just wishing for a cure would send me into my trip's first full-on paralysis. Then I thought: *You are not alone in this.*

"I forgot to do the biting-the-top-off thing," I said to the kid.

"I wasn't gonna bring it up. Happens to everyone."

"Why is burning your taste buds the worst feeling in the world?" I said, scowling and making a show of how weird my tongue felt at the moment, trying to sell the fact that I believed what I'd just said.

"At least now you can wish your tongue a speedy recovery."

I laughed. "How does food-wishing work in America, anyway? I know how it works in Montenegro, *obviously*," I

joked. "But I forgot to research this. Do I get, like, one wish per meal? One per food item?"

The kid showed his palms. "I don't make the rules," he laughed.

I placed another dumpling onto the flat spoon, then leaned down and bit off the top peak. Steam billowed out, along with a little bit of broth. I followed the steam as it rose and disappeared into the air, the way my body eventually would, the way the planet would, time itself. I closed my eyes as my heart rate started climbing, then took a deep breath. *Not now,* I thought. I urged myself to stay just in the restaurant, stay in the food, stay in the moment.

"Here you go, man." The waiter reappeared, this time holding the not-soup. "Damn, boy, feeling hungry?"

I peered at the bowl, which was piled high with shrimp and vegetables, little cubes of what looked like meat or fish. The broth was a beautiful golden color, with little circles of orange oil floating on the surface, near the edge of the bowl. My heart rate slowed, oblivion averted. "More chances at wishes. But also, this looks damn good."

I realized I was still holding the spoon with the dumpling, the steam not wafting out like a volcano anymore. So I closed my eyes again and readied myself for another bite.

This time the heat took a step back and allowed everything else to come forward. The savory richness of pork, a bite of ginger and scallions, the broth. Oh, man, the broth. I hadn't ever tasted anything quite like this before. I chewed the dumpling, which was starchy but also managed to melt away, not letting its texture dominate. For a moment, I wanted to reach for something beyond the flavor, but failed. Would I recognize the taste of magic, if magic even had a taste? Then I let the flavor itself take over.

"Wow," I said.

"Good?"

"So good." I prepared another dumpling, forgetting about wishes for the time being. On this one I drizzled a tiny amount of chili oil into the hole I bit off the top. It was hard to wait for the heat to dissipate, hard to resist the gratification of another bite.

By the time the fifth dumpling had disappeared, I was starting to sweat from the heat and the spice. I took a long gulp of water and turned my attention to the not-soup. I dipped the chopsticks into the bowl, grabbed the first morsel I could hang on to—something that could have been cabbage—and let the oil drip down like I'd seen the other customers do. A satisfying crunch, followed by the velvety, rich feel of whatever this heavenly liquid was.

It was the spiciest thing I'd ever eaten, and I had to keep asking the waiter to refill my water, causing my new friend to crack jokes.

"You know you don't have to eat that whole thing, right? You are bright red right now."

I went to respond but ended up coughing instead. Ice cubes in water had never felt better. I just shrugged and dug deeper into the bowl. A piece of shrimp, something unidentifiable that was fatty and chewy, a texture I'd never cared for but could now appreciate, maybe because of the potential fear-erasing promise within it. I took a bite, intensely attuned to the motion of chewing, wanting to sense anything that was different about this meal from all the others. I phrased the wish in as many ways as I could, in as many languages as I could remember. Each time I wished, it was with added desperation, a plea to the food, to the chef, to whatever magic existed in the world. And when the desperation threatened to overwhelm me, I took another bite.

There had been a few times in my life when I'd honestly devoured a meal. The last time was that day a few summers ago when Miljan and I swam across the bay. We'd been sitting in front of our home, bored out of our minds and sticky with sweat from a heat wave passing through. Even inside we couldn't get away from the heat without the boredom compounding. Then Miljan pointed at Old Town and asked how long I thought it would take to swim there. Five minutes later we were in our trunks and jumping off the cement into the water. About halfway across the bay, my thighs and arms were already throbbing with pain and fatigue. I looked up from my paddling and saw Miljan a few meters ahead of me, the edge of the water an impossible distance away.

I thought that if a cramp hit in that moment, pulling me under, Miljan would keep swimming and not look back until he'd reached the shore. I thought about the way the bay had been shaped by glaciers thousands and thousands of years ago, about how little time, in comparison, it would take me to drown. My life itself was such a brief flash in comparison. The thought that I could die in this situation entered my mind, that the universe had granted me a life but could take it back at any moment. I started swimming harder. I imagined sharks in the water, rip tides, though neither of those exist in Kotor and had never been a fear of mine and never would be again.

Forty-five minutes later we dragged ourselves onto the shore, panting and wishing we'd brought enough money for a taxi back. Miljan lay down on the gravelly rocks, his hands on his forehead, his face turned into a tired sneer, calling us idiots for not staying within our boredom. I panted, wondering why I couldn't catch my breath, why my thoughts were glued to oblivion.

We found an overpriced restaurant in Old Town and sat down in our swim trunks on the patio of a plaza, eating mounds of spaghetti in tomato sauce and drinking water in the shade, people-watching and gathering our energy. The air cooled within the high walls of Old Town, and I remembered thinking that it would have been a perfect afternoon, absolutely glowing in beauty, if not for the fact that the swim had put death in my mind. The stain on the day was there and wouldn't leave.

The dim-sum meal felt kind of like that perfect afternoon, though this time I'd managed to push thoughts of death away before they could ruin my appetite. I scooted my chair back, tossed my cloth napkin onto the table. The waiter came by and cleared my plates, leaving behind a check in a leather booklet. I usually get out of restaurants as soon as I can, since I like post-meal walks. Now I lingered, though, not wanting to part with the restaurant quite yet. I fumbled with my wallet as if I couldn't find the bills within it, finished my water. I dipped my thoughts into the realm of death to see if I'd get pulled under.

I looked over at my neighbor, noticed that his food had been gone for a while now, but he was still around. "My name is Joko," I said, reaching my hand across the table. "Thanks for helping me figure the food out."

"Leo."

We shook hands, and again the din of the restaurant stepped in. I wiped my sweaty brow and bit my lip. I looked around the restaurant. Quite the crowd had built up by the hostess stand, some people on their phones, some looking hungrily into the dining room. I waited for a terrifying thought to come but felt the fullness in my stomach and forgot.

"So," Leo said. "What'd you wish for?"

I chuckled as a response, since I still remembered the look on Miljan's face when I'd told him, the squint in his eyes that made me feel like I was a fool for fearing something so simple and inevitable. I looked out the window. The sunlight coming in had turned a rich gold, and I suddenly longed to be outside in the beauty of Rowbury. I started gathering my things, and Leo stood with me, saying he was heading out too.

We stood on the sidewalk in front of the restaurant for a

moment, the sun on our faces. I closed my eyes, taking in its warmth. When I opened them again, Leo was still standing there, a smile turning his lips. I remembered that I was on this trip as a cure, that I had left Montenegro behind, and that I could leave the secrecy of my fear behind too.

"I wished that I could stop thinking about death. Or at least not care about it," I said.

Leo's eyebrows went up for a second, and I wondered if my confession had made things weird. Then he nodded and said, "I guess it's too early to tell if it worked."

I shrugged. "Probably."

We lingered in silence another moment, watching people walk by. The food rested heavy and warm in my stomach, and if nothing else, I knew I'd at least eaten well. "For what it's worth," Leo said, "I always think about how things aren't canceled out by the fact that they ended. Life ends with death, but that doesn't erase all the moments leading up to it."

Something like hope bubbled within me.

It could have been my momentary friendship with Leo. Or it could have been the meal, could have just been the fact that the neighborhood looked cool, the ideal stuff of a traveler's daydreams. This, the dust America tried to keep hidden under the carpet variety. Skin colors, cuisines, cultures, all within the umbrella of that damn flag. The whole world gathered on its land, embraced the history it repeatedly wiped clean, and still America wanted to only sing of its

European roots. And yet the dust rose in the air, resisting. It lingered and fought, and I was here as its witness.

I could smell spices in the air, couldn't even identify any of them. A sort of magic, that, right? Mysteries the world would continue to hold no matter how long I lived. Even if the dim sum wasn't wish granting, these snippets of magic would still exist. And I was given a life with which to discover them.

I decided in the moment that I would eat in this neighborhood every day I was in the city. A full week, but short in the wider scope of my travels. I'd go on to Mexico City, then farther and farther south. Until then, I'd give myself a chance at the magic the Swede and the Internet had talked about. I would look for snippets of magic, whether death came for my thoughts or not.

Food, everywhere. There were so many spots I could walk into and be served a plethora of dishes I'd only ever seen on TV or the Internet. Food that my brothers would make fun of me for wanting. Food that they would sneer at, call it foreign bullshit.

Again I thought about how I'd been touched only by luck. Like the meal I'd just had. Like this street here in front of me. Indian food on the corner nearest to me, an Italian restaurant right next door, roasted chicken across the street, people living above, basking in the smell.

Hell, if there were some magic in the world, why wouldn't it be here? This place that I'd arrived at only by circumstance, because of the chance encounter with a tourist and an unusually cheap flight, a crazy Internet theory. That meal had been magic, regardless of how long I felt this way. I put my hands in my pockets and slowed my gait, kept an eye out for beautiful things as I made my way down Pepper Street.

When I passed a bakery, the smell lured me in, and a girl named Lila sold me a cardamom roll, which I picked at while sitting on a bench in Mallow Park, even though I was still stuffed to the point of discomfort. Eating had brought me joy for a moment, and I wanted these moments to keep coming.

To my right were three food carts, each selling a different cuisine. Straight ahead of me, a halal cart, the girl working it smiling at her customers as she passed them their plates of rice and meat, her body language changing entirely as soon as they walked away. Her shoulders slumped, and she pulled her phone out, put it away again, grabbed a rag and half-heartedly ran it over the counter in front of her. She puffed her cheeks out and exhaled, then caught me watching her and blushed, smiling to herself while avoiding eye contact. I laughed, then looked away so as to not make her uncomfortable.

A sweet little moment, which I would have to hand back to the universe one day. For now I could set it on my tongue and taste it, forget about anything else. It was possible.

The Slender One

BY CAROLINE TUNG RICHMOND

Mr. Ingersoll died from a heart attack four years ago, but that didn't stop him from drifting into the Happy Horse Convenience Mart every morning to ask Charlie if the coffee was ready yet.

"Pour me a cup, won't you, kiddo? All black. None of that decaf stuff," said the ghost of Mr. Ingersoll, who looked exactly like the living version of the fifty-six-year-old German American, from the bald head to the spotless slacks that he'd worn to his job of three decades, running the Button & Sew dry cleaners on Pepper Street. "I'll take one of your mom's tea eggs, too. Big day ahead, you know."

Charlie glanced up from restocking the ramen noodles. His family had run the Happy Horse for eighteen years, and it was his job to take the early shift until he caught the city bus to his private school on the other end of town. The store was quiet at this hour, and Charlie was alone, save for Mr. Ingersoll, who showed up at 6:03 a.m., like he'd done when he was alive. Ghosts were predictable like that, even if it meant ordering a coffee and Chinese tea eggs that they could no longer touch or consume.

Charlie had been able to talk to ghosts for as long as he could remember. It was a trait passed down on his mom's side of the family, although it tended to skip a generation, which explained why he and his grandma could see Mr. Ingersoll, but his mother could not. *It's a gift,* his parents often reminded him. *You've been given a great honor.*

But Charlie wasn't so sure of that. Most of the time, his "gift" made him feel like a weirdo.

Mr. Ingersoll waved a hand in front of Charlie's face. "Don't tell me you forgot! The gates are opening tonight, remember?"

"I know," sighed Charlie.

The gates of heaven and hell, of course.

He hadn't forgotten; he just didn't want to deal with it anymore.

Every year it was the same. During the seventh lunar month, the underworld's shadowed entrance would break open and allow spirits to roam the earth. Charlie's grandma had told him everything when he was a little kid, explaining that there were different types of ghosts. Some were friendly, like Mr. Ingersoll, who remained on earth to watch over loved ones, while others entered the underworld after death, eager for a long rest. But sometimes those ghosts would grow bored. A few even became angry, due to past slights or regret. As soon as the gates reopened, they would rush back to earth, and it was the Mas' job to placate them with food and entertainment— but not all could be appeased by a juicy pear or Chinese opera.

"Did your grandma order enough mangos for the festival?" asked Mr. Ingersoll. "Her shaved ice always sells out fast."

Charlie glanced at the poster hanging on the door, which announced the store's annual Hungry Ghost Festival, just four days away. It used to be Charlie's favorite holiday, from the puppet shows at the community center to the paper lanterns that his mom hung outside and to the food—especially the food. Sautéed pea shoots. Roasted duck. Pineapple cakes that fit into the palm of your hand. Then there was his grandma's shaved ice with all the toppings—chopped mangos, condensed milk poured on thick, and her famous mung beans in sugary syrup. He could eat a whole bowl of those.

"You're sure your grandma can handle everything in her condition?" Mr. Ingersoll went on.

"I think so," replied Charlie, although he wasn't sure at all. A month ago his grandma had gotten clipped by a Honda Civic—Waipo had cursed out the driver even as the paramedics treated her—and she had been laid up in bed with a broken foot ever since. Despite doctors' orders, she was still taking customers at her astrology business, but over the phone instead of in person.

Mr. Ingersoll drifted closer, and the whiff of a campfire drifted into Charlie's nose. Ghosts always smelled like smoke to him.

"What will we do if a ghost gives us trouble?" asked Mr. Ingersoll. "Your grandma always handles them, like that time four years ago."

Charlie shuddered at the memory. On rare occasions, a spirit would arrive from the underworld inconsolable, desperate to fix something that they couldn't fix in life. Their pain—so sharp—would eventually affect the living, and only Waipo knew how to help them.

"We're going to need your help. Your grandma can teach you," said Mr. Ingersoll.

Charlie ducked down his head. His parents had been hinting too that he should take over Waipo's spiritual duties, but he changed the subject every time they brought it up. Over the summer he'd gotten a full ride to Alabaster Prep, one of the top five high schools in the state. None of his new classmates knew about the old Charlie Ma, the one with the glasses and the scrawny build of a scallion, not to mention the odd family. He wore contact lenses now, and he was lifting weights at the Y three nights a week. And nobody teased him about his eccentric grandma, because none of them had met her.

Charlie winced at his own thoughts. He loved his waipo

so much, but he wished that she wasn't so different.

That *he* wasn't so different.

"There's something else," Mr. Ingersoll pressed.

Charlie pretended not to hear and rang up a girl at the register buying a tin of black tea and a jar of kachampuli. He hated ignoring Mr. Ingersoll, but if he wanted to fit in, he couldn't keep whispering to dead people.

Mr. Ingersoll, however, wasn't going away. As soon as the customer left, he said, "Listen to me, kiddo. I've heard that there's a ghost already at the gates, screaming to get out of the underworld and into this one." He leaned closer, the campfire scent overwhelming. "They're calling it the Slender One."

A chill nipped down Charlie's spine. He had never heard of a spirit doing that before.

"Our families could be in danger. We need your help, Charlie," Mr. Ingersoll said.

I can't. I'm sorry, Charlie thought, but he said instead, "We'll talk later, okay?" He shrugged off his apron to reveal his uniform underneath, and he yanked open the door that led to his apartment upstairs.

"Ma! Ba! I'm leaving," he said in Mandarin.

His mother appeared at the top of the stairs. "Did you eat yet? Waipo is asking for you."

Guilt tugged at Charlie's gut, but it wasn't enough to get him up the steps. "I'm going to be late," he said before bolting.

"Charlie!" his mom said. "When will you get home?"

"Charlie!" Mr. Ingersoll said. "What about tonight?"

Charlie didn't turn around. If he wanted to become the new Charlie Ma, then he had to leave the old one behind.

The city would be fine.

That's what he told himself anyway.

Forty minutes later, Charlie hurried onto Alabaster's pristine campus and headed to the next meeting of the Cultural Exchange Club. He'd signed up for the early morning club to round out his extracurriculars, but the reason he kept coming back had nothing to do with college applications.

Charlie claimed a seat in the Latin classroom, where the club was held, while the club's president, Andie Bellin, jotted notes in her bullet journal. She finished her s'mores Pop-Tart while a few more members trickled in.

"Let's get started!" said Andie. She was a sophomore, like Charlie, who always wore her brown hair tied with a ribbon. "I had to cancel our service project at the Rowbury West Library because its basement got flooded, but—"

"Sorry, I'm late!" A petite girl glided in, with her blond hair flowing behind her like a cape. Every male in the classroom straightened at Helen Overton's entrance, including Charlie, who silently cheered when she sat next to him. "What did I miss?"

"Fortunately, not much," Andie said with a smile and a little shake of the head, like she was used to Helen's tardiness. The two of them had grown up together on the same block of historic brownstones in northeast Rowbury.

"Anyway, I signed us up for a new service project. . . ."

Andie kept talking and passed around a stack of flyers, but Charlie wasn't listening. With Helen sitting so close, he could smell her shampoo, and it smelled like coconuts.

"Hey, did you finish our pre-calc homework by chance?" she whispered, leaning toward him with her bright eyes locked onto his.

Charlie's pulse thrashed. He managed a nod.

"Could I borrow it? I forgot my textbook at my dad's place and—"

Within seconds Charlie had handed over his worksheet. It was against school policy to copy homework, but Helen's parents were getting a divorce, and her grandmother had died unexpectedly last spring break. It made total sense that she needed a little academic boost.

Helen's smile brightened a few watts. "You're the best, Charlie Horse."

Something twinged inside Charlie. Something sharp. His last name meant "horse" in Chinese, and the ensuing nickname had followed him from his old school to this new one, thanks to the many students enrolled in Mandarin. But with Helen smiling at him and smelling like a tropical beach, he decided to let it go.

Andie cleared her throat. "We can meet at the community center around eleven thirty. We'll help the kids make dumplings, so wear something you don't mind getting dirty."

Just then, the fliers reached Charlie's desk, and his face paled.

The 14th Annual Hungry Ghost Festival

Hosted by the Happy Horse Convenient Mart &

the Hungry Heart Row Community Center

It was the flier that his dad had posted on the store's website. Andie must have found it and printed it out.

The Cultural Exchange Club was volunteering at the festival.

His classmates would be going to his neighborhood.

Helen would see where he worked, where he lived.

She might even run into Waipo.

A soccer player named Ross snickered in his seat. "Do you think they'll sell dog meat at this place? I've always wanted to try golden retriever." He barked twice, and three freshmen girls giggled.

Charlie flushed red. *Say something,* his brain shouted at him. *Tell Ross to eff off.* But his mouth felt mealy, and all he could do was slide down in his chair.

"That isn't funny, Ross," Andie said tightly, her voice cutting through the laughter.

The classroom went quiet.

Ross waved her off and motioned at Helen. "Back me up, Hel. I was kidding!"

Helen glanced up from Charlie's homework. "Don't drag me into this, please."

"And don't bother coming to the festival if you're going to say 'funny' shit like that again," Andie added. She flicked a sympathetic glance at Charlie, and he wished he could disappear into thin air. *Poof*, like Mr. Ingersoll. But he wasn't a ghost, so he had to sit there and stew, wishing he had the courage to punch Ross in the nose.

As soon as the bell rang, Charlie was ready to run across campus, but Andie walked up to him first. "Sorry about what happened earlier. I told Ross not to come to our meetings anymore."

Charlie's cheeks turned pink. "No worries," he said, trying to sound nonchalant but failing.

Beside them Helen laughed nervously. "Don't let it bother you, Charlie Horse."

Charlie winced again at the nickname, but then she gave him a little side hug when she returned his math homework, and he forgot what he was thinking.

"I know you two have to run to class, but can you make it to the service project?" Andie asked, thumbing through her journal.

Charlie glanced at Helen and thought, *Please be busy, please be busy.*

"Totally! We should carpool, Andie," said Helen before she tossed her hair over her shoulder and strolled out.

Charlie's heart wilted. This meant that Helen would see him wearing his bright orange festival T-shirt and ringing up orders on Saturday. She would undoubtedly notice Waipo, too, talking to the empty air while insisting that she was chatting with a ghost.

"What about you?" Andie asked him. "Can I put you down as a yes?"

"No!" he said too forcefully before he dialed himself back. "I mean, I have to work."

"Gotcha." Andie reassured him with a smile, revealing two dimples on her cheeks. "Where do you work, by the way?"

The warning bell rang, and Charlie hustled out the door with a wave instead of a reply. His American history class was on the other side of campus, so he urged his legs faster, pumping them into a sprint and trying not to think about his worlds colliding in four short days.

If he went fast enough, maybe, just maybe, he could outrun the shadow of his old life.

After school let out, Charlie spent the commute plotting ways to hide from the Cultural Exchange Club during the festival. His armpits felt damp. He didn't know how to separate his school life from his home one, and once they crashed into each other, he was sure it would be a catastrophe. Helen would think he was a freak.

As he turned onto his block, he was so miserable that he didn't look up until he got to the store. He reached for the door, dreading the restocking he had to tackle, but it was locked.

His eyes shot up.

The Happy Horse never closed early, not even on Chinese New Year.

Within seconds, he'd unlocked the door and run up to the apartment. His mom was in the living room, pacing.

Questions tumbled out of Charlie's mouth. "Why's the store closed? Why didn't you call?" His gaze skidded toward his grandma's bedroom. "Is Waipo okay?"

The corners of his mother's mouth tightened. "She fainted earlier."

"She *what*?"

"She snuck outside when I was at the bank. The girl from Pop's Deli found her on the sidewalk. Baba and I took her to see Dr. Gupta, and he's getting her prescriptions now." She sighed. "Waipo will be fine, but only if she rests."

Charlie released a tight breath. "Where was she going? To see a customer?"

"She wouldn't tell me, but it must have something to do with the gates."

"But they're not supposed to open until tonight—"

A familiar voice called out from his grandmother's room. "Charlie-ah?" Waipo said crisply. "Bring me some water."

"You need to sleep, Ma!" said Charlie's mother.

"Send in my grandson. With my water," came the reply.

Mrs. Ma frowned but knew there was no use arguing. So she filled a mug with water from the kettle and handed it to her son. "Tell her to rest. Please."

Charlie entered Waipo's room, which was barely big enough to fit a bed and a dresser. The walls were empty, aside from a Chinese zodiac calendar that his grandmother had picked up for free somewhere, but the space had always felt cozy to him instead of cramped.

Waipo lay in bed, one foot propped on a pillow. She was tiny, even more petite than Helen, and her permed hair had long since turned white. She wasn't alone, either. Mr. Ingersoll stood at her bedside.

"It was the Slender One," Mr. Ingersoll announced as soon as Charlie came in. "Your grandmother went out to face it. Alone."

"Puh, don't scare him!" said Waipo in accented English. She beckoned for Charlie to claim the folding chair next to her bed. "Sit, sit."

Charlie didn't move, though. "The Slender One was here?"

"It slipped out of the gates somehow," Mr. Ingersoll explained, hands on hips and pacing. "Thank God it didn't stay for long. It stalked off somewhere, but your grandmother got hurt nonetheless. What were you thinking, Shirley?"

Waipo frowned furiously at him. "Ai-ya, I was out for two seconds! Doesn't even count."

"Tell Charlie what it looked like," said Mr. Ingersoll.

"This type of ghost? Always the same." She shrugged and patted her throat. "Long neck."

"Like the one four years ago," Charlie whispered. He shivered at the memory. The hungry ghost had looked like an ordinary businessman in a pinstripe suit from the collar down, but its neck had stretched into a frighteningly thin arc, with its head dangling at the end and its mouth wide and toothless. Waipo had tried every trick to appease it—burning incense, offering paper money—but nothing worked until she pored over the local obituaries. That was where she found a photo of an Italian-American chef, wearing a pinstripe suit and standing outside his Sicilian restaurant. He had drowned in a boating accident, leaving behind a husband and a young daughter. That gave Waipo the idea to offer the ghost a platter of caponata, the restaurant's specialty. The gamble worked, and the chef had moved on, but the ordeal exhausted Waipo for days. She couldn't repeat that in her current state.

Waipo, however, wasn't flustered. "Don't worry so much. It gives you pimples, Charlie."

"You should let us worry," Mr. Ingersoll said. "You can't keep the city safe on your own. You have to teach Charlie what to do."

Charlie froze under their gazes. He wanted to be a good grandson, but he couldn't do what Waipo did every seventh lunar month. She was the one who sought out the unhappiest ghosts, the ones who knocked over trash cans and made the neighborhood lights flicker. She would talk to them and puzzle out what pained them. A ghost who died brokenhearted might need the comforting aroma from a pot of chicken ginseng soup. A soul who died estranged from his children might be soothed with an offering of Waipo's pineapple cakes. When Charlie was younger, he would join her on her excursions, and he'd feel a glowing pride whenever they helped a spirit find peace.

But he was older now. Almost sixteen.

Was it so wrong for him to want to be normal?

Waipo cleared her throat and said to Mr. Ingersoll, "Charlie needs to focus on school. He worked so hard to get into Alabaster."

Charlie looked up, surprised, while Mr. Ingersoll swooped in to protest.

"He can study hard *and* protect the city."

"If the Slender One returns, I'll be ready," replied Waipo.

Shame crept over Charlie. He couldn't ask her to placate a hungry ghost alone. "Hold on—"

"Do your homework like a good boy. I need to talk to Mr. Ingersoll."

Charlie knew a dismissal when he heard one, so he shuffled out. As he shut the door behind him, he thought he'd feel relief. Waipo had given him the go-ahead to concentrate on school—on his new life, on the new Charlie.

This is what you wanted, he reminded himself.

But he never thought that getting his wish would leave him feeling so awful.

The day of the festival arrived before Charlie knew it. By five in the morning he was tossing on his orange festival shirt; by seven thirty he was setting up catering tables on the sidewalks; and by ten forty-five he was starting up the shaved-ice machine while telling a guy visiting from Montenegro that the event wouldn't start for another fifteen minutes.

His mother brushed past him with a tray of noodles in hand. "Remember to set out three bowls for the spirits like Waipo does," she said.

"I will, Ma," said Charlie. His parents had decided not to sell their usual pineapple cakes—because none of them could bake like Waipo did—but the shaved ice was still a go, and the responsibility fell to Charlie this year.

As he adjusted the machine's settings, he glanced guiltily at his grandmother's window. His mother had slipped a sleeping pill into Waipo's tea the night before. Charlie didn't like being sneaky, but his mom held firm. She told him that Waipo would never get better if she didn't take it easy.

After Mrs. Ma hurried off, Charlie tested the shaved ice and glanced at the spirits drifting into Hungry Heart Row. They'd been pouring in since dawn, wandering through the stalls that each participating restaurant had set up, clustering around a fragrant Crock-Pot of ash-e-reshte and platters full of pumpkin tamales. Across the street, Lila from the local pastelería was unboxing dozens of conchas and novias, each one more brightly colored than the last.

Charlie got to work setting out the fixings. Assembling a bowl of shaved ice was a lot like making an ice cream sundae. Just replace the ice cream with slivers of ice and cover them with toppings that take on a special Asian flair—grass jelly, chunks of mango or sliced strawberries, and Waipo's mung beans in syrup. He and his mom had spent the night preparing the mixture, but they couldn't get the recipe quite right. The beans were a little too firm and a touch too sweet. They lacked Waipo's expert touch.

Guilt sliced through Charlie like a chef's knife. He wouldn't have to worry about Helen bumping into his grandmother today, but thinking that only made him more miserable. He'd never celebrated a Hungry Ghost Festival without her before.

Soon, the first batch of festivalgoers arrived, and he was scrambling to get the silverware in place when two customers stopped at his table.

"Is this dessert? I love mangos!" said a voice that sounded very familiar.

"I'm not sure. What's that black jiggly stuff over there?" said another voice that made Charlie's heart take off sprinting.

He thought about ducking into the store really fast, but that was when Helen noticed him.

"Charlie Horse?" she said, confused. "Is that you?"

Charlie's face went up in flames as he turned around to face her and Andie. He thought he was prepared to see them, but not this early. He'd even gone over what he would say, *Oh, I'm helping out with the festival*, capped with a nonchalant shrug, but now Helen was here, looking like a pretty summer's day in a flowy sundress.

"Is this where you work? You should've told us! We wanted to come before the service project started to look around," Andie said. She peered down at the festival flyer she was holding and glanced up at the Happy Horse sign. Something seemed to click in her eyes. "Oh! It says here that the Ma family has been hosting the Hungry Ghost Festival for over a decade. I didn't realize that you were related."

"So neat," Helen said weakly as she looked at the various food stations. Charlie couldn't help but notice that her nose scrunched at the sight of the stewed chicken feet sold at the Emperor's Way food stall, a dish that the restaurant made especially for the festival.

Maybe she doesn't like spicy food, Charlie thought, but that felt like an excuse.

Andie motioned at the shaved ice. "So how does this work? Do we choose the toppings?" She elbowed Helen to take a bowl too, but Helen blinked at the mung beans and shook her head.

"Gosh, I'm not hungry," said Helen.

"You said you were starving on our way down here," Andie teased.

"I totally did not!" Helen said with a nervous laugh, the same one Charlie had heard when she tried to brush off Ross's racist joke.

Something deflated inside him. Helen had looked at the mung beans like they were mung beans. She wouldn't even try a bite.

More festivalgoers streamed onto the block, and Charlie told himself to get to work. He explained each of the toppings to Andie, from the condensed milk to the grass jelly (aka the "black jiggly stuff," as Helen called it).

"Wow, this is *good*. You're missing out, Hel," Andie said, three spoonfuls into her shaved ice. "How much do I owe you, Charlie?"

"It's on the house." He glanced at Helen. "You sure you don't want any?"

She smiled too politely. "That's so sweet but—"

All three of them went quiet as a chilly breeze brushed over their skin. Charlie shivered in his T-shirt. He looked up to see if a storm was coming, but the sun was shining brightly overhead. There wasn't a cloud for miles, and yet it felt like one had wrapped around his heart, blocking off every speck of warmth.

"Weird," Helen said. "It got really cold all of a sudden."

Andie grimaced. "I don't feel cold. Just . . . not quite right. I think I need an aspirin."

But that wasn't the worst of it. An awful stench soon overwhelmed Charlie's nose, like steaming garbage and burnt hair rolled into one.

"Oh no," he whispered. He turned toward the scent, but he already knew where it was coming from.

The Slender One had returned, and it was coming straight down Tansy Street. It looked like a twisted version of a human being, with limbs stretched into skinny ropes and with fingers bent and broken.

"Olenna," it said in a gravelly whisper that only Charlie could hear. Its neck had elongated into a frighteningly thin arc, and its dangling head possessed no eyes or nose, just a gaping mouth.

Terror claimed Charlie's body. He might've been the only one who could see the horrifying ghost, but the festivalgoers could definitely feel its presence too. All around him, people shuddered and fell silent. A baby cried while a young boy sat down on the pavement, wrapping his arms around himself.

"Olenna!" the Slender One cried. It barreled toward the shaved-ice station, right toward Helen.

"Watch out!" Instinct took over, and Charlie pushed her out of the way. He whipped around to face the angry spirit, but there was someone blocking the way, protecting him and Helen.

"Run, Charlie!" said Mr. Ingersoll, his sleeves rolled up to his elbows. Without blinking, he grabbed the Slender One by the middle and wrenched it away from the shaved-ice table, grimacing as the hungry ghost shrieked and scratched at him. Through gritted teeth he shouted, "Bring your grandma to Mallow Park! I'll keep this one there as long as I can."

Charlie watched Mr. Ingersoll haul the Slender One down an alleyway and out of sight. He didn't know how long Mr. Ingersoll would last; he needed to hurry.

"What was that all about?" Helen said, staring at Charlie the same way that she'd looked at the mung beans. Like he was a weirdo.

A week ago he would've wilted under her gaze, but right now he found that he didn't care that much. The city needed him and only a weirdo like him knew how to save Hungry Heart Row from the Slender One.

"You should go home," Charlie said once he found his voice. "It isn't safe."

Helen went white and backed away from the shaved ice. "You mean food poisoning?" She reached into her purse to search for her phone. "Where's Andie? She's my ride. Wait, do you have a car? My mom's place isn't far."

He glanced over his shoulder. Helen Overton was asking him for a ride. He'd been waiting for this moment since the first day of school. He had dreamed about it. Yearned for it. This was everything the new Charlie wanted.

But, now, Charlie wondered what he'd been thinking.

"There's a bus stop down the block," he said before he ran into the store to find Waipo.

Without another thought, he scrambled inside the Happy Horse and made a beeline for the back when a shadow stumbled toward him.

He lurched back, convinced it was a ghost, but it was Andie. And she didn't look well.

"Can I buy some Tylenol?" she asked, her fingers pressed at her temples. The Slender One was likely blocks away, but she looked like she was still feeling its effects.

"We have some upstairs," Charlie said quickly. He was about to grab her a few, but she swayed into him, and he caught her before she fell. He knew he couldn't leave her alone. "Take my arm, okay?"

He led her up to the apartment, where she promptly slumped onto the living room sofa with a groan.

"It sounds crazy, but it felt like there was a Dementor outside," she said, leaning her head against a pillow.

That isn't too far from the truth, Charlie thought. He glanced at Waipo's bedroom door, then back at Andie. "Stay as long as you want, but I have to check on my grandma."

He left her with some aspirin and a glass of water before stepping into Waipo's room. He thought he'd find her conked out in bed, but he should've known better. His grandmother was already dressed and hobbling toward him, her broken foot in a boot.

"Did your mother give me a sleeping pill?" she demanded. "Never mind, I'll speak to her later. The Slender One is back. I can feel it."

"Mr. Ingersoll dragged it to Mallow Park, but I don't know how long he can keep it there."

"That's where we'll go. I have to find out what it wants."

"You could faint again." He blocked her path. "Tell me what to do, and I'll handle it."

She swatted at his shoulder. "Charlie-ah, move."

"This isn't like four years ago! It's so much worse."

That made Waipo go quiet, but she pressed on. "What did the Slender One say?"

"Promise me you'll let me go after it."

"Ai-ya, answer the question! We need to figure out why this ghost is so angry."

Charlie had to admit she had a point. "It said 'olenna,' but I'm not sure what that means. Maybe it's a place."

"Or a name. I need a computer."

Elbowing Charlie aside, Waipo grabbed her crutches and tottered toward the ancient Mac in the corner of the living room, but she stopped when she saw Andie on the couch, sitting wide-eyed with her glass of water and looking much more alert.

"Oh. Hi," said Charlie. He'd forgotten about her for a minute, and he wondered how much she had overheard, but he relaxed when he remembered that he and Waipo had been speaking in Mandarin. "This is my grandma."

"Nice to meet you. Charlie and I go to school together." Andie set her glass down shakily. She sounded nervous. "I'm so sorry, but I overheard what the two of you were saying."

"You speak Mandarin?" Waipo said in English.

Andie flushed. "I was in a Chinese immersion program until the eighth grade."

Oh, great, thought Charlie. He waited for Andie to scuttle out of the apartment, whispering "freaks" on her way out, but so be it if she did. He had to protect his neighborhood.

But Andie didn't leave. "There's obviously stuff going on that I don't understand, but I also know that what I felt outside wasn't normal. The two of you said something about Olenna, right?"

"Look, I can explain later—" Charlie started.

"Let the girl speak," Waipo said, and nodded at Andie. "Go on."

Andie swallowed. "Olenna means 'Helen' in Ukrainian. It's what Helen's grandmother called her.

"Who's Helen?" prodded Waipo.

"Our classmate," Andie replied. "Her grandma died last year."

"Were they close?"

"Very. Her grandma even moved to Rowbury when Helen's parents separated." Andie bit her lip, as if she shouldn't say what she wanted to reveal next. "The Overton's divorce has gotten really messy. I don't know what Helen would've done if her grandma hadn't been there."

Waipo nodded along. "How did Grandma die?"

"She went back to Ukraine for a wedding, but she got sick and passed away at the hospital. The doctors think it was meningitis."

Waipo's eyes fluttered shut as she mumbled to herself, switching between Chinese and English. "Unexpected death . . . a granddaughter left behind. Grief turned into anger. Anger became bitter." Then her eyes shot open, and she gripped Andie's elbow. "What did Helen's grandma like to eat?"

Andie looked a bit baffled, so Charlie stepped in.

"Did she have a favorite food?" he said, understanding his grandmother's intent.

Andie chewed her lip as she racked her memories. "She

always had diced pineapple in the fridge whenever she stayed at Helen's house."

Waipo's eyes brightened like birthday candles. "We have to preheat the oven." To Andie she asked, "Do you bake?"

"Um, I've made brownies before. From a mix."

Waipo clucked her tongue. "Good enough. What's your name?"

"Andie Bellin."

"Do you want to help us, Andie Bellin?"

"I think you and I can handle things from here, Waipo," Charlie cut in, wanting to give Andie an out.

But the two women ignored him.

"Give me a job, and I'll do it, nǚshì" Andie said, addressing the older woman in Mandarin.

Waipo cracked a smile. "You can call me Waipo."

The three of them barely fit in the apartment's galley kitchen, but that didn't stop Waipo from barking out orders like they were in a Michelin-starred restaurant. While Charlie rolled out the pastry dough and Andie heated up two cans of crushed pineapple, Waipo called her daughter to explain that Charlie's dad needed to take over the shaved-ice station because Charlie was busy.

Andie stirred the fruit mixture to keep it from burning. "What are we making?"

"Pineapple cake. A bitter ghost needs something sweet," said Waipo.

formed an assembly line to fill each mold with dough and sweetened pineapple before pinching the edges together and placing the little cakes onto a cookie sheet that slid promptly into the oven. They crowded around to watch the squares turn golden until Waipo deemed them ready. She let them cool a touch before cutting one into thirds for them to taste.

"They're hot," she cautioned.

Andie took the smallest of bites. "Holy cow. This is incredible."

The filling burned Charlie's tongue, but he had to agree. Waipo's pineapple cakes were the stuff of legend, and this particular batch tasted extra special. The crust was perfectly flaky, and the filling had hit that sweet spot of not too sugary and not too tart.

His grandma swept the cakes into an empty cookie tin. "They're ready. Let me get my shoes."

"You should stay home. I'll go," said Charlie.

"Stay home and do what? Watch television?" Waipo replied in a huff.

"You fainted the last time, and something ⁓
happen now. Waipo, please." Ch⁓
on his grandmother's shou⁓
the Slender One alone, but⁓
health. She was far too imp⁓
that he had ever been embarra⁓
eccentric? Sure, but so was he⁓
how to do this."

"You think Helen's grandmother turned int[...] Andie asked, paling a shade.

Charlie paused from rolling the dough. "It's [...] plicated."

"Not complicated! Very simple," Waipo [...] to interject. "We live, we die, and then we bec[...] its. Some spirits are happy; some are sad. I he[...] ones—make sense? I feed them the food they [...] that makes them happy again." She pointed And[...] the stove and instructed her to simmer the pin[...] their juices. "You understand?"

"I think so." Andie stirred the fruit conco[...] stole a glance at Charlie. "Do you see ghosts too[...]

Charlie's face warmed, but the truth was t[...] wasn't it? He'd been trying for months to hid[...] that he was a scholarship kid who could talk to [...] but it had been like cutting himself in half. He [...] to his bones, eccentric waipo and all.

Maybe being normal was overrated.

"Yeah, I can see spirits," he said to Andie at[...] voice cracking slightly. "I got it from my grandm[...] of runs in the family."

Andie blinked at the revelation, considered it, [...] "Balding runs in my family, so that's a lot co[...] [the]y shared a grin, but the moment was brok[...] [sn]apped at them.

[...]k, more rolling!" she snapped.

[...]hip adequately cracked, the three

"You think Helen's grandmother turned into a ghost?" Andie asked, paling a shade.

Charlie paused from rolling the dough. "It's . . . complicated."

"Not complicated! Very simple," Waipo was quick to interject. "We live, we die, and then we become spirits. Some spirits are happy; some are sad. I help the sad ones—make sense? I feed them the food they like, and that makes them happy again." She pointed Andie toward the stove and instructed her to simmer the pineapples in their juices. "You understand?"

"I think so." Andie stirred the fruit concoction and stole a glance at Charlie. "Do you see ghosts too?"

Charlie's face warmed, but the truth was the truth, wasn't it? He'd been trying for months to hide the fact that he was a scholarship kid who could talk to the dead, but it had been like cutting himself in half. He was a Ma to his bones, eccentric waipo and all.

Maybe being normal was overrated.

"Yeah, I can see spirits," he said to Andie at last, his voice cracking slightly. "I got it from my grandma. It kind of runs in the family."

Andie blinked at the revelation, considered it, and nodded. "Balding runs in my family, so that's a lot cooler."

They shared a grin, but the moment was broken when Waipo clapped at them.

"Less talk, more rolling!" she snapped.

With the whip adequately cracked, the three of them

formed an assembly line to fill each mold with dough and sweetened pineapple before pinching the edges together and placing the little cakes onto a cookie sheet that slid promptly into the oven. They crowded around to watch the squares turn golden until Waipo deemed them ready. She let them cool a touch before cutting one into thirds for them to taste.

"They're hot," she cautioned.

Andie took the smallest of bites. "Holy cow. This is incredible."

The filling burned Charlie's tongue, but he had to agree. Waipo's pineapple cakes were the stuff of legend, and this particular batch tasted extra special. The crust was perfectly flaky, and the filling had hit that sweet spot of not too sugary and not too tart.

His grandma swept the cakes into an empty cookie tin. "They're ready. Let me get my shoes."

"You should stay home. I'll go," said Charlie.

"Stay home and do what? Watch television?" Waipo replied in a huff.

"You fainted the last time, and something worse could happen now. Waipo, please." Charlie pressed his hands on his grandmother's shoulders. He didn't want to face the Slender One alone, but he couldn't risk his grandma's health. She was far too important to him, and he hated that he had ever been embarrassed by her. Was she a little eccentric? Sure, but so was he. "It's time for me to learn how to do this."

Waipo went speechless for once. Her chin wobbled as she reached up to pat Charlie on the cheek.

"You can't go out there by yourself," she said finally.

Behind them, Andie cleared her throat. "I can go with him."

"That is a good idea," Waipo said before Charlie could protest. "Now, listen to me carefully. Find the Slender One and offer it the cakes. Remember: It can't touch you, but it can make you feel its pain. But you're stronger than it."

Charlie pecked his grandma on the forehead. "We'll be back soon."

And then he and Andie took off.

Down the stairs, down the street, the two of them raced through the thickening festival crowd. More than once, Charlie looked back to make sure Andie hadn't fallen behind, but she kept pace with him step for step as they entered Mallow Park. The weather was sunny and warm, and the park should've been filled with couples strolling by the riverfront and families out barbecuing. But the place was eerily empty, and Charlie knew exactly why.

"Over here!"

Charlie sprinted toward Mr. Ingersoll's voice. He and Andie reached a line of willow trees not far from the water, offering a view of fishing boats and the Carraway Bridge. Mr. Ingersoll had cornered the Slender One between himself and the river, but Charlie could see that his friend had gone translucent, worn down from exertion.

"Do you see it?" Andie whispered. "I can feel it."

"Me too," he said, his hands trembling. "What's Helen's grandmother's name?"

"Mrs. Honcharenko."

He repeated it softly. "You can hang back for now, but go get my grandma if I tell you to, all right?"

Charlie forced his feet to move, and he approached the closest willow tree, where he saw the Slender One through the wispy branches. For a second, he was tempted to make a run for it, but then he channeled his grandmother's grit. She wouldn't turn back, and neither would he.

"Mr. Ingersoll, I've got this!" he said, and his friend nodded at him gratefully and slumped by the river to rest.

Charlie swung his full attention at the Slender One and tossed off the cookie tin cover. "Mrs. Honcharenko?"

The Slender One swiveled its neck toward him, and Charlie's knees honestly went weak, but he stood his ground.

"We made you something!" he said.

The ghost inched toward Charlie, its mouth moving toward the tin. A skinny tongue darted out, right by Charlie's fingers, and he dropped the box.

The Slender One lurched back and let out a horrible screech, followed by a distraught "Olenna!" inches from his face.

Charlie backpedaled, terrified, but then he felt someone yanking him to his feet.

"Come on! Tell her about Helen. Tell her that her

granddaughter is okay," Andie urged. She swept the cakes back into the tin and pressed it into his clammy hands. "You've got this."

Her words buoyed Charlie, and he thrust the box at the Slender One once more. "Your granddaughter Helen goes to school with us."

Then something strange happened, right after Charlie spoke Helen's name. Two slits appeared on the Slender One's face, like a primitive nose, and they sniffed at the cakes.

"Tell her that Helen got named captain of poms, and that her mom is giving her driving lessons," Andie whispered urgently.

Charlie repeated what she'd told him, and the Slender One drew closer, its claws reaching for the tin, its nose inhaling deeply.

"Helen misses you," Charlie went on. "But she's doing all right."

The Slender One's head bobbed up, tilting toward him. "All . . . right?"

"She's safe."

"Safe," the ghost said, like a sigh.

Slowly, right in front of Charlie's eyes, the Slender One started to change. Its neck shrank, and its body filled out. Its claws retracted into delicate fingers, and its nakedness was covered by an ankle-length dress in a red-rose pattern.

"Olenna," it whispered again as its transformation completed.

A petite old woman stood in front of them now, her silver hair held back in a bun and her posture as straight as a dancer's. Wrinkles lined her face, but Charlie could still see the resemblance. Helen had her grandma's cheekbones.

The woman blinked, disoriented. "Where is my Olenna?"

Andie might not have been able to see the ghost, but she seemed to sense a shift in the air, the emptiness gone.

"What do you see?" she asked. Charlie described the woman in front of him, and her eyes went big. "That's Helen's grandma. I went to the funeral, and she was buried in a dress with roses on it."

Mrs. Honcharenko drifted toward Charlie. "You know Olenna?"

"We're classmates. You don't have to worry about her anymore," he replied.

"I will always worry about my granddaughter, but I cannot remain here." She tried to touch his shoulder, but realized she couldn't. "I am tired. Very tired."

"There's a place where you can sleep. I think you know the way," Charlie said. He was unsure how everything worked after death, but he had a feeling that most ghosts were able to find the path to the underworld.

Mrs. Honcharenko began to fade, like a photograph left out in the sun. Just before she disappeared, she said one last "Olenna" and was gone.

Charlie's hands dropped to his sides, and he realized he was out of breath. The past few minutes had drained him completely, and yet he couldn't help but grin.

They had done it.

"She's gone, isn't she?" Andie marveled. "It's like someone opened a window and chased out all of the bad air. Does that make sense?"

"It does," Charlie said softly. Now that Mrs. Honcharenko had moved on, he was realizing how much he had revealed to Andie in the last hour. No one outside of his family knew that he could see ghosts. For so long, he had made sure to keep it that way, but now his secret was out there, and he felt shy. Exposed. "You're probably super freaked out by all of this, huh?"

"I mean, a little," Andie admitted, and Charlie felt his walls go up. But then she looked at him, and there wasn't fear in her eyes. Only curiosity. "Mostly I have questions. Like, there really is life after death? And what does that make you? A ghostbuster?"

That made Charlie laugh out loud, and all of a sudden he felt that everything would be okay. "I don't know. Maybe more like a ghost whisperer."

Andie nodded, as if this made perfect sense. Then, out of nowhere, she went white and began patting her pockets for her phone.

"What?" Charlie got anxious, wondering if he had said something wrong.

"I totally forgot about the service project! We have to make two hundred dumplings—remember?"

He groaned. He had forgotten about it too, although they had a pretty good excuse for being late, appeasing an angry spirit and all. "If we run to the community center, you can still make it. I'll take you there."

"You sure?"

"As long as you don't tell anyone about my ghost whispering."

"Deal," she said, and they hurried out of the park together.

Later that night, long after the crowds had dispersed, Charlie volunteered to close up the Happy Horse. The festival had been a big success, minus the visit from the Slender One, and his family had celebrated over a dinner of dim sum. Afterward, he had told his parents to rest while he helped Waipo into bed.

"You made me very proud today," she told him as he drew her covers over her legs, like she used to do for him when he was little.

He flushed. "Thanks, Waipo."

"But don't get big head. I have a lot to teach you."

He chuckled, but she looked dead serious.

"We'll start tomorrow morning," she added.

Charlie chuckled. Waipo would always be Waipo. "Yes, ma'am."

Downstairs in the Happy Horse, he filled the mop bucket and was about to lock the door when one last customer came in.

"You got any tea eggs, kiddo?" said Mr. Ingersoll.

Charlie went over to greet his old friend, wishing he

could hug him. "Thank you for what you did today."

"You did the hard work. Well, you and that new friend of yours. What's her name?"

"Andie."

"There's something special about that girl." Mr. Ingersoll winked, and Charlie fidgeted. Andie *was* special. And brave. And all-around cool.

"How's Lou? Did she have a good time today?" Charlie blurted, changing the topic to Mr. Ingersoll's daughter before he started blushing. Louisa and her boyfriend had stopped by the festival earlier, thankfully *after* the Slender One's visit.

"She's wonderful, actually. Her boyfriend proposed."

"Whoa, really?"

"David was waiting until Christmas to pop the question, but I think Hungry Heart Row made an impression. Lila gave him a special pastry." He got a glint in his eye. "And Shirley pulled him aside and told him to get on with it already."

"That sounds like my grandma," Charlie said, chuckling. "Lou must be happy."

"She's over the moon. I only wish that I could walk her down the aisle."

"You can still do that, even if they can't see you."

Mr. Ingersoll shoved his hands into his pockets. "I don't think I'll make it. It's time for me to go."

Charlie gripped the mop handle. "Go where?"

Mr. Ingersoll looked around the Happy Horse,

inhaling its soy sauce scent. "I need to move on."

"But—" Charlie stopped himself and took a breath. He wasn't ready for this good-bye, not by a long shot, but if anyone deserved to rest, it was his old friend. "I understand, Mr. Ingersoll."

"I'll be back for the festival next year. Haven't missed one yet." He placed a ghostly hand on Charlie's shoulder as Charlie blinked back tears. "Go get a tissue."

That made Charlie laugh.

Mr. Ingersoll gave a little salute before he began to fade. "See you next year, kiddo."

Charlie lifted a hand. "See you, Mr. Ingersoll."

The shop went quiet. A lump formed in his throat, and it wouldn't go away no matter how hard he tried to swallow it. So he stood there in the store, alone, mop in hand, thinking about how lonely his mornings would be without Mr. Ingersoll bugging him about coffee and eggs.

A ping from his phone made him jump. He went to turn it off—he didn't feel like texting anyone—but the message was from Andie.

Boo! I'm texting you from the great beyond.

Charlie's heart did a little flip-flop. He wasn't sure how to reply when another text popped up.

Random question–do you know a good dessert place in Hungry Heart Row? My friend Fiona and I are a few blocks away. Want to come with?

His thumbs hovered over the screen. He needed to mop the floors, but then out of nowhere he heard Mr. Ingersoll's voice over his shoulder.

"Take her to Butter. Order the sweet potato pie. Trust me."

Charlie whipped around. There was nobody there, only the fading smell of a campfire. He smiled to himself and looked down at his phone.

I know a place. He sent Andie the address. Meet you in 10?

His stomach fluttered when she texted back:

Sounds good! My treat, Ghost Whisperer.

Charlie called upstairs to his parents that he was heading out for an hour. Then he stepped into the night, ready for the ghosts that he might encounter on his path and excited to see the girl waiting for him down the block.

Gimme Some Sugar

BY JAY COLES

"Leo!" I hear Momma scream for me upstairs.

I rush up and into her room, hoping right now isn't the moment, *that* moment, the moment she's spent the last few months warning me about. My mother is dying and just three months ago was given the ultimatum of paying a shit ton of money for surgery or having a handful of days to live. Momma doesn't make a whole lot, so we survive mostly on whatever checks she gets for disability, and I've not been able to find a job either. So, I take comfort and find solace in cooking.

"Hey, Sugar," Momma says, her head wrapped up in gauze, legs elevated like she's been in some really bad accident. Doctors say she has a brain tumor and has to keep her legs elevated. Sugar is her nickname for me. It's better than Stretch, which some people call me at school because I'm six feet tall. "Help Nurse Nicki real quick." Nurse Nicki is Momma's nurse who lives with us. And right now Nurse Nicki wants me to hold Momma's feet in place while she adjusts the sheets underneath her body. I've had worse jobs, so I don't even hesitate with assisting.

After helping, I head downstairs to the kitchen, take out all the ingredients I need to make this Cap'n Crunch French toast recipe I found on the Internet last night. I cook when I'm anxious. I see the flyer on the counter next to the stove and microwave—the one that I found on the subway last night. An ad I couldn't believe, it was almost like an omen or something, about a food competition in Rowbury with a five-thousand-dollar prize. It occurs every three years and is happening in five days. It's a televised event for the whole world to see, too, which has me a little nervous, but I can't let that distract me. This year, the flyer says it's being held at the community center.

I have a two-, three-, four-, maybe even five-second crisis with myself. I want to go so damn bad. I want to challenge myself. I want to visit Rowbury again, where my grandma lives and owns a soul food restaurant. I miss it there. The last time I was there was two summers ago, and I tried Korean food for the first time. Grandma's probably the most respected person in our family and rightfully so. Grandma's hard working and has been through so much and is still standing strong. I want to see her and taste her fried chicken again. But none of my wants are as big as my *one need*. I *need* that money. It could pay for Momma's surgery and could save her life. And besides all that, I'd get to do something that I really like doing: cook. Even if I don't win that moment, which would be absolutely devastating, and I wouldn't even know what to do or how to feel, I think it could be good for me. I've been so caged up here in Muncie, Indiana, and haven't really done anything as thrilling as this competition sounds.

But.

I don't know.

I try to distract myself, cranking up the music I'm playing. "No Regrets" by Lecrae is blasting through my cheap, bulky headphones. I crack open two eggs and beat them in a bowl with some rice milk, pouring a few tablespoons of cinnamon and sugar, then some brown sugar and nutmeg.

After putting some Cap'n Crunch cereal into a small sandwich bag, I take a frying pan and beat the bag until the pieces are all smashed and powdery, like a great dry rub.

I pick up a piece of bread and dip it in my French toast mix. Then I dip it in the crushed Cap'n Crunch and cook it in the frying pan until it's a nice, golden brown and ready to flip on the other side. While my French toast is cooking, I make a small fruit salad with some leftover strawberries and blueberries and some seriously ripe bananas that have been sitting on top of the fridge for over a week now.

I don't know what it is, maybe the smell of the sweet maple syrup heating up in the microwave or what, but I'm suddenly remembering back to when Momma was well and

Dad wasn't drinking so much, back to when things felt right and normal, and I felt whole and didn't have to deal with anxiety or panic attacks or pills, back to when I could go to Knight High School and feel like my friends and live a normal life. Momma used to make me French toast and fruit salad. Now I'm doing it for her.

The flyer.

I'm gazing at it, thinking about all the possibilities. I've always wanted to do something with food. I've always wanted to show off the skills that have been passed down to me from my ancestors.

This could be *it*. Right? But what if everything fails, and I actually, like, burn the whole place down from a grease fire? Or what if I put something in my food, and someone has an allergic reaction and, like, dies? What if I disappoint Grandma or, hell, myself by losing with one of her recipes—one of her recipes that I know is worthy of every damn award in the world? What if I get there and I . . . lock up on camera, if it's televised? I can see it now—me, frozen in place and dead faced, like a deer in headlights. Oh, God. What if I faint?

Ugh.

A billion other what-ifs float around in my head, banging up on one another, causing nothing but chaos upon chaos, like that time I thought it would be a good idea to try out for my school's play of *Peter and the Starcatcher* and fainted before saying my first line.

I gasp and hold in a breath until I can clear my

thoughts. I crank up my music a bit more. Music is such a powerful thing, and a few months ago I realized how music was like water in the way it drowns out things you don't want to deal with or things that are hard. For me, listening to music helps me mellow out and eases the anxiety.

After I finish cooking the French toast, I slap on some butter and drizzle the warm syrup on top of it. I scoop out some of the fruit salad onto a plate and take it upstairs to Momma. I have to feed it to her since she's lost some of the movement in her hands.

I show her the flyer. I place it on the metal tray that's connected to her medical bed in her bedroom. She can control it with the push of a button and brings it closer so she can read the flyer.

"Hungry Heart Row Food Competition, huh?" She pauses and looks up at me, then goes back to reading. "Wow. That's a lot of money at stake."

"Yeah," I say. "I need to do this, Mom." The way the words fall out of my mouth almost sounds like a desperate plea more than just asking for permission, and it's like she picks up on that.

She starts crying. And when she cries, no matter why, I do as well. I'm a watery mess, and it's way too early for this. It's in this moment, though, that I notice her skin. Up close, I can see that it's not the familiar brown that I remember. Up close, I can see that she's becoming more of a sick gray, turning into something that will one day no longer be Momma, but just a shadow of her that's slowly drifting away from me.

"I'm so proud of you," she says so sweet and slow, sweet and slow like the maple syrup running down the side of her hand. Her eyes tell me she thinks I should do it.

She pulls me into a hug. I squeeze, but not too tight. I wish the two of us could stay like this forever and ever. "I love you," I say, the words coming out with a breath. I can't imagine a universe where she doesn't exist or even one where she did exist and then stopped existing.

"I love you more, Sugar." I can smell the maple syrup on her.

A pause. I can almost feel the world spinning.

"I want you to go," she whispers through tears sneaking into her mouth. "I want you to go and do your thing, and I'll be here cheering for you." She's the most supportive person in the world.

"I'm going to win the money for you, Momma," I say, a lump in my throat. I blink the tears away, which takes more than one attempt.

"No, no, no, no," she goes. I imagine her shaking her head like she used to be able to. "It's not about the money. You're gonna go and have fun, and you're gonna feel alive. That's all I want, Sugar."

I move, and her automatic-sensor lights cut on. I was hoping she couldn't see my face, but I'm sure she does. She doesn't say anything, though, and I guess in some way, we're both enjoying the place we're resting in, a place between deep sadness and bittersweet hope.

* * *

I go online and register for the competition, feeling beads of sweat fall into my eyes. My heart beats hard inside my chest, but I'm ready for this.

After a while, I begin to pack, taking little breaks to cry or slow down and shut my eyes when I need to, throwing everything into a suitcase, not even caring what's in there. I'm filled with too much excitement and also anxiety right now—so much excitement and anxiety I might even have a panic attack. I end up calling Grandma to let her know I'm coming and that I'm doing the Hungry Heart Row Food Competition, and before we hang up, she screams with enthusiasm for about two minutes straight.

The next day, I'm so insanely happy, I wake up with butterflies fluttering in my stomach. I've never felt like this before.

I get showered and change into a pair of jeans and the Black Panther T-shirt I preordered when the movie came out, grab my headphones and my suitcase. I wave good-bye to Nurse Nicki and give Momma a good-bye kiss, a light peck on the forehead that lasts longer than usual, and then I'm out the door, headed to the train station for Rowbury, something heavy and churning in my stomach. I've not left her alone like this in years. And I'll potentially be gone for a whole week.

The entire nine-hour train ride I bought with money I saved up, I flip through my phone for all the things I could make for the competition. I scroll through so many websites and so many recipes, but none feel right, none feel good enough, none feel like winners, none fill me with that fluttering feeling in my stomach that tells me when a recipe is . . . *special*. And that's just what I fucking need, man. The thought that it's happening so soon, this week, and not later on in the month has my chest constricting and my jaws on fire again.

I inhale, taking the deepest breath, hands shaking. It's yet *another* strategy I read about online in some anxiety forum to help train your body to fight back against the symptoms of a panic attack. Sometimes it works. But most of the time it doesn't. I pop in one of my pills and try to nap on the train, listening to the new collab album by Beyoncé and Jay-Z.

I arrive in Rowbury and take yet another bus to the heart of Hungry Heart Row. I almost forgot how amazing this place really is. It's certainly a lot different from the ghetto where I live, mostly because the only shops we have are run by either white folks or black folks, but here—here there are so many other cultures and cuisines and histories, and I love it.

A breeze blows, and I grasp my elbows. I forgot the weather was like this this time of year. One time I was here in Rowbury for grandpa's funeral, and it was humid as hell for autumn. The weather gods have blessed me this time around. I'm walking down the sidewalk, and it hits me that I don't really even remember the way to grandma's restaurant, since she moved to a new location this year. It's called Butter.

There's a white boy with red hair and a thin, red mustache holding a sign that says TOUR GUIDE. He's passing out brochures about Hungry Heart Row and maps of all the wonderful places to eat. I notice he's got a Hungry Heart Row Food Competition flyer pasted on his sign.

He locks eyes with me, and I immediately look away. *Shit.* Eye contact with strangers has to go in the top five weirdest things about life. He's walking over to me.

Shit. I have to look at him now. And I can't slip my headphones on like I don't hear him. I mean, I could, but that would be hella rude right now that he's standing so close.

He smiles. "Hi. Welcome to Hungry Heart Row. Brochure or map?"

"Map, please," I say.

After stopping at some really awesome halal food cart by the park on my way to Grandma's restaurant and getting probably the most delicious chicken gyro I've ever had, I stop by a few restaurants just to smell around. The smells are my favorite and make me feel more at home sometimes than in Indiana. I linger inside a few places to maybe even get some inspiration for what to make for the competition, including a dim-sum place and some delicious pastry shop, too. Along the way I take in everything—the food carts, the restaurants, the architecture, the smells again, the

people, hell, even the trees that are a plethora of colors—
everything is so beautiful, and I didn't know how much
I missed it here. The girl in the pastry shop is wearing a
name badge with the name Lila and a shirt that says HUN-
GRY GHOST FESTIVAL and the dates; it's happening in a
couple of weeks. She seems like she really likes it around
these parts. I buy a blue concha before heading out.

Once I find my way to Grandma's restaurant, after
what feels like a zillion wrong turns and dead ends, I walk
in and smell all the bomb soul food—her famous fried
chicken with all the creole seasonings, thyme, rosemary,
and tarragon. I even get a whiff of her famous sweet potato
pie, and I'm practically drooling.

Grandma is cleaning off a table with a wet rag when I
creep up behind her to surprise her.

I hug and squeeze her from her back. She smells like
fresh rolls and cinnamon butter.

She gasps at first, spooked out, and then whips around
fast. "Grandson!" she shouts—so loud half of the restaurant probably stops eating and ordering. "Gimme some
sugar!"

She kisses me on the cheek. It's a wet, gross-feeling
kiss, but really shows me just how much she's missed me.
Up close, I can see all the stress wrinkles and gray-white
hairs that have appeared since the last time I saw her.

We hug a second time. "Good to see you, grandson.
Saturday, you gon' blow Hungry Heart Row outta the
park. You just better 'member everything yo' granmammy

taught you." She knows about the competition and she knows about Momma and she knows why I'm here, and she thinks I'm using one of her recipes. I've not even decided on what I want to make yet, which is probably terrible to admit. "Hey, you just 'member it's all in the butter. I keep trynna tell your cousins that, and they don't listen for the life of 'em."

Butter is probably Grandma's favorite ingredient, and she puts it in nearly everything. I believe she'd put it in her raisin bran in the mornings if she could.

One year, she made deep-fried sticks of butter and dipped them in chocolate sauce and melted peanut butter. I'm not gonna lie. It was pretty flame, but I'm sure at least one of my arteries clogged up.

Grandma takes me into the kitchen of the restaurant and introduces me to all the workers. For many years, it's just been a family-run restaurant; my cousins were the bussers and waitresses, aunts and uncles did the cooking, and grandma just did the managing and taste-testing. I'd apprentice with her some summers I spent here, which were mostly when I was a little kid. That was long before grandpa died. Ever since he died, grandma had to hire other people—people outside the family, but still people she could trust, people who could handle a stick of butter, I'm sure.

I'm looking around the kitchen and see Hungry Heart Row Food Competition flyers posted everywhere and posters of past competitions pasted along the walls too.

There're first-place trophies from the early nineties and eighties.

"Grandma, you won these?" I ask. Of course she did. I remember that she won the Hungry Heart Row Food Competition, but I didn't know she'd won it *this* many times. As much as I'm impressed, it's extra pressure for me.

She looks at me and just offers a warm smile, the wrinkles on her forehead lifting as she cocks her head back and closes her eyes, like she's reminiscing or transporting herself to back in the day.

She grabs my hand and places one of the trophies in it. "It feels just like yesterday I was cooking up almost-butter chicken and steamed asparagus, and all those other family foods."

I don't say anything back. I stand still and listen, feeling the weight of the trophy, feeling the weight of pressure on my shoulders so suddenly.

"Y'know, I never entered with the intent on winning. I went in with the intent of cooking something good, putting a piece of my soul in the food—something that'll explode the expectations of the people tasting it."

It feels like all the stars have brightened and aligned. Maybe I *should* use one of her recipes. Ha. They've won in the past; maybe they'll win again.

"Oh, yeah?" I backpedal in my thoughts.

"Mm-hm. Every year, the judges were blown away. You see, there'll be a lot of folks there. Korean folks, Thai folks, Persian folks, Muslim folks, African folks, black folks, white folks, and a bunch of others—all making different things, but all with the same goal. Not all of them are gonna know to put their soul in the food and become one and the same with it. But you know how. It's in your blood, grandson."

Grandma opens the book of secret family recipes and flips through it. "Any of these look good to you?"

"That one," I say, pointing to something that looks like glazed chicken with cheesy potatoes.

She goes to the back to retrieve the ingredients and returns. "Ready to try it out?"

My heart stops and then starts again. I really need this practice. If I really want to win this money for Momma, I better get to practicing. I mean, it'll only maximize my chances of winning, right? I nod at Grandma and accept her offer to make the recipe.

"No other person in the world outside of our family knows this recipe, kiddo," she says. "This one is extra special. My great-great-grandmother created this one."

I watch her begin washing the chicken breasts and flouring them up, adding tons of different seasonings. "Pass me that paprika."

I watch in awe at how fast she's doing everything, trying to memorize every move she makes. Just in case.

I'm creating a mental checklist, searing this moment— this training montage—into my brain for future reference. Suddenly there are so many spices in the air, and I'm trying my hardest not to sneeze. Sneezing would mean I'll blink and miss a moment.

She takes a metal bowl out of the cabinet above the stove and then begins flattening the chicken breasts with it before frying them. She shows me how to prepare the potatoes and how to properly season them—how to know how much seasoning is enough. She even makes a joke about the white folks who will be in the competition. "They won't know how to season anything," she says, slightly chuckling. "Poor babies."

I bust out laughing too.

"You know yo' momma didn't used to know how to season either. I used to have her in the kitchen cookin' all the time. And she would drown the food in seasoning. Mashed potatoes would turn green from how much parsley she would use. Mac and cheese would be black from all the pepper. It was a mess."

I laugh some more. I like this. I miss times similar to this one with her so, so much and to have them back so briefly means everything to me. I take in everything, holding this moment close to my heart, like a Polaroid picture.

"Glad she learned. And I'm glad you're here learning from me too. I dreamed up this day. But I didn't dream up her getting sick." Everything stops for a brief moment. I watch as a tear or two streak down her cheek, she rubs her face with her sleeve and continues to chop up a red onion. I know Grandma feels bad about not getting to visit her daughter because of the restaurant tying her up all the time. I know every night she talks to Momma on the phone, she feels worse about not being there. "She's gonna be a'ight, though. I've been telling myself that everything is going to be a'ight. My baby will be okay. The Lord isn't gonna take her away from us like this. He won't."

I sigh, trying to blink back the tears now, but I'm too late.

"The pan needs more butter," Grandma murmurs, like she's trying to keep her voice down or like the tears she's holding back are lowering the volume of her voice.

"More butter?" I ask.

"Not actual butter, honey," she says, and chuckles at me. "The butter in the soul. It's an expression from the South. It means, as you're cookin', try and feel more in tune with what you're makin'. If you feel it in your soul, the taste will be amplified. Sometimes, though, things just need more butter, literally."

Whoa. I'm so confused. I need some time to think about this.

"Grandma, why aren't you entering the contest too?"

"I would, baby. I really would. But I turned seventy this year. Sixty-nine is the maximum age."

"Oh."

"It's your turn."

"But I'm scared and nervous," I say, feeling those things even right now. I don't make eye contact with her, until she lifts my head up with her finger like I'm a little kid again.

I expect her to say something like, *Ain't nothing to*

be scared of, boy. But she doesn't. Instead, she says, very calmly and sweetly, "That's okay. Being scared and nervous are things you're supposed to feel, but you gotta be brave, baby. Being brave means going on while you're scared and nervous, keeping up that fight inside your beating heart. I promise you'll eventually end up winning that fight."

My heart feels real full right now, and suddenly I'm not worrying as much, because I have the best teacher in the world—a multi–Hungry Heart Row Food Competition champion. I don't have to worry about anything. At least, not in this moment. The thing about anxiety is that it creeps up on you whenever it wants to. Sometimes when you are least expecting and sometimes in those moments you're trying to be the most present— the most *you*.

We take the chicken out of the fryer and melt some white cheese over it before pouring the already cheese-infused potatoes on top. Her soul-smothered chicken, smothered in potatoes and love.

One whiff of the air, and I'm in heaven. It smells so damn good, my mouth is watering, tongue tingling.

We finish cooking within half an hour. It's a relatively fast dish, Grandma reminds me, hoping that I use it, and then we eat up.

I feel warm and fuzzy and like everything is going to work out and in my favor. After all, it sounds like my destiny, right? And I even think I know exactly what I'm going to make now. Already. I missed the deadline for turning in what I'm going to cook to guarantee my ingredients would be there, but their website has all the ones they're providing, so I'll just have to work with those.

"I'm gonna start cleaning up 'round here. You go on and get some rest." She hands me the key to her apartment, where I'll be staying, to put my luggage in, and she makes sure she gives me the book of secret family recipes, and my eyes get really wide, my chest gets really tight. I grab a slice of apple pie before heading there. Her apartment is literally across the street, so I don't have a far walk at all. I don't even need to use the map. As I'm eating the apple pie with one hand, trying to imagine all of the ingredients before I read about them later, I'm transported back to when I was just a little boy. Suddenly I'm just ten years old, in the kitchen with both Momma and Grandma, making Thanksgiving pies.

Before bed, I FaceTime Momma just to check up on her and let her know how things have been going since I got to Rowbury. Once we hang up, I flip through the book of family recipes, seeing things I only vaguely remember from my childhood. I'm going to make Grandma's soul-smothered chicken. It's the perfect thing to try to recreate—a classic that Grandma made me that time the lights were off in our apartment and the gas bill was overdue and Momma and I lived with her. I'll grab some ingredients from the restaurant before I head to the competition. I'm pretty sure I can do that without getting disqualified. Before I fall asleep, I make sure to go online and register what I'm going to make, and I keep Momma's smile seared into my eyelids for motivation.

A few days pass by and suddenly, it's Saturday. I wake up in the morning choking on anxiety, a familiar sourness in my gut, and at any moment, I just may throw up. I'm hoping it happens before tonight—before the food competition.

Grandma drives me to the place where the competition is being hosted at the Rowbury Community Center, and I can see lines of people filing into the red-brick building once we pull in. I don't know if this is all my competition or also people who will be watching me, but my anxiety is starting to act up. My chest feels tight; I can't really breathe right.

I rush into my backpack and pull out my headphones. I put them on and play the first song on my playlist. There's something about the bass in this Drake song that calms me, makes me feel like I'm not drowning anymore. I can squeeze my eyes shut and work on my breathing.

In.

Out.

Slower.

In.

Out.

Grandma probably has no clue what's going on with me, and she doesn't ask, so maybe that's a good thing so

I don't get distracted. If she were to ask, it would be all I could think about.

Finally we arrive at the community center. Eagerly, I rush in and a gasp slips out of me from how much this is exactly what I pictured it would be. I look back, and Grandma's waving me to come back to her.

She hands me a clipboard for signing in and then escorts me to my cooking station before wishing me luck. When I get to my little station, I scan the room again and see all of my competition, a lump burning up in my gut. My throat is dry like I've eaten an entire thing of salt, and my chest is tight, and these are some of the signs of one of my panic attacks.

The five judges take turns counting down, each saying one number, before they start the timer overhead.

Five.

Four.

Three.

Two.

One.

Everyone darts and zooms. Pots clinking and pans smacking. Stoves sizzling and butter caramelizing, funneling in the air like a sweet fog. The world spins faster around me. My chest feels so damn heavy. I pull out my bottle of tiny round saviors that continue to help me over and over again in times of need like this moment right now where I feel like there are a zillion fire ants in my gut and a shit-ton of grenades going off in my stomach and head, bringing on a panic attack.

I squeeze my eyes shut for a moment.

I put on my headphones so I can stop feeling like at any second I'll burst into flames. I'm going through my "mellow out" playlist, keeping the volume down low enough so I can hear the judges and the timer.

The timer above the cooking stations is blinking at me in huge red numbers how much time I've got left. It's such a sad and depressing reminder of the amount of time Momma probably has left to live. Unlike Momma, at least I know exactly how much time I've got left. And looking at the timer, that's one hour. At the end, no matter what, I know *I'll* be alive. That's more than I can say for Momma.

I'm about to make Grandma's recipe, but with my own twist. I will need to put my own soul into this dish.

I gather all of the ingredients from a large pantry that the competitors get to choose from.

5 chicken breasts—one for each judge

¼ teaspoon of salt

¼ teaspoon of lemon-pepper seasoning

¼ teaspoon of paprika

2 tablespoons of olive oil

3 sticks of butter

1 onion, sliced

½ cup of Colby–Monterey Jack, melted

½ cup of pepper jack cheese, melted

10 strips of maple bacon

Some sort of green garnish

I cut the chicken breasts into halves, season them with the dry seasonings, and bake them. When they're ready and cooked all the way through, I wrap each half in bacon and fry them with onion slices until the bacon's a nice, crispy, golden brown and the onions are soft and cooked through and through. The whole time they cook and simmer, I run the stick of butter around the chicken halves for even crispier edges and that buttery taste that brings anything to the next level—a strategy probably everybody black knows, and I guess it's to my benefit there's not many black people in this competition. I scan the crowd once more and lock eyes with Grandma. She's got these big, alert eyes and a smile that stretches from ear to ear. I can tell she's proud of me.

It hits me that I'm cooking in a cast-iron skillet. Cast-iron skillets are important where I'm from—commonly used for corn bread there. They're symbolic, if you will. Symbolic of our ancestors, but also symbolic in the sense that people are a lot like them. The way they can be absolutely resilient and multifaceted and complex and able to take the heat. Kind of like Grandma. She's all those things and then some. She's someone I aspire to be like some day. She carried an entire family on her back, started up her own restaurant, and became a professional cook without even having to go to school, and she's epically won this competition almost every time she entered, proving that she's capable of doing anything she really sets her mind to.

Who knows, maybe this is that next step I need to take

to be more like her. I tell myself that I've got to do crazy, hard, and brave things, like Grandma's done all her life, to be anything like her.

It's all in the butter. Grandma's voice suddenly gets stuck in my head, like she's the Holy Ghost, and she's guiding me through all this, showing me just what to do.

I look around again. I see a mother and son cooking together—or at least this is what they appear to be. I see a husband and wife cooking together. I see two friends cooking together. And I see people who're all by themselves, relying on family recipes or their own creations, like me.

Focus, Leo.

Don't get intimidated.

Don't back down.

More butter.

There's something about the smell or the sound of the bacon sizzling or something else that makes me think of Momma, that sends me swimming, no, drowning in memories of life with her healthy, growing up with a mom who knew she had a life timeline that had fewer days than her own son. I imagine buttering soft, fresh bread with her for holiday feasts. I imagine her warm smile and laugh—her usual smile and laugh, not the one she has now—the one she had back when we'd tell each other jokes as we'd cook together. It's the thought of never ever getting any of this back that has me shaking as I let the plastic covering of the stick of butter fall into the pan. I can't breathe all of a

sudden. I crank the volume up on my headphones and fish out the wrapping and toss it in the trash.

I force myself to release the tongs in my hand, to back away, just for a breather, a second that feels more like forever. Squeezing my eyes shut, I slow my breathing and crank the music a little louder, still not too loud, though.

I walk back over to my station, the timer is closer to 5 minutes now. I make sure the cheese is melted perfectly before pouring it over my bacon-wrapped chicken breasts.

I put the food onto a plate as fast as I can, still trying to be all neat about it, but remembering how Grandma used to always say that no soul food is ever "neat," because it's messy putting your soul into something. I just hope these judges are thinking the same way when they taste the food.

HOLY SHIT. HOLY SHIT. HOLY SHIT.

Oh.

My.

God.

My eyes widen as I stare at the plates in front of me. Wow. Wow. I did that. I did THAT! It's beautiful, and it looks like the way Grandma used to serve it to us, even with the fancy green garnish on the side.

Suddenly the timer blares, and everyone who's competing shoots their arms up, like they're surrendering or reaching up high in the sky to collect victory stars. I let my headphones fall on my neck, keeping my hands up, high and still.

Everything is done. This is it.

The world is still spinning.

My chest hurts. *That money.*

Heart pounding and I struggle for breath.

Fingers numb.

Blood hot.

Anxiety.

Anticipation.

I don't even notice I'm crying until I feel little droplets roll down my chin, drying there. The stop siren is still buzzing and blaring for another few seconds, and all the judges come forward, weaving throughout the different cooking stations inspecting all the food for plating and style. I probably don't get any points this round, especially since I notice I spilled a little melted cheese on the side of one of the plates. *Fuck.*

The judges come over to my station, writing notes on their clipboards. Some of them have smiles. Others don't. Some of them look at me. Others don't. One of them even kinda rolls his eyes. I can feel my heart nearly palpitating in my chest.

I can still hear my music playing around my neck, and it's so bitterly quiet in this room, I'm sure everybody can hear John Mayer.

Oh shit.

Next is the tasting round. *I need that money,* I think.

Trust in the butter. Trust that my soul is enough.

Some people made extra food, so we can try their

dishes before the judges do. I walk around and taste all
kinds of food—food I've never even heard of or thought
of. Some of it tastes so damn good; others don't.

Eventually, I make it back to my station and wait for
the judges to come over again.

The first judge who does is a short, white man with red
hair. He takes a fork and sticks it directly in the middle of
a chicken breast.

"Tender. Perfectly cooked all the way through. Nice
and soft." He doesn't look at me when he says this.
Just writes something down and takes a big, cheesy bite.
"Excellent."

Yes! I celebrate in my head. *Point for me, right?* He's only
one judge, though. There are four others. If he likes it and
the others don't, his compliment would suddenly mean
shit. So I stop celebrating and wait for the others to come
around to my station. I stare at my brown hands, messy
and greasy-looking from giving this meal my all, until I
notice two people in front of me, both in casual clothes.
The next two judges.

They are both women—one's Latina, and the other is
black, with her natural hair out and proud, reminding me
of Momma, catching me off guard for a split second. They
both compliment my work and smile. Something about
this makes me feel warm and fuzzy inside.

The last two judges finally make their way to my station and try my soul-smothered chicken, and they're
both reactionless, like they're somewhere between Simon

Cowell and Gordon Ramsay on the judge niceness scale.

The judges huddle together, maybe to compare whatever they wrote down on their clipboards. Minutes slip past—agonizing minutes that make me feel clammy all over.

I interlock my fingers and say a quick prayer. I don't know what I'm even praying or who I'm even praying to anymore, but it's my desperate attempt at hoping I win this.

The judge pulls out the big check for five thousand dollars. It's one of those huge ones you'd see on a game show. Everyone gasps. One even slips out from deep within my gut.

They announce third place first. It's an Asian girl who made some form of moo shu pork with noodles. She walks over to accept the bronze trophy and shake the hands of the judges. They even take a photo for her. The whole room erupts in applause.

The Latina judge is getting ready to announce the next winner. She's talking slowly, describing how much she enjoyed this next dish, how it reminded her of her honeymoon to Italy a few years ago. A yelp comes from the back. A mother and son who made some sort of Italian dish win second place.

I don't even notice that my fingers are crossed until I go to clap for them.

"And finally, for first place in this year's Hungry Heart Row Food Competition, we've got a new champion."

The room falls silent.

I imagine a drum roll going on in the distance, so much hope trying to beat, beat, beat its way out of, or into, my chest.

I clasp my hands together tighter.

"Leonelvis Watkins." My name falls out of the judges' mouths simultaneously and in different pitches.

"That's me." I have to convince myself, the words coming out in a weird glob. "That's me. That's my name!"

I gasp and gasp and gasp deeper. It's in this moment that I realize that my hands aren't shaking anymore, my chest isn't so heavy, my jaws aren't burning up. I'm standing in shock at just how far I've come, from once upon a time being an anxious mess who would've never even entered the competition to growing a pair and not only signing up but also winning, and the tears are nearly pouring from me now.

There are so many butterflies fluttering in my stomach right now. And I feel frozen for a moment. Suddenly my face is a watery mess, and everything is blurring in front of me. I have to force myself to take tiny steps toward the judges, where they are holding up the first place trophy and check. I'm so happy right now, and there's an entire Fourth of July celebration inside me. A celebration's going on in my chest, not only because I won—holy shit, the more I let that sink in the more it feels huge—but because I didn't let my fear or anxiety stop me or destroy me one bit. I own my anxiety; my anxiety doesn't own me.

After taking the photo while holding the trophy and check, I see Grandma in the audience with the biggest smile on her face. Immediately I think about Momma, and the tears keep coming.

I call her up. I can't wait to tell her the news. My heart is racing, and I don't think it's a panic attack coming out.

She answers, her voice a little croaky, like she's waking up from a nap.

"Momma," I say through the phone, hella excitement probably evident in my voice, "I'm coming home. You're gonna live."

And I will too, and I wish I could live inside this moment forever.

The Missing Ingredient

BY REBECCA ROANHORSE

Mom's screaming again.

Top of her lungs, with enough f-bombs to send the kitchen staff scurrying for cover. Something crashes against the tile floor, the high, tinny sounds reverberating through the empty restaurant like the cymbal solo in my favorite Peaches song. Heather, the bartender, flinches. I take another sip of my Diet Coke.

"Kelsie!" my mom screams. "Get in here!"

Heather shoots me a sympathetic glance. "You don't have to go in there, Kelsie."

I slide off the barstool. "Yeah, I do. Or she'll bring the drama out here. And no one wants that."

Heather grimaces. She knows I'm right.

"It'll be fine," I tell her. "She's just fired up because

a review of the restaurant came out in the *Rowbury Times* today." I tried to beat my mom to the paper, taking the one that lands on our stoop every morning and tossing it in the recycling out back. I even made sure no one coming in for the lunch shift brought a copy with them. But somehow she'd gotten hold of one anyway.

"Was the review bad?" Heather asks.

"Not as bad as the last one. Three stars, I think? They liked the drinks." I give her a weak smile and start back toward the kitchen. I can hear my mom still muttering at volume, but I haven't heard anything else break, so the angry is probably passing into tears by now.

Behind me, Heather says, "It's hard running a restaurant all by yourself like your mom does. It's a lot of stress since . . . you know. Your dad. Your mom's lucky she has you. That she has someone who loves her."

I pause, look back. Heather's a nice person, but she's only been working at the Indigenous Gastronomist a few weeks. I know she means well, but she doesn't know anything. She sees the slick modern décor, the glass wall up front, the hip antler chandeliers that drop soft, gauzy lighting over the intimate clusters of tables, and she thinks everything is beautiful here. She hasn't caught on to the rot just underneath. The stink of failure hiding behind the pretty plating. She doesn't know that the restaurant is failing, and my family is failing along with it.

I think about telling her. Telling her that I hate this place, and more than that, I hate my mother, and my mother hates me. But I know normal families don't hate each other, so people like Heather always react with some platitude about how that can't be true and how my mom really loves me and I just don't realize it because I'm only sixteen, so I just smile and say what she expects me to say.

"Yeah, we're both real lucky."

"Oh, there you are!" Mom says, grabbing my arm, her fingers digging into my bicep, as soon as I come through the swinging door. "Did you see the paper today? Three stars! We won't survive on three stars." She literally spins me around to face the newspaper.

The restaurant section of the *Rowbury Times* is spread out on the stainless-steel cooking counter. I rub at the red marks she leaves on my arm and, with my other hand, turn the paper around to face me. Skim the articles. There are three reviews for this Sunday. A new Mexican restaurant on Tansy Street, a halal food cart in the park that I tried last week and loved, and mom's restaurant, the Indigenous Gastronomist. The other restaurants have good to great reviews. Ours is by far the worst.

"You shouldn't read—" I start before Mom cuts me off.

"Did you see this?" she demands, turning the paper back toward herself and stabbing a finger at the print. "Did you see what they said?" She leans over to read: "'The innovative restaurant, serving fusion Native American cuisine, was once the most promising newcomer on Hungry Heart Row. But after the sudden death of its founder, Franklin

Tenorio, the dishes seem to be missing something. Call it heart. Although the endeavor has been nobly carried on by his wife, the Indigenous Gastronomist fails to live up to the hype' . . . blah, blah . . ." She huffs. "They don't even mention me by name. Just 'his wife.' My name is Jeanette." She stabs at the paper again. "Jeanette!"

"Well, Dad did start the restaurant," I say. "And you're not even Native."

She stares at me so hard I take a step back, worried I've gone too far. But somebody had to say it. It's not like nobody's thinking it.

"Mind your mouth," she spits at me. "You're part white too."

"I never said I wasn't. I'm just saying that this was Dad's dream, and he's the Native one so . . ."

Mom's face turns a dangerous shade of red, and her words come out hot and fast, grease popping in a sauté pan. "Your father was a line cook when I met him. A cook! A nothing. I'm the one with the culinary degree. I'm the chef. But because I'm a woman . . ." Her fingers curl into fists, and it takes her a moment before she can talk again. When she does, her voice practically seethes. "I work my fingers raw for this place. Who plans the menus? I do. Who hires the staff? I do. Who makes sure every plate is perfect when it goes out that door?"

"Well then don't read—"

"But even I can taste it," she says, looking down at the paper again, "what Mr. High-and-Mighty Reviewer calls 'heart.' Your father had a gift, and I just don't seem to be able to . . ." She trails off.

I want to say something comforting to my mom, but the truth is that this is not a new conversation. Every time a review comes out in the paper, or on Served, or even on some rando blog, we have this talk. Because they all say the same thing. Beautiful restaurant, great presentation, but something's missing.

I watch as Mom's shoulders heave, and before I can say anything more, she's crying, heavy and hard. I have to wait a few minutes for her to get herself back together. When she finally does, she looks at me with red-rimmed eyes. "I just want the restaurant to do well, Kelsie. Is that so awful, for me to want that? Am I a bad mother for that?"

Yes! I want to scream. Not because this was Dad's dream before it was yours, and not because you talk about him like he's trash even now, but because you are obsessed with your stupid five-star review. Because you love this restaurant more than you love me. *Yes, that makes you a bad mom! Yes!*

But instead I say, "No, Mom. I'm real lucky to have you."

"We're lucky to have each other." She smiles through her tears and comes around the corner of the table to hug me. She's wearing short sleeves, and the skin on her arms is cold against my own. The hug is suffocating, but mercifully brief. She lets me go and turns back to the newspaper.

"We should have dinner together tonight," she says absently. "Something simple. Just the two of us, maybe at that Persian place . . ." Her voice drifts away as her eyes are drawn to the review again. I can see her lips moving silently as she reads it. Twist to bitterness on "his wife." The feel of her arms around me lingers, and I realize that I can't remember the last time she hugged me. Maybe not since Dad's funeral two years ago. Against my better judgment, I feel a little hopeful. Enough to make me say, "So we'll have dinner together tonight?"

She looks up, confused. "What?"

"You were saying maybe we could do something, just us."

She rubs at her forehead. "Did I? Hey, could you ask Heather to come in for a sec? I need to tweak that cranberry-sage martini recipe before brunch starts. If I can get the balance right, I'm sure it's going to be a winner. Maybe even worth another star . . ."

She's still talking when I slip out the door.

I don't think she even notices.

It's the lull between brunch and dinner rush, and I'm out by the Dumpster smoking a joint and texting my best friend Morgan when the kitchen door slams open. I jump up, put out the J against the wall, and tuck it into my shirt pocket. Pull out a stick of gum with the same quick move and drop it in my mouth before I turn back around to see who it is.

Seth, one of the busboys, is dragging trash out. He heaves it up over the edge of the Dumpster lip and drops it in. He's got his uniform on—black pants and a black button-up shirt with a generic tribal pattern across the chest. In small turquoise letters across the pocket it says making more of myself! in some obnoxiously optimistic font.

Seth's a Fresh Start kid. Fresh Start is the program my dad began to bring teens from the reservation to the city to work at the restaurant. My mom hates Fresh Start, but she can't get rid of it; it's written into the incorporation documents for the restaurant or something. I don't know why she would care. It costs her almost nothing, since the Fresh Start kids all live below me and mom in our basement apartment across the street from the restaurant and work for minimum wage. But maybe they remind her of Dad. And if they remind her of Dad, I can only imagine what looking at me every day does to her. No wonder she hates me.

Seth hasn't noticed me yet, and I try to act causal, hoping he won't. But he sniffs the air dramatically and looks my way, eyebrows raised. "Didn't figure you for a bad girl," he drawls in his Texas accent. "Does your mama know?"

I roll my eyes, annoyed, but mainly worried. Seth's pretty new, and I don't know if he's cool like that, yet. He's from some small rez in southwest Texas; I can't remember his tribe, and he's only been here a month or so. He's never spoken to me. In fact, he's pretty much gone out of his way to avoid me. I figured it was because Mom is his boss. Some of the kids don't mind it; some like it and try to get me to do favors for them or put in a good word with Mom. But Seth has never even seemed to notice me. Until now.

"She doesn't care," I say, trying to sound cool and collected. "She's got other things on her mind."

"Poor thing." He tsks as he pulls a cigarette pack from his pants. He shakes out one and tucks it between his lips. "What was your nice white mama yelling about?"

"The restaurant got a so-so review in the Sunday paper. I mean, it wasn't terrible, but it wasn't good, either. Mom wasn't happy."

"'Mom wasn't happy . . .'" He stretches the words out long and slow, like they mean more than I'm letting on. His match flares as he lights the tip of his cigarette. "Sorry to hear it."

"Yeah, well, it's nothing new. You're not working at Le Cirque, you know."

He tilts his head. Flicks the strand of black hair that's escaped from his ponytail out of his eyes and gives me a look. "This is the best job I've ever had," he says. "Three meals a day. A roof over my head. My own bed that I don't got to share unless I want to. Maybe you take a place like this for granted," he says, jerking his head to indicate the restaurant, and maybe Rowbury as a whole, "but you ain't ever lived on the rez."

Heat rises on my face, making my ears burn. "You shouldn't smoke cigarettes," I say. It's kind of a blurt, and I know I don't have any business telling Seth not to smoke when I indulge in the occasional joint, but I don't like the way he's looking at me, like I'm some kind of stupid, rich, half-white girl who doesn't get it.

He exhales, smoke curling around his head. "Tobacco is pleasing to the Creator. Didn't your daddy teach you that before he died? Creator don't mind as long as it's that clean mountain tobacco you're smokin'. Which this is." He lifts the cigarette in a kind of salute.

"Tobacco's sacred," I say, remembering exactly what my dad taught me. "You should be using it in ceremony, for prayers and stuff. Not just standing around smoking it."

"My life is a constant prayer," he quips.

"To who? Lord Voldemort?"

He raises an eyebrow at that but doesn't say anything.

"Sorry," I mutter, already regretting my stupid Harry Potter joke. Now Seth probably thinks I'm not only spoiled, but a total nerd. This is turning into the worst conversation ever. "I better go inside," I say, pushing off the wall. "Dinner rush starts soon, and Mom wants me up front at the hostess station."

"She's an ambitious one."

I pause. "Who? My mom?"

"I can guess her story. A lady like her. Probably went to one of them fancy culinary schools and graduated top of her class. Real smart. But things didn't work out like she expected. Thought her smarts would be enough to get her what she wanted. She underestimated."

"Underestimated what?" I don't really know Mom's story before she met Dad. It's something she only shares in snarls and bursts of rage.

"I bet having a baby put a real knot in her plans," Seth

continues. "Bet someone like your mama was thinking she'd be a chef in New York City or maybe one of those celebrity places in Las Vegas. But here she is, in Rowbury, a single mom with a teenage daughter and mediocre restaurant reviews. That must really chap her hide."

I wince. Even without knowing Mom's whole story, I can guess that Seth's real close to the truth. I always suspected I was a burden, but to hear someone else say it stings more than I care to admit.

"You ever get tired of it?" he asks.

"Of Rowbury?"

"Of your mama. Doing everything your mama wants even when it's never gonna be enough to make her happy."

"It's not like that."

Seth's face says he doesn't believe me. And he shouldn't, because, yeah, he's right. But he doesn't even know me, or my life. He can psychoanalyze my mom all he wants, but I'm not going to let him do it to me. I fold my arms across my chest. "My mom's problems don't affect me. I do what I want." I pat the pocket with the leftover weed in it to make my point.

Seth leans against the wall, lets that cigarette hang loose in his mouth. "And what is it that you want? Besides hiding out here and getting high?"

"None of your business."

"People want things," he says. "No shame in that. Problem is, they're not willing to sacrifice for them. Not willing to give up something to get something. That's the trouble with your mama, too. For all her ambition, she's not willing to sacrifice."

"And what have you sacrificed in your life?"

He exhales blue, fixes me with dark eyes. "You couldn't take it if I told you."

The way he says it makes the little hairs on the back of my neck stand up. I shake it off, swallow down a sudden urge to get out of here. I plant my feet instead, stubborn, not willing to let Seth intimidate me. "You're full of it."

He shrugs one shoulder. "Okay, then. Think what you want. I'm not telling you what to do. I'm just saying that everything comes at a cost. The bigger the cost, the bigger the reward. Where I come from, there's people who can help with things like that. And maybe I learned a thing or two from those people. So maybe I could help you, too."

That same little voice that made my hair stand up whispers in my ear to beware, and my courage falters a bit. I remember that I don't know this guy. And that what he's saying . . . well, it's a lot. But then I remind myself that he's only eighteen, not that much older than me, and he's probably just big talk, trying to prove he's cool.

"We have those here, too," I say, voice sarcastic. "They're called criminals."

He shakes he head. Squints at me through the smoky haze that surrounds him. "Not like that. More like . . ." He makes a sort of abracadabra motion with his hand. "Harry Potter."

"Magic?"

"We don't call it that back home." His eyes linger on

mine as he takes a long drag. I rub at my arms, chilled. I look up, expecting a cloud to have passed between me and the sun, but the sky is still that bright late-spring blue.

"This is the weirdest conversation I've ever had," I say. "You know you sound completely wack."

He grins. "Think about it, city girl. What is it white people say? 'There's on more things in heaven and on earth'?"

"You know Shakespeare?"

He straightens, stubs out his cigarette under his foot, clearly done with the conversation. "Just think about it." He slips his hands into his pockets and turns for the door.

"Wait!" Because I do want something. And I believe in witchcraft. Sorta. But I also think Seth is the kind of guy who might know a guy who could make things happen, magic or not. So I have to know. Even if my stomach is doing a flip-flop and my heart is pounding a mile a minute.

Seth stops. Cocks his head expectantly.

"Let's say I did want something, and I was willing to . . . sacrifice. What would I have to do?"

His grin stretches a little wider. "For starters? Cook for me. But not just any old thing. It's gotta mean something to you. You do that, and I can make sure you get anything you want."

"What do you think he meant by all that?" Morgan asks the next day as we make our way between classes. Morgan's got trig right next to my AP History class, so we usually walk together, stopping at my locker before crossing the court-yard to the honors buildings. It's my favorite time of the day besides lunch, because it's the only time we get to talk.

"I don't know. It was weird, though. Like, I could swear it felt . . . real."

"What do you mean 'real'?"

"Like what he was saying was important. The truth." I shiver, the memory enough to raise goose bumps. "I can't explain it, but it was heavy."

"Yeah, but you were smoking weed, Kels. Being high will do that to you."

I shrug. I'm sure she's right, and I'm just being paranoid.

"But let's say he could make things happen," she says, surprising me with the one-eighty. "What would you want?"

I've thought about it ever since our conversation last night. In fact, it's all I've thought about. "I would want my dad back. But if I couldn't have that, I would wish that my parents never opened that restaurant."

"Well, neither of those are going to happen unless Seth can go back in time."

I groan. "I know. I mean— What's this?"

Morgan's holding a pink bakery box out to me. I open it and take a look inside. The smell of cinnamon and anise tickles my nose.

"Lila dropped them off," she tells me. "She said to give them to you, and that you should take some to your mom, too. She said it would help."

"Help with what?"

Morgan shrugs. "Make you sweet?"

"Yeah, right. No thanks." I shake my head, and stuff Lila's box of sweets into my locker. The last thing I need is more sugar. "I just need to accept that the restaurant means more to my mother than I do and keep it moving. Stop thinking things are going to change."

The bell rings, and Morgan gives me a quick hug. "We'll talk more later, okay? Don't do anything rash until we talk. And stay away from Seth. Honestly, Kels, he sounds like bad news. Promise?"

I give her a faint smile. "Promise."

"You decide you gonna cook for me?" Seth asks.

I freeze three steps in front of the door to my apartment, one hand outstretched for the doorknob, the other digging through my bag for my keys. Seth is coming out, and, my mind focused on the lock, I almost run right into him.

"What are you doing in my house?!"

"Actually, I'm just leaving your house," he says as he pulls the door closed. He's got his sleeves rolled up, and there's a long gash on his forearm that looks like it's only recently stopped bleeding. He sees me notice and pulls his sleeve down, not like he's embarrassed, but like it's none of my business.

"Having trouble handling the knives?" I joke, my tone a little more mocking than I mean it to be.

"I never had trouble with a knife," he says, one of his weird little grins leaking across his face.

"You say the creepiest things—you know that?" I say, an involuntary shiver juddering through my body. I lean to the side to look around him. The lights are all on, so Mom must be home.

"Were you just in there talking to my mom?" My heart ticks up a beat, worried about what he could tell her about our conversation.

"Your mom is my boss," he says, spreading his hands, grin still in place. "I kind of have to talk to her. Restaurant's closed today, so she asked me to come here. To her house."

"Oh, yeah. That makes sense." But it doesn't make sense. I've never known Mom to have a Fresh Start kid in our house.

"Besides, I already know what Jeanette wants." His smile falls sideways. "I've tasted her cooking."

I blink. "Were you . . . were you helping her with recipes?" I mean, weirder things have happened, but not many.

"You think about what we talked about the other night?" he asks, not answering my question.

"Not really," I lie. "Look, I need to go."

He steps out of the way, and I move past him, half expecting him to reach for me or say something creepy as I pass. But he lets me by, unbothered. I look back as I close the door, and he gives me a little salute. So weird.

Once I'm inside, I turn the lock. The bolt lock too. I swear I hear him laughing.

"Kelsie?" Mom calls from the kitchen. "Is that you? Come in here, will you?"

I dump my stuff by the front door. "What is it?" I say, stomping into the kitchen.

"Try this," she says, sliding a plate across the counter toward me.

"What is it?"

"Pumpkin compote in a masa shell," she says. "It's a new recipe I'm going to try this week."

"So, a pumpkin tamale? You know you can just call it a pumpkin tamale. Nobody's going to be impressed because you used some fancy words."

Her mouth turns down. "Thank you for the editorial. Just try it."

I take a bite. It's good. Better than I expected. The balance of cinnamon and nutmeg is perfect, a hint of allspice. And some ingredient I can't place. Almost . . . coppery? But it works. "Did Seth help you make this?"

Mom's hand freezes, reaching for the produce in front of her. Just for a second, but I see it. And then she's picking up an onion and positioning it on the cutting board. "Who?" she asks, her voice an octave too high.

"The Fresh Start kid. He was just here."

"Oh," she says. "No. I was just giving him his schedule for the week. That's all."

I put my fork down. As long as we're on the subject, I might as well ask. "I was thinking," I begin, trying to ease into the conversation.

"That sounds dangerous."

"Ha-ha. So . . ." I hesitate, already feeling unsure about it.

She gives me a tight smile. "Spit it out, Kelsie."

Might as well. I can always change my mind if I decide to chicken out. "How would you feel if I had someone over?"

She raises an eyebrow. "Someone?"

"A boy."

"Someone I know?"

"Weird coincidence, but Seth. From the restaurant."

This time her whole body freezes. I can see the muscle in her jaw tighten. "No."

"Mom."

"I do not want you spending time with the Fresh Start kids, especially him." Her knife cuts through the onion in front of her, the blade a sharp rhythm against the wood cutting board. "They're a bad influence. Did you know he smokes?"

"Half the restaurant industry smokes."

Her mouth tightens. "I said no, Kelsie."

"I just want to cook for him."

She looks at me, eyes wide. A thin layer of sweat sheens her forehead. "Cook? Then definitely no." She laughs, light and breathless. "You can't even cook."

My stomach tightens, and something inside me feels like falling. "That's not true," I say, sounding as hurt as I feel. "I used to cook with Dad all the time."

Her mouth turns down, disgusted. Not a bit of nostalgia in her face, just distaste in the way she wrinkles her brow. "Oh, we were so poor back then, trying to get the restaurant off the ground. Besides, what do you remember about your father? You were a child when he died."

"Mom, it was two years ago. I remember everything."

She exhales heavily. Slams the knife down hard enough to make me flinch. "Oh, Kelsie, you know what I mean. Why do you always insist on misinterpreting me? I just . . ." She sighs. Checks the clock on the wall. "We'll talk about Seth later. Right now I have to finish this recipe, and I can't get it done with you sitting there pestering like that. I'll take everything to the restaurant kitchen. You can stay here." She starts to gather her supplies.

"Wait, you're just going to walk out on me?"

"Don't be so dramatic."

"How is that dramatic?"

"Look, you may think I'm not working right now, but I'm always working. Do you know how hard it is to run a restaurant all by mys—"

"Yes, I know. Because you are always telling me! I know. I fucking know."

"Kelsie. Language!"

I shove off from the counter, knocking the plate with the tamale onto the floor. It shatters, the sharp sound of porcelain breaking into pieces making me cringe. The perfect tamale splatters into mush against the hardwood. I pause, stunned. "I'm s-sorry . . . ," I stutter out.

"Just go," she says, her voice one step from disgusted. "I can't deal with you right now."

"Can't deal with me right now?" I shout, unable to

control my frustration. "You never deal with me! You care more about that fucking restaurant than you do me!"

And that's when it happens.

She hits me. An open-handed slap across my cheek that whips my head to the side. My skin burns, half from the sting of her hand, and half from the humiliation. And rage.

"I wish it had been you instead of Dad!" I scream, tears already hot in my eyes.

Her jaw pulses. "You don't mean that."

"Oh, I do. I really, really do."

"Well, if that's how you feel," she says, her voice as cold as a February snowstorm. And there's something about her eyes. Something dark and hurt and unforgiving that I've never seen before.

And for a minute I want to take it back. I want to take it all back. But it's too late for that.

I run for the door.

"Where's Seth?" I say, bursting into the Fresh Start apartment.

A girl I don't know looks up from playing a video game. "Second room on the left."

I throw her a grateful nod and run down the hallway. I don't even knock, just fling open the door. Seth's sitting on his bed, headphones on. I can hear the tinny music coming out of the cheap speakers. Something loud with a heavy bass line.

He sees me and sits up, wary. Slides off his headphones.

"Now," I bark, before turning and stomping back the way I came.

I don't turn to see if Seth's following me, but I know he is. The kitchen here is small, just a wall of shallow cabinets and a two-burner stove, but I don't need much. I start opening cabinets, looking for ingredients. Lard, flour, baking soda. Basic stuff that any house of Native kids would have.

"Hey," the video game girl calls from the couch, "what are you doing?"

"Get out," growls a voice from behind me, and it takes me a moment to realize it's Seth. The girl mutters something that sounds like "whatever, freak," grabs her bag, and leaves. Seth follows her, locking the front door behind her.

I stop for a minute, my eyes on that locked door. My breath catches, and a tiny thread of fear trickles down my spine. Logic tells me that the door locks from the inside. It's not like I can't open it if I want to leave. So why do I suddenly feel trapped?

"Just so nobody will bother us," Seth says, his accent thick. "I'm not locking you in."

"Right," I say, shaking off my paranoia. I square my shoulders, determined. "Let's do this."

I gather all my ingredients on the table. It's been a few years, but I remember how to make frybread like I was born to it, and maybe I was.

I measure out the ingredients, dump them all in a bowl.

"Water," I tell Seth. "Warm. Not too hot."

He fills a measuring cup with warm water and sets it beside me.

"Lard in the pan," I command him. "Burner on high." He does as he's told.

My dough is mixed, and I add the water in bits, just enough to keep it thick and sticky, adding pinches of flour as I go. And as I work, I feel something inside waking up, something that's been dormant since I lost my dad. My hands push through the dough, and I put all my grief, all my rage, all the emotions that I'm feeling into the bread.

When I'm satisfied with the dough, I pull out a section and shape it into a ball. Stretch the ball and drop it into the hot lard. It sizzles like rain against a tin roof, a sound that makes me smile with memories. I watch it cook, turning it once, and when it starts to fry golden brown, I use tongs to pull it out. Place it on the paper towel Seth's set out for me. I reach for the powdered sugar and cinnamon on the shelf, but he stops my hand.

"Not yet," he says, his voice eager and his dark eyes shining. "Like this, first. Pure."

I nod, feeling it too. Feeling there's something sacred in this moment, some magic in what I've made. As weird as that sounds, I know it's true.

He gingerly tears a corner of the hot bread off with his fingers. Puts it in his mouth. I catch a glimpse of his teeth, his tongue. He chews, eyes closed, and for some reason I'm stupidly nervous. I want him to like it. No, I want him to love it.

After a moment, he opens his eyes. Smiles.

"Good girl. I didn't know if you had it in you, but you do." His dark eyes are intense, his voice no more than a whisper. "What do you want, Kelsie? What do you really want?"

"I want it to be the way it was before my dad died. I want . . ." I take a breath. "I want my mom back."

He nods, like he's considering it. "Now what are you willing to sacrifice for it?"

"Every single brick, every chair, every table, every damn chandelier. Every pot, every pan, every martini glass. Take it. Take the whole restaurant. I want you to tear the Indigenous Gastronomist to the ground."

I wake up feeling great. Better than I have in forever. I practically skip downstairs to the kitchen for breakfast. Mom's left already, probably to meet the delivery truck or hit the farmers market early. I make sprouted-wheat toast, the only bread Mom keeps in the house, slathering it with cream cheese. Wash it down with orange juice before heading to school.

Last night runs through my mind. The feel of my mother's palm against my cheek most of all. But also cooking for Seth, making my dad's frybread. The feeling of the dough in my hands, and the memories of my dad filling my heart. I don't really understand why it meant so much to Seth, but I know it meant the world to me, and now, in just a few short hours, my world is going to change.

Seth and I agreed that it would be done by four o'clock. A perfect time, since the restaurant's closed from two to five p.m. Even the staff won't be there. I want the place destroyed, but I don't want anyone to get hurt.

The day zips by in nervous anticipation, and before I know it, it's final period. Morgan's waiting for me in the usual spot, and we walk across the courtyard together. I think about whether to tell Morgan about my deal with Seth, but decide against it. I don't want her trying to talk me out of it.

"What is going on with you?" she asks after one look at my face. I should have known I couldn't hide a secret from her. But I try to play it off anyway.

"What do you mean?"

"Your mom called my mom last night?"

"My mom? Why?"

"Girl, they weren't going to tell me. But I've got eavesdropping skills. Seems your mom was doing the laundry and found, and I quote, a 'bud of marijuana' in your shirt pocket."

"Oh, shit." The roach I put in my pocket when Seth caught me in the alleyway. I'd totally forgotten.

"How you going to be so thoughtless, Kelsie? Getting caught smoking weed? From what I heard, your mom's going to be there waiting for you after school, and you are going to be grounded for life."

I groan.

"Oh yes," Morgan says. "And I heard your mom say something about night shifts during the week at the restaurant so she can keep an eye on you?"

"You don't understand. Last night my mom and I got in a fight. I said—" I flush, embarrassed just thinking about it. "I told her I wished she had died instead of Dad."

Morgan blinks. "Oh no, Kels. You didn't."

"It gets worse."

"Worse than wishing your mother dead?"

"I went to see Seth."

"The creepy magic dude? You guys aren't . . . ?"

"No, nothing like that."

"Oh good. Wait, you didn't tell him to hurt your mom, did you?"

"No!" I take a deep breath before I say, "I told him to destroy the restaurant."

Morgan stares at me, chewing on her lip. "Well, that's a little better," she finally says. "But not much. Did he say how he was going to do that?"

"I didn't ask," I admit. "I'm not sure I want to know the details. For all I know, he's already put it in motion."

"Kelsie, think. This is not smart. What is he going to do?"

"I imagine he'll burn it to the ground. That's what I would do. Make it look like a gas leak in the kitchen or something."

"But your mom will be in there! You don't really want to hurt your mom. Do you?" She has a look of horror on her face.

"Of course not! I'm doing this because I want my mom

back. Once there's no more restaurant, everything between us will be fine."

"But she's going to be there."

"No, Thursdays are her farmers market days. She never gets there earlier than five p.m. on market days. No one does."

"I just told you. She's sending Heather to the market so that she can be there when you get home at three to talk to you about your drug problem."

My stomach drops to my feet. "Oh God, Morgan. I didn't know. What do I do?"

"You go back there right now and you stop Seth before you ruin your whole entire life!"

She's right. I'm so stupid. How could I have been so stupid?

"Go!" Morgan says, pushing at my shoulder. "I'll cover for you. Just, go!"

I shove my heavy backpack at her and take off running.

"Mom!" I scream as I come through the heavy glass doors. The restaurant is empty, silent as a graveyard at this time of the day. Nobody here. I checked Seth's room first, to see if I could catch him before he started whatever he has planned, but he wasn't there. And then I went upstairs to our apartment, but it was empty too. So I came to the restaurant last.

The doors of the restaurant are unlocked, so someone has to be here.

"Mom!" I yell again, striding across the dining area floor

toward the kitchen. Part of me is relieved to find the restaurant intact, nothing wrong. But the other part of me feels uneasy, the air too still, like it's holding its breath, waiting. Watching.

I'm almost to the kitchen when Mom pushes the swinging door open.

I sob with relief. "Mom!" I cry, rushing forward to hug her. I wrap my arms around her. She's shaking, and she holds on to me so tightly I have to peel her away. Her face crumples, tears streaming down her cheeks as she looks at me.

"I-I'm sorry," I say, feeling awful about how upset she is. "I won't smoke again. I didn't know you would care."

But she shakes her head back and forth, no.

"Then what?" I ask, confused. "If you're not upset about me smoking weed, then what?"

"Hey, bad girl," Seth says, stepping out from behind my mom. I hadn't even noticed him there. My stomach plummets. He must have told her about our plan.

"I can explain," I say in a rush.

"You cooked for him, Kelsie," Mom says, her voice cracking. "Why did you do that? I told you not to. I told you no. I would have made it work with just Seth. But now he knows. Now *I* know. And I can't . . . I can't walk away from that."

Fear skittles down my back. "It was just frybread."

"We both know that ain't true," Seth says.

I want to protest that it *is* true, that it was just flour and baking powder and a little bit of salt. But he's right. It was more, and we both know it.

"You were right last night," Mom says, still crying. "Seth came to the house to help me with my recipes. He figured out what's missing."

"What are you talking about?"

"The missing ingredient? Remember what the review in the *Rowbury Times* said? What they all say?"

"They just don't appreciate you."

"No, no. They're right. I know it. We all know it. A white woman trying to cook indigenous foods. No matter my years at school, my prestigious internships, my hours in the kitchen. I just couldn't get it right. But Seth explained it to me."

I eye Seth warily. He lifts his arm up, showing me the wound on his forearm. "It's either in you, or it's not." I take a step back. My eyes dart between the two of them, trying to understand.

"All I had to do," Mom says, "was want it bad enough. Be willing to make a sacrifice."

"But you've already sacrificed so much for the restaurant," I say. "Everything!"

Mom's blue eyes soften. "Oh, Kelsie. Not everything."

And that's when I notice Seth's holding a knife in his other hand. The big butcher's knife that's used for quartering beef. Slicing through muscle and tendon. It flashes bright in the light from the oversize windows. And I remember how he said he's good with knives. But there's nothing here to butcher.

"Mom?" I whisper. "What's going on?"

"I need this," she says, her voice a whisper. "Please understand. What you're doing for me, it means everything. My dreams. Your dad's dreams. You're going to make them all come true." Tears spill down her cheeks, but her eyes are hungry, and she licks her lips, excited. "I'll name my new dish after you, I promise. I won't forget your sacrifice."

"The new dish?"

"The one's that's going to get me five stars."

"I told you this was the best job I ever had," Seth drawls, twirling the knife between his fingers. "All I had to do was figure out what your mama's recipes were missing. If I did that, she'd move me on up to the kitchen. No more trash, no more busboy. Ain't that right, Jeanette?"

Mom nods through her tears.

"Blood is good and all," he says, taking a step closer to me. "But why stop there when you can do better? Your mama's recipes need more than I can give her." His smile spreads. "They need heart."

Hearts à la Carte

BY KARUNA RIAZI

It was a slow night, up until this guy fell from the sky.

No, not merely fell. He plummeted, as harshly uprooted and roughly swept away as a shooting star, sun streaming and teary eyed. He fell, and he brought with him several dislodged pigeons, a handful of tinsel, and one or two errant balloons with their stomachs glutted on dirty city exhalations and gutter backwash.

I mean, I could have stopped his fall.

Maybe. Well, honestly, I value my life.

And maybe I'd have had more sympathy and thoughtless altruism if it hadn't been the hundredth time this month that some rich partygoer had toppled off a balcony in his attempt to imitate a YouTube parkour video.

Also, and more reasonably, it was Christmas Eve, and

the police probably had better things to do than field their hundredth call of the year from King of Kuisine ("the food you hate to love from the people you love to hate," according to my youngest aunt, which was met by no end of snickers and scolding depending on which generation she said it in front of).

In any case, it also wasn't as though a man falling from the sky was unprecedented. Our cart had the misfortune of being parked next to a historically protected and ridiculously ostentatious water fountain, which drew teen boys for ill-advised stunts any time of the year. I'm not sure what I could have done, honestly, besides hustling out of the cart and holding my arms up like I was a Ghibli character.

And the last time I checked, I was not.

So floating guy got a face of concrete. This was unfortunate and made a very unpleasant sound reminiscent of the spiced-mutton patty currently working its way toward a good burn on the grill.

I winced and gripped the hem of my apron a little tighter. Yes, I'd seen falling men before, but that sounded like a particularly rough landing.

"Um . . . excuse me . . . ," I started.

The gray lump on the sidewalk shifted a bit, and then let out a pathetic cough.

"Um . . ."

I reached back without looking away, fingers fumbling and triumphantly clamping down once they met with cool metal.

I held up my weapon to the light, and deflated.

My greasy spatula. It figured.

Still, there was no time for hesitation or doubt. I inched my way out of the cart and down the stairs toward the lump on the ground.

"Um, sir . . ."

I prodded at him with the spatula. He shifted and groaned again, rolling over with a grimace.

Okay. Here's the thing. When you're the daughter of a dad who still remembers his Casanova of a college roommate and the five girlfriends he managed to have at a relatively conservative campus, and said dad pretty much flatlines at the mere suggestion of the word "date" out of the context of Ramadan and the innocuous dried fruit, you don't see many guys in your social circle—or admit to having many guys in your social circle—who are, well, second-glance material.

I know some of my friends are not as choosy, but for me, cousins do not count.

But this guy was more than second-glance material. I'd hazard to put him at a 10.5 out of ten, along with a tossed-in giggle with a close female companion and a bumbled attempt at a sly candid to post on Snapchat: *I DIDN'T KNOW ALLAH MADE THEM THAT FINE IN THIS AREA.*

Looking down at his wild shock of dark hair, the blue-black eyebrows perfectly arched as though drawn with the steadiest hand, and the mouth that already had the gentlest laugh lines forming at the crease, I won't lie: I finally knew what it meant to be thirsty.

Seeing the glass in front of you and needing to reach out for it just to reassure yourself it was sitting there.

It is a moment I am not 100 percent proud of, but I readily own it.

You wouldn't have raised your eyebrows at me if you'd seen him. That's all I'm saying.

I blinked, and the boy had managed to peel himself off the stain-studded pavement with more grace than I expected from someone who had hit solid concrete. He leaned his weight on the cart, reaching down to inch a sneaker up his foot. I opened my mouth to ask if he wanted me to call 911, and my jaw hung there.

His sneaker was smoking.

And his hand was glowing.

There was no other way to describe it. Later, it would be easier to pass it off as my own shock, but for a moment, his fingers glistened as though they dripped stardust and deferred dreams. And then I blinked, and there was a handful of wadded bills and brown, callused fingers.

Had I really seen that?

"Did you just . . . ," I started, and then blinked rapidly as he shook the bills directly in my face.

"As-salaamu alaikum. Sorry, should have led with that once I saw the hijab. Emergency services aren't needed. Just give me whatever carbs you got on hand."

Two minutes later, I was leaning on the counter,

watching as he dug into a layered bowl of Egyptian-style kushuri—pasta, fresh tomato sauce, lentils and rice— digging deep for the flecks of onion I'd snuck in and humming to himself. I wasn't the biggest fan of kushuri on our menu myself, mainly because my memories of it had the bitter aftertaste of disappointment and deception.

Time for a quick flashback. So, we were in Egypt, circa . . . well, whatever year it was when I was thirteen and moody and wanted to have time to myself and skulk through the pyramids, where surely the atmosphere would be dark and dank enough to reflect the tortured depths of my soul.

But Ma didn't want that to happen, because "that's a huge tomb and you don't know WHAT might be waiting in there," and Baba had somehow sweet-talked his way into a dinner invitation with our cab driver at some hole in the wall, and the way his eyes were glinting as he pored over menu items, I knew my ideal sightseeing day was going to be given up for the greater good of King of Kuisine, as always.

And I hated it. I hated Egypt. I hated its food. And then Baba leaned over the table, went, "You have to try this!" and shoved a good spoonful right into my sulking mouth.

It was amazing. But I wouldn't admit that, even now.

Apparently, though, I was really easy to win over. The sight of this guy totally devouring kushuri—my kushuri, the type that always seemed a little sloppier in execution compared to my father's efficiently tiered bowls—almost had me understanding my dad's obsession with watching the customers eat, which was scary.

"Good food should temper the shock of the fall, but you really should get medical assistance."

"This is good enough. Wait, scratch that. This is amazing enough," he said, and gave me a devastating smile. I didn't even know those were real, but he had one. There was even a hint of dimples.

I flushed. "Freshly made every day," I managed. "But hey, your sneakers . . ."

He waved it off. "It happens from time to time. I'll live."

Obviously, I wasn't going to get much more out of him. So I settled. And watched him eat. He polished off the kushuri and a few fish patties that weren't on the official menu but more like Ma's personal gift to our regulars. Those were more of our usual home fare, the type of thing that felt warm in my mouth and grounding and that I often selfishly "vanished" rather than share with the customers. I separated categories in my head: cart food and our food. I knew other friends whose parents had restaurants, but I still balked from asking them if they had similar feelings, ways in which they drew the line between the business and them, what territories they could have to themselves.

Watching him gulp down several of the browned and spiced patties, though, oddly didn't sting. I didn't even argue when he claimed the rest of the baklava I had triumphantly shaped and filled under the guidance of Aunty Busra up the block (all the while bitterly realizing that my father's pride meant it would end up on the counter at work and not in the house). He eyed the empty pots longingly, and, with a sigh, I passed a white paper bag over the countertop. He raised his eyebrow at me inquisitively.

"One of my friend Lila's special pastries," I explained. "Consider it a complimentary gift for spending more than any customer I've had in a night and effectively clearing out the rest of our inventory."

"I can't tell if this is heartfelt or sarcastic, but thanks anyway." He pressed it into his shirt pocket and patted it. Something about the gesture made my heart melt.

For a moment, as he smiled at me and finally passed back the plate I found behind the counter, he seemed entirely normal.

And then he slid off into the night when I paused in the middle of clearing away his containers to take a call from my mom.

(That wasn't embarrassing at all: trying to fumble through the usual "yes, I'm fine," "no, there's nothing going on," "yes, the big butcher knife is under my stool" and awkwardly turning my back on another flash of dimples.)

All that was left was a large wad of money—I'm talking a good stack of twenties, from the peek I took—and a note.

For the next meal!

There was a smiley face, too. I smiled back at it, if you want to know how low I fell over a guy with cute eyebrows and a healthy appetite and some foolish ideas of how to spend his night.

And then I got on my phone and tried to figure out if we were really free of liability since he had fallen in front of the cart.

Not to sound all jaded or anything, but I really expected that would be the end of it.

It was one of those nights, in that type of city.

And at least for that moment, I had felt bemused and bedazzled and almost magical. Something bizarre and curious had happened to me, in a city full of other people's dreams. He had been that change, that taste of something else that I needed for just that moment. And now it was over. I would never see him again.

As it turned out, Falling Boy—or, well, Hasan Mahmood—came back for that meal he had alluded to in the note. And another one after that. And another one. You would think that all that time spent together would have lifted some of the fog of mystery around his shoulders. But it only deepened.

When I asked where he went to school?

"Rowbury High."

"That's where I go!"

"Well, then, there you go."

I mean, he's the type of guy you would remember seeing in the halls, though, at *some* point.

Then again, I'm not always the most observant person at school. I spend a great deal of time shopping around the previous night's leftovers and using my friends' enthusiasm for my ventures into spiced kofte and pistachio-laced rice pudding cups as a reason to eat something different for once, even if it was bland hamburgers off the hot lunch line and not face the whole "what do you want to do with your life" question that everyone in high school seems to want you to grapple with.

Anyway, Hasan and his appetite were always a good distraction.

And even when he was eating, or waiting hungrily for something to come off the grill, those eyes were always fixed on me—smiling, gleaming brightly in preparation to tease me, but just . . . there.

Present. Actually caring about what I had to say.

It was different.

It was nice.

We didn't agree on everything. That was the best part sometimes.

Tonight, though, we were back on his favorite topic to needle out of me—well, everyone's favorite topic to bring up as soon as they saw my face, apparently: what Munira plans to do as a career. In the future. For the rest of her life.

Cart not included.

It was the type of topic I usually shied away from with even my closest friends, but Hasan just knew how to work it in and make me talk about it as well as he could sniff out whatever was left in the fridge that he might devour.

I ended up telling him about the internship application I had taken out of the guidance office—one I hadn't even bothered showing my parents while I considered my own feelings about it.

The internship was in event planning, which was a little skip of the stone away from my usual, to be honest, but not so detached that I'd have trouble getting past the door. It was a boutique setup that focused on intimate weddings and bridal showers, and honestly, I watched enough *Say Yes to the Dress* and *Cheapest Weddings* in my downtime that I thought I could dig it: arranging color palettes, making bouquets, and . . . well, setting out the food.

But at the same time, it wasn't the cart. It wasn't what I was always told I was good at. And I guess that scared me. A little.

Well, a lot.

"I like the sound of the internship, but being a wedding planner doesn't sound like a career where you can just blend into the background. Maybe I'm meant to be a photographer. Your name's at the bottom and you're credited, but at the same time, you're not necessarily as awesome or as remembered as the person in the frame."

"I won't argue with that," Hasan said, "but I will point out that a lot of photographers are burdened with awards

and recognition, so if you want to skulk in the shadows for
the rest of your life, I might not go that way."

"Okay, fine. I'm just not sure why it's an issue if I just
stay with the cart for the rest of my life."

"I'm not saying that you can't. You seem to do pretty
well in the food cart. I'm surprised that you're planning
your future around it but not seeing yourself as, like,
co-owner or taking over for your dad when he retires."

"And how is that different from skulking in the shadows elsewhere for the rest of my life?"

Hasan didn't respond for a moment. He seemed to be
staring into the distance as he bit into his lamb skewer. It
was his second of the night, which made me a little proud.
Apparently I was getting better, toeing the line between
entirely charred and perfectly scorched. Not that Hasan
ever complained about my food.

It helped that I was working with a pretty awesome
recipe. Baba had this way of drawing out the tender in his
meat, marinating and using delicate pinches of spice that
he dusted gently over the hills and valleys of slices and
rolled balls and rural-hewed chunks destined for gyros
or meat trays or to be garnished with salad within a deli-
ciously sloppy naan sandwich.

He always seemed so confident that, if I just watched
his hands, if I took the same small pinches, my fingers
would learn the same movements and be able to result in
that same welcoming taste. I always kept my eyes down as I
rolled ground chicken between my palms and formed fists

in bowls piled high with raw, marbled goodness, hoping that if I focused on it as passionately as I tried to concentrate during prayer, I would *feel* something close to the way he seemed to feel about it. I wanted to. I really did. But it never seemed to work.

I absently knocked over one of the glasses on the countertop when my elbow stretched out too far, and Hasan— who had up until that moment been nursing his glass of sour cherry juice—sat up straight.

"What was that?"

"That was my fault! Sorry!"

I tugged the glasses back in line, watching out of the corner of my eye as Hasan glanced both ways on the quiet, dark street before he settled back down.

Recently, he had been really . . . well, it sounded like wishful thinking, but Hasan was acting almost *protective* over me.

It had started when I said I thought I saw the same guy lurking near the cart on the evenings Hasan tended to turn up. I'm not an alarmist, so I was willing to write it off the first few times, but Hasan nearly jumped out of his skin.

"Where? When? What does he look like?"

He'd never been that forceful, so I freaked out a bit myself. It must have shown on my face, because he cooled down, apologized, and said he was a little on edge due to the rumored increase in crime plastered all over the papers: kidnappings, bank robberies, and the stray appearance of some creepy guy in nineties flasher gear menacing girls in lonely alleyways.

"You're here by yourself most nights," he ended. "And you're important to me. I don't want to see anything happen to you."

I didn't understand most of his concern (city life pretty much equals crime and the occasional holdup while you're browsing an aisle at your local deli), but I was mostly stuck on that whole "you're important to me" line he snuck in as subtly as raisins in a platter of Afghani rice. That was enough to make me nod and smile, probably a bit gooey around the edges.

After that, for a few weeks, Hasan had turned up a bit earlier, glowering at the gathering shadows around the cart, and the guy's appearance turned more sporadic. It was probably a coincidence, but I didn't point that out. Hasan's company was worth it.

"Anyway, don't change the subject." Hasan raised his eyebrows at me and took another bite. I scowled and then realized he had white sauce stuck to his collar.

"Um . . . you've got a little . . ."

I reached for a napkin as he eyed me bemusedly.

"Thanks, Mom."

I flushed. It was rare that Hasan even made a reference to family outside of my own. He didn't like talking about his family. Like, at all. Any mention of them was small— "Oh, my mom cooked something like this once"—and tended to be hastily curtailed. It was odd, but I could get a hint: There was some painful backstory there, and he wasn't ready yet.

To be honest, and I'm not too proud to admit it, I had other things to focus on besides Hasan's family. The thought that he was dressing down to be as comfortable as possible for his outings here—getting cozy for these marathon feasts, these moments shared with *me*—made my cheeks warm, as did the idea that he actually enjoyed listening to me ramble on about my family problems.

It took me a good minute, caught up in this reverie, to realize that Hasan's cheeks seemed similarly flushed, and that my hand had foregone the napkin to pluck absently at his decidedly clean and crisp collar.

"Oh!" I dropped my hand like it was touching a hot pot handle. "Sorry!"

"No harm, seriously. I'm good for a laundry run anyway." Hasan cleared his throat.

"Oh, you're going now?" I couldn't keep the disappointment out of my voice. It wasn't entirely over Hasan leaving—well, there was a lot of that. It was just that, even if that weird guy hadn't appeared recently, I'd had the feeling I was being watched. Maybe those headlines had gotten to me after all.

But I didn't tell Baba. And I certainly wasn't telling Hasan. He obviously had other problems.

Hasan's devastating smile made an appearance. "I could stay, if you're really that lonely."

Tempting. Very tempting. But it was getting later, and

the street was quiet enough, and I didn't want to be that big baby who was jumping at shadows, so I let him go.

Maybe I shouldn't have.

A few minutes later—or maybe it was just seconds, long enough for him to make it around the corner and out of sight—I turned away to wipe down the counter and clear off the empty containers like I always did.

And then I was thrown forward.

And my only thought was, *Ow, who rammed their car into the cart?*

Maybe that wasn't my first thought. Maybe it was just *Ow, ow, ow.* Because it hurt. I could feel the sticky damp of hot sauce seeping into my jeans, and my head was throbbing. And then I realized the reason I hadn't stood up and started taking down a license plate was because the cart was on its side.

And there was a man standing in front of it.

I dazedly dragged myself out, a hand to my head.

"Um . . . can I help you?"

He just stood there, looking at me.

He had on a fedora—a *fedora*—and a pinstriped suit. He really didn't look like a paying customer for King of Kuisine, so my odds were on him being the jerk who'd just toppled over my father's babies—both of them, literally. And then, before I could even wrap my head properly around that, he sprang *up*, physically, onto the capsized counter and planted his knee into the steel until it gave under him, just melted down and into a meek shelf for him like it was dollar-store plastic.

"Girlie, you've got five minutes to tell me where the Comet is."

I grasped my ridiculous spatula and just stared at him, even as a scattering of would-be customers gaped from a safe distance. My hesitation was a mistake. He reached out, and before I could even react, he had hold of my arm.

And then, in a slick judolike move—no, that made it sound realistic, human, like something a person actually did without it being impossible and scary—he lifted me off the ground and then smacked me back down. Hard.

The city lights scattered about my head like bobbing, filmy stars. I, the girl who was supposed to protect King of Kuisine and my father when they both reached their middling ages, sat there on the ground and held my head and whimpered over my scraped elbows and watched as that creep trashed my life as I knew it right in front of me.

That was the last thing I could focus on: that cart, my family's trust in me, being crushed under his heel.

No. That's wrong.

All of a sudden, there was something else. Someone else. There was a boy, in an incredibly unflattering yellow suit with a lightning bolt across his chest and a cliché mask over his eyes. And he fell from the sky like a star, in such a familiar plummet that I felt sure that this time he was going to land on the cart and get his body egg-scrambled and die and come back to sue me for not having a softer place for him to land.

But he didn't. He landed quietly, like a cat on velvet paws, and he saw me on the ground, and our eyes met. He rushed over to me, and he lifted me in his arms, and that was the moment when I was sure that I had succumbed to a concussion around the time the creep had slammed me to the ground, because the way he said "Munira," so gently, like his breath alone would find all the places I was cracked and make me come entirely undone . . .

It sounded like Hasan. And I wanted it to be Hasan.

And even with my brain dazed and my legs aching, I was focused enough to feel guilty that I could even think of that.

And then the fedora guy caught sight of him and snarled, and I watched as the boy in the yellow suit . . . no, it *was* Hasan—the boy who tried to devour me out of house and home, the boy who laughed with me and listened when I needed him to, the boy who was apparently a superhero—neatly caught what was left of our side cooler in his right hand and crumpled it and tossed it back, ablaze with a near-heavenly fire.

And then there was this huge battle, where the Comet screamed a lot of things about how I shouldn't have been brought into this, and the fedora guy screamed back about how he decided who was brought into it or not, and then apparently I managed to drag myself upward and bean him in the back of the head with a frying pan while shrieking, "King of Kuisine isn't your personal playground!"

I wish I couldn't remember this happening.

I also wish I could forget what happened afterward, later that night in the hospital, after my teary-eyed parents kissed my brow and tucked me in and I closed my eyelids against the raw, open devastation on my father's face, when the boy who was the Comet and also who I thought was becoming my best friend slipped through the hospital window.

And we fought.

"I was careless," Hasan admitted. "I don't have a family who worries in the same way, and I felt that when I was with you, I was close to that. Apparently, I got too comfortable and settled into a pattern. I'm sorry, Munira. I really am."

"I wish I could say I get that," I seethed back, "but unlike you, I don't play pretend with other people's lives when I know there's a risk of them getting hurt."

"I already said it was my fault. I already said I knew he was looking for me. I don't know what you want from me. Would you rather I left you there to die?" Hasan roughly tugged at his hair. "Don't make me apologize for not being able to. I couldn't do that to you. You're the last person I could ever leave behind like that."

At any other time, those words would have been everything I wanted to hear, but my drama-heroine quota had run dry for the day. I was in pain, I had a needle stuck in my arm, and the boy I was starting to realize I had more than a crush on apparently was some mask-wearing, high-flying vigilante in tights who had ruined everything my parents had worked for.

I didn't want to admit that I might have been angrier with myself than with Hasan: for the relief that washed over me when I remembered that, even if tomorrow was a working day, there was no shift to miss. King of Kuisine was a goner.

"No matter what is going on with you and I assume your . . ."—I waved a hand toward the costume, the glimmering arches of his brows, his whole terrible, brilliant self—"mission or saving the world or whatever . . . you should have been honest with me from the beginning that something like this could happen."

"Would you have believed me? If I just went, 'Oh, hey, Munira, guess what? I'm a famous superhero, and there's this whole organization after me because they don't like the thought of some caped wonder boy foiling their schemes!'"

"I would have tried! If you had at least done more to keep my family out of it, I would have tried." I shook my head, both out of dizziness and to fend off tears. "And now I can't."

"Munira . . ." His voice turned tender, pleading.

"You said you didn't know what it was like to have a family who worried about you," I bit out, roughly. "And you're right."

It wasn't kind. I'm not proud I said it. He had all the earmarks, looking back, of the privileged but pushed-aside kid: the kid who was told he was loved, but not shown it outside of high-tech trackers and a supersuit that came with its own baggage. Afterward, I could remember how his face had crumpled down the middle and hate myself for it.

But in that moment, I pressed on.

"You jeopardized us. I know you'll try to laugh this off and say something about not being able to resist the free baklava." I raised my chin and tried to keep it from quavering. "Unfortunately, I don't have one to give you for the road. Because, you know, our cart is down for the count."

"Munira," he said again, but it sounded more defeated this time.

And then the nurse came in, and I had to pretend that the reasons for my one-sided dialogue and tear-glazed eyes were, respectively, the soap opera rerun on my TV screen and the lack of morphine in my veins.

End scene on our not-breakup breakup.

End scene on my friendship with the boy who fell like a golden star.

And of course, again, I assumed that was the last I would see of Hasan.

Or the Comet.

Whatever.

Fast forward six weeks. I was grumpily hanging out in my aunt's café. It was no King of Kuisine. There was a lot I was finding I hadn't properly appreciated about our little truck until it had been smashed to smithereens and had to be slowly coaxed back into the world of the living by a dedicated team of mechanics, like the fact that it didn't involve time spent cooped up with relatives who think that seventeen is far too close to old-maid status and who you can't tell that the last boy you were interested in turned out to be a superhero and ruined your life.

Well, not entirely. If you must know, I got the internship.

It probably helped that Baba was still so dazed over King of Kuisine that when I brought it up at the dinner table, he blinked and nodded and went, "Well, that's a good way to fill your time for now, sweetie."

Which I took as approval.

Ma was a bit more reticent. She went in with me the first day and smiled and nodded along with the bubbly receptionist who gave me my "very own badge!" and a "brand-new locker!" and assured me that I was going "to love it here!" And then she went home and got on the phone and bragged to all her friends that her daughter, the eldest one, is now a wedding planner, and all their kids should keep her in mind for their future nuptials.

That would probably bring up its own set of problems, but it was good to realize that the world wasn't going to cave in and my parents didn't really care that I was doing something outside of the cart and away from a stove. They really just wanted me to be happy. And make good money, which was why Ma instantly tried to haggle up the monthly transportation stipend I was offered.

And a lot of the food cart regulars—well, not customers now, but friends—still came around, whenever they could. I still had Lila's sweet confections in my life, and her friendship, which was just as sweet. Some guy actually wrote into the local newspaper trying to get a fund going for our repair fees, complaining that he had lost access to the one good halal place on Hungry Heart Row, which was flattering.

I did a lot of eating instead of serving those days, when I wasn't at my internship. That particular afternoon, I was seated at my aunt's counter with a plate of rui fish and rice: a beloved Bengali dish that seemed like a good antidote for heartache. Besides, working out the bones between my lips and pressing my finger against their sharp edges was cathartic. I couldn't beat up the guy who ruined the cart, but I could show a fish who was boss.

I doubt I was reassuring any of the other wary regulars, who had all been informed by my aunt about my sensitive state, by gnawing on the bones.

"Um. You seem to be very engrossed there," a familiar voice broke in tentatively.

Of course. I should have known better than to expect that he would vanish from my life that easily. I kept my eyes on my plate and took another generous bite of fish, making sure to scoop up the fried onions and a bit of the fat that had soaked up enough of the turmeric, ginger, and garlic sauce. "I'm calling on the strength of my ancestors."

"Is it working?" There was a smile in his voice. It hurt.

"Considering that you're still here, not the way I want it to."

Hasan exhaled.

"For what it's worth, I'm sorry."

"I've heard that before."

"I've apologized to . . . well, my family, you could call them. They warned me I was living dangerously, and they were right."

I nodded. "Good. And, to be fair, I guess I wasn't reading enough into all your extracurricular, altruistic activities."

Hasan offered me a weak smile. "I guess you were too busy enjoying the fact that I bought three trays of your meatballs and chased it down with two shakes, huh?"

The words almost slipped from my lips, the words that his puppy-hopeful expression and subtly clasped hands made me want to say: *No, I enjoyed seeing you. I enjoyed being with you. You eating my food without making faces or tugging bone shards out of your mouth was a bonus.*

I sighed and pushed the plate back, swiveling to face him properly.

"Okay, listen. I'll be upfront because I believe in transparency and honesty. I don't want you to grovel. I don't want you to bend at the knees and promise me you're shipping off to madrasa or something to learn the errors of your ways. I just . . ."

My voice trailed off for a moment.

"I just wish you had found some way to let me know

besides, you know, waiting for some weird macho guy literally wearing a fedora to trample all over my dad's hopes and dreams."

"Yep, he's literally crying a river right now," my aunt piped up. I'd almost forgotten she was there, and I glowered at her as she studiously slid a cup of coffee in front of an equally uninvolved customer, who I suspected was one of her gossipy masjid friends.

"Totally heartbroken upstairs in my apartment. It's amazing my brother can even be so engrossed in the cricket match right now when he has a tissue stuffed up each nostril and pressed against his eyes like he watched the ending of *Devdas* on repeat."

Hasan let out a suspiciously stifled sound, but when I whirled back to face him, he was fidgeting with his collar.

"I just want us to be cool," he said quietly. "I mean, I don't want this to be awkward, but . . ."

We both glanced at my aunt. She sighed, shook her head, and gestured to her friend. They both stood, perhaps with a little too much whispering and head craning between them, and headed out to the terrace.

Thank God.

Almost as soon as she left, though, I wanted her back there. The shop suddenly felt larger, and so did Hasan's presence next to me.

"Okay, listen." Hasan looked me straight in the eye. "I want to be honest now. I like you. I really like you."

I like you.

I really like you.

There was a boy, a cute, Muslim, superhero boy standing in front of me and telling me that he really, really liked me. And he wasn't done.

"You didn't find it weird when I was always hungry. You spilled your guts about your family and made me feel like I was part of it. You always smiled at me. I really like the way you smile." And then *he* smiled. "I definitely like the way you cook."

Okay. Things were getting out of hand.

"Um . . . uh . . ." I swallowed hard. "I appreciate your honesty. But . . ."

"We're going to pay for the truck." I didn't have to ask who *we* were. "We're going to stay out of your family's affairs. I promise, I promise, I promise we will."

"But you . . . want to stay in mine." I regretted the phrasing as soon as it escaped my lips, particularly when it made that smile so much wider.

"If that's the way you want to put it."

And then, bold as a Bollywood hero, he reached out, grasping my hand. Just the fingertips, nothing brash enough to tempt the Haram Police into bursting into the shop and gasping in horror over the extreme skin-to-skin contact. But I could feel myself flare up and flush.

This was happening.

He was here, and he was holding my hand and smiling at me and telling me he *liked me*.

But I just couldn't make my mouth form the words

back. King of Kuisine was gone, but I could still feel that presence behind me of the warm stove and the crowded cooler with its soda cans and syrupy juices. I could remember learning how to count off the coins in the drawer and the first time Baba cut open one of my burgers and said, chest puffed out with pride, "This is *well done*."

For all the nights I had kicked at the wheels and tugged down the shutters to study for the SAT in peace (and shamefully stuck a few bills in the tip jar to even the balance), I loved King of Kuisine in my own way. And, even if it wasn't Hasan's fault, even if it wasn't what he meant to happen, that life—those nights—weren't coming back. Not quickly, at least, and they would never be the same.

"Hasan, listen," I said. "This is not something I ever thought I would say. You changed my life. And there are ways in which I would never take that change back, whether it was making up alter egos for the street pigeons or that time I tried to make firni."

"I thought we weren't talking about your attempt at making firni."

"You're right. We weren't. But I'm super nervous, and I want you to know that I do like you."

"There's a but there."

"There is. But I don't know how to deal with you right now. We can joke about it, but King of Kuisine was a big part of our family. Even if your people—whoever they are—replace it, that's going to be changed for us now. We're going to have to adapt, start back up, gather up our regulars, and maybe change locations so that we aren't as easy a target."

"I don't want you to think of yourself as a target," Hasan protested, grasping my hand a little tighter. "I just want you to think of yourself as Munira."

"That's what you want, but I don't think that's what your world will be satisfied with. And I'm not sure if you're ready to stand against them."

His grasp loosened from my fingers. And then he pulled himself up and squared his jaw, and I could see—in that moment, even without the incredible costume and the emblem across his chest—where the hero was in him.

"I think it's more of them not being ready to stand against me," the Comet said, and his voice reverberated through the shop and its walls and my skin and my bones.

I exhaled and nodded once. "Okay. Wow. I can believe you. But I just can't tell you what you want to hear right now. I'm sorry."

I almost hated myself, watching him as the light ebbed out of his eyes, as he tried to smile and nodded once. But I knew that I would hate myself more if I stepped over my resolve—over what my family meant to me, over all we had to rebuild and scrape back into normalcy—if I seized back his hand and promised him my heart when it just wasn't there yet.

It took me a moment to realize he was headed for the door.

"Wait!" I called, and he paused.

"No offense, Munira, but if this is the moment where you ask if we can still be friends . . ."

I winced. "It kind of is. But I really mean it. Not awkward tense friends, not friends who can't forgive each other for everything that's happened. But friends who build past it."

For a long moment, I held my breath and watched Hasan as his face shifted. And then, though I couldn't see out the window, the sky cleared as he broke into a smile.

"Define what the end game is, and you'll have a deal."

"All of it, except . . ." I gestured to both of our hands—currently not grasping each other—and felt my cheeks flare. "That can wait for later. Much later."

And though I wasn't sure if I could hold to that promise myself, an hour later—laughing as Hasan gulped down a glass of water and fanned his mouth, an open container of spicy ramen on the counter—I could live with a little less steamy Bollywood and a little more open, honest time.

That's the thing about fairy-tale, neatly tied happy endings. They don't exist, even for heirs apparent to huge family food dynasties (or, well, one very singed truck currently in repairs) and bright, beaming, currently sweaty-faced boys who fall from the stars.

But the ones you have to share, with everyone you love around you and good food spread over the counters and the city you love spread out before the open window with all its glimmering magic and promise?

Those I could live with.

And plan to.

Bloom

BY PHOEBE NORTH

Every morning at Pop's Deli is the same. That's what I like about it.

The sky cracks gray and hazy no matter what kind of day comes after. The air is cold even in the dead of summer. It's autumn now, but I don't care. The leaves, brick red and brown and gold, all look like a dull cloud of sepia before the sun comes up. I throw on my jeans, a white T-shirt, my apron, and my shoes. I decide I'm not going to go to school today. Pop won't care. When the office calls, he'll tell them I'm sick, like he always does, and I won't even have to ask.

When I go downstairs, Pop has just lifted the metal door that covers the storefront. It rattles on its way up and sends light all through everything, the deli case and the floor I mopped till it shone last night before closing. I go to get the chopped liver and the whitefish from the walk-in fridge, shielding my hands with a second skin of latex, then scoop them into the containers. I slice up onions and lettuce and tomatoes. I set out orange-pink lox on a platter and lay down a sheet of saran wrap over it. Pop and I work beside one another, not talking, not needing to. This work is all that's necessary.

Eventually, our rhythm is broken by the jangling bell on the door. It's Chava, the butcher's girl. She gives a wink to me, greets me quickly—"Hey, sweetness"—like she always does, and I'm silent, like I always am. Then she sets about arguing with Pop about what he's going to take for the day. Roast beef or turkey? Sweet white round slices of chicken breast? Soon they're bickering about Chava's tattoos again. It's the usual topic of conversation.

I watch them, listening. I don't talk to Chava, not yet. It's not that I don't want to, but I don't really know how to draw myself out of myself, to pretend I'm an ordinary person. When you've lived through what I've lived through, it marks you just as permanently as any tattoo.

She's interesting, though, with her pushed-up sleeves and crooked mouth. Like someone who has seen things, felt things, and tucked them inside her back pocket for safe-keeping. There are tattoos you show, and ones you keep hidden. I think we both understand that.

"How could you do that to yourself?" Pop says, gesturing up and down at the whole package that is Chava. A dangling bullish nose ring and colorful sleeves that snake out beneath her work shirt. Letters in Hebrew and vivid splashes of color. Dragons. Fish. "A Jewish girl should not be tattooed."

"A *nice* Jewish girl?" Chava teases. Pop waves his hand at her dismissively, but she presses on. "Whoever said I was nice?"

"When I was in the army, they wanted me to get tattoos. They said everyone in our division had to get tattoos." Pop was in Vietnam. He hardly ever talks about it, I've learned, except the same handful of stories, over and over again. Like this one. I don't look up from my work. "Fighting bees. You think I did it?"

"I don't know," Chava answers. "You tell me."

"No. I told them, get out of here! They tattooed my family in the camps. My father would roll in his grave. Besides, what would the rabbi say?"

"He'd say, 'Haven't seen you in years, Arthur,'" I pipe up, hardly raising my eyes from the bagels I'm setting out in their basket.

My grandfather grumbles. I guess you could call him a Passover Jew, but not even that. He hasn't set foot in the synagogue since my parents' funeral, five years ago.

"Enough," Pop says sternly. "Chava, you're a beautiful girl. I just don't know why you'd do that to yourself."

"Why don't you ask me?" she asks him, with challenging eyes. My grandfather doesn't say anything. Chava's smile is wily. "Thought so. Do you want the roast beef, or not?"

Pop looks at me. I shrug.

"Sure," I say, speaking to Pop and not Chava. "Sold well last week."

He asks me, because he knows I understand. I understand, because I work. It's what we do in my family. It's how life moves forward. Soon the sun will come up in earnest, and Pop's Deli will be busy, and the rhythm will wash the world away.

It's days like these I never want to give up.

It's lunch hour, and time passes in a flash if you let it. I'm busy slicing sandwiches and toasting bagels and pouring customers steaming paper cups of coffee, asking them if they need room for milk. At first, I don't see the boy who shrugs under a trench coat, his dark hair tousled into his eyes. And then I do see him, but it doesn't matter. I'm too busy to pay him any attention. Until he makes me.

"'Mr. Leopold Bloom ate with relish the inner organs of beasts and fowls,'" he's saying, bending over to gaze down into the deli case. His breath is fogging the glass. I'm watching it suddenly. Watching him. "'He liked thick giblet soup, nutty gizzards, a stuffed roast heart—'"

"'Liverslices fried with crustcrumbs, fried hencods' roes,'" I say, and I'm sure I sound a little stunned. I'm not used to boys coming into the deli to quote some of my favorite modernist literature. Even I can't resist that. A boy like him, who, from the first moment, seems to love the things that I love. With his hands in his pockets, he stands up, grinning at me. His teeth are kind of crooked, like his parents could never afford braces.

Or at least that's what I'm imagining. My family could never afford braces either.

"You know *Ulysses*," he says.

"Yeah, of course," I tell him, my head still spinning. Reading is the only thing I care about besides the deli. "I love James Joyce."

"That's rare," he tells me. "You must still be in high school."

When people look at me, I blush. I hate it, hate how it makes me look like my feelings are open to everyone else. I'd rather be a cipher, tough, hard, unreadable, just like Pop. But I'm blushing furiously right now, right into the white collar of my T-shirt.

"I'm a senior," I say to him. I glance over to where Pop is busy with Mrs. Feldman, arguing over the cost of lox. "Hey, are you going to buy something?"

"I thought I might try the liver," he says, tapping the glass. Smudging it. I'll have to clean it later, but suddenly I don't mind. I'm grinning instead. Grinning and blushing. I don't think I've ever seen a guy under fifty order the liver before.

"We don't make it fried with crustcrumbs."

He's looking at me, a smile in the corners of his mouth.

"How would you recommend it?"

"Oh, I hate liver," I say, and then laugh. He's laughing too. It's remarkable, how we're laughing together. I'm not much of a laugher. "But if you have to do it, I'd go classic. You can never go wrong with a bagel."

"Sure," he's saying, watching me. Watching me blush. "Sesame. Toasted. Black coffee, too."

"Sure thing," I say.

I'd be lying if I said that I didn't think about the boy after that. The one who quoted *Ulysses*. The one who ate chopped liver and wore a wrinkled trench coat like it was some kind of statement. Or maybe he isn't a boy; maybe he's a man, but a youngish one. College, I think, thinking about it too much, a freshman, no more than a sophomore. Something about his hands. I think about it at school the next day, when I decide to go in for no particular reason, and I think about it over dinner while me and Pop eat and watch the news. I think about it when my brother calls and nags me about college. I think *college* for the first time. And for the first time it sounds vaguely palatable. Do boys read James Joyce in college, or do they read him all on their own, like I did?

"You need to get your applications together," my brother tells me. "High school doesn't last forever."

"I'm working on it," I say, and for the first time in my life, Ethan goes quiet. He always thinks he knows what's best for me—doesn't understand that I've always known how to take care of myself. I follow signs when I see them, tea leaves in a particular pattern, birds crossing my path on a certain day. It's not religion, not exactly, but my own strange sort of faith.

I know already that that morning, that conversation, that boy—it means something. It's a disruption from my usual life, which usually I would hate. But I don't mind it. Don't mind him. I'm dreaming, which feels big and dangerous. At the same time, I don't expect to ever see him again. He may have gotten me to pick up *Portrait of the Artist as a Young Man* for the four-thousandth time, but he's a symbol. I think that's all he'll ever be.

Until he appears two weeks later, just before we close for the day—when the only people who are there are me and Pop and the old men who always linger over their newspapers until nearly three thirty, closing time. I'm mopping when the door jingles open and in walks the boy, the smell of autumn all around him.

"'Mr. Leopold Bloom ate with relish the inner organs of beasts and fowls,'" he says, grinning at me. It's a nervous grin.

"You're back!" I say, wondering if I can ignore the way my face heats so that we can both pretend it isn't happening.

"I came back a few times," he says. "But you were never here."

"You must have quite the taste for liver." I look down at the floor, mopping furiously.

"Where were you?" he presses.

I shrug, still not looking. "You know. School."

"But not today?"

I shrug again. No, not today. Today, I needed the deli. The humming lights. The customers. The whitefish.

"Listen," the boy says, like school or not, it doesn't matter, "I want to take you out."

Me. Out. I eye him. I am not the girl boys "take out."
I am not a creature with a body, with feelings. And those
are things boys like, right? Except this boy. This boy likes
James Joyce.

"Don't look so offended," he says, letting out a small,
nervous laugh. I like that laugh. It's like his rib cage is
opening up right in front of me, his beautiful pink guts
spilling out.

"I'm not offended!" I say, too loud. "I'm just surprised."

"You shouldn't be. I know this place that makes great
Persian food. It's called Manijeh's. C'mon. Please?" There's
a longing in his face, sad and a little intense, and normally—
like if I were at school and saw a boy looking at a girl like
that—I'd roll my eyes. But I'm just blushing, wondering, *Has
he been thinking about me like I've been thinking about him?*

"Um," I say, "I have to ask Pop."

That's a lie. I don't *have* to ask Pop anything. We don't
really have rules in my house. My older brother Ethan was
nearly eighteen when we moved in and only stayed that one
summer. And I'm a pretty boring human being. I don't drink
and I don't smoke and I've never dated before. But it feels
right to check in with him, to ask him, in a way, *Do you see
what's happening here too?*

I glance over my shoulder to find that Pop's been watching us, paused in cleaning the counter. Both of his bushy
white eyebrows are raised, and he glances at Mr. Schneider
and Mr. Walton at their table, and both seem to let out
silent chuckles before going back to their newspapers.

"Go," Pop says. "Be young. Have fun for once."

If I were a different girl, I'd go and kiss my grandfather on the cheek. But that's not who I am, who he is. So I turn back to the boy.

"Okay. Okay, then. I'm Naomi, by the way. But I guess you know that." I take off my name tag, my apron, leave them both at the counter. The boy is watching me, looking amused.

"Simon," he says, finally breaking out into a grin.

We walk to the restaurant, our knuckles brushing, but not exactly touching. There's a little buzz in the back of my head: *I'm on a date I'm on a date I'm on a date.* I'm not sure if I'm thrilled or terrified, but either way, it makes it hard to keep up with the conversation.

"So Pop is, like, literally your pop?" Simon asks.

On a date I'm on a date . . . It takes me a little too long to answer. "Yeah, my grandfather. Everyone calls him Pop, though. Forever. He was raised by his aunt and uncle, and they said that he was a little old man even at like nine years old."

"I can get behind that," Simon tells me, pausing to straighten the lapels of his trench coat as if for effect. I laugh.

"What's with the old-man getup, anyway?" Maybe I asked a little too boldly. He frowns, but doesn't look all that upset.

"I often feel like I was born in another era. Back in the time of your pop, maybe."

I stuff my hands down in my pockets.

"I'm glad I wasn't."

"Oh?"

"Well, you know. There's the fucking Holocaust. And 'Nam. Separate water fountains. Rampant sexism. No birth control."

I don't realize that I've said it until I do, and I blush worse than ever, bright, bright red, like a rash all over my neck and ears and face. Simon's looking at me. But he only nods.

"I guess you're right. I've never thought of it that way before." It's as if for Simon, life has always been the same privileged pleasure for everyone. He holds the door open for me. I feel myself blush even worse than before.

"Ah, sorry," I say. But I'm not sure why I'm apologizing.

I'm so nervous that I hardly eat and speak even less. Simon seems comfortable enough talking for both of us, though he's nervous too. He never even bothers to take off his coat, and he keeps talking with his mouth full and then apologizing.

". . . so my mom and dad wanted me to major in something useful, like accounting. Sorry. But I said that there's nothing more useful than literature and—excuse me—philosophy. My mom got my dad on board."

"That's good," I say as I swirl my food around my plate. I try to imagine what it's like to be Simon, majoring in philosophy and literature, taking night classes, drinking black coffee, and scrawling notes longhand in his Moleskine. It feels like a world away.

"Sorry. I'm talking too much." I smile a little bit more to hear him admit it. He smiles back. "How about you, Naomi? What are your thoughts on college?"

I shrug, pushing my collards back and forth on my plate. I remember my fantasies, what I told Ethan. *I'm working on it.* But I haven't really done anything. Just fantasized. Even those fantasies feel far away—almost impossible. "I like to read. Not just James Joyce. Everything, I guess."

"Do you think you'll join me in the army of unhirable English majors?"

I grin. But then the corners of my mouth twitch a little. The other night I stayed up late, googling colleges like other kids might google porn. Nothing fancy. State, or the reach schools I've heard the other students talking about in the cafeteria. The entrance requirements made my lungs feel like they were collapsing. "I don't know. My grades are pretty bad right now. They've been for . . . a long time, really."

"High school sucks," Simon says with all the wisdom of a college freshman. "It's not just you. It sucks for everybody."

I look at him, and for a second, I swear I see a flash. Simon, getting his head slammed into a locker in the hallway. Simon, reading all the wrong books under his desk in tenth-grade English class. Simon, in a wrinkled suit and suspenders that are stylish but stylish in the wrong way, getting called into the principal's office over a letter he wrote to the high school paper.

"No," I say. "It's not like that for me." Actually, sometimes it is like that. But quieter, and with more internal screaming.

"What then?" he asks, and for the first time in a long time I have the sense that someone is really listening to me.

"School used to be really easy," I say, tearing my eyes away from him, because it hurts to talk about it, which is why I never talk about it. "I was in TAG—talented and gifted, you know? All through elementary school. And then my parents . . . well, they croaked. When I was in middle school. A car accident. I sort of started to wonder what the point was."

"I'm sorry," Simon says. "I can't imagine."

I don't say anything. I guess I'm supposed to say *thanks* or *it's okay*, but I can't. Because he can't imagine. And I don't have to. I lived it—the long, crushing days before and after.

"My parents are pretty great," he admits, almost like it's another apology. "I'm . . . really, really lucky."

"You are," I agree. I look at him and can feel the tears in my eyes, even though I don't want them. Fuck. Crying is worse than blushing, isn't it? I'm not supposed to be like this, but something about Simon has everything on the surface, breaking through.

"Let's talk about happier things," he says gently. I feel myself exhale. I am distilled relief. "Tell me. What was the last book you read and hated?"

This is easy. This I can talk about. I tell him about *Nine*

Stories, and he looks like I've just committed sacrilege, but it's okay—I can tell.

And that's when I decide Simon is okay too.

We're together after that. We don't discuss it, but we just *are*. My days are more or less the same as they always were, school, or not school. The deli, or not. But my nights—my nights are full of Simon.

His hands, broad and cool, and his body, which is nearly hairless, and his hair, which is straight and dark and he is always pushing out of his eyes, until I learn to push it out of the way for him. Until I learn he doesn't mind. He leans his cheek into my hand, his lips on my palm. We kiss and I'm rattled and I feel something. I feel a lot.

We move fast, and maybe it's scary, but maybe it's the only way it can go for me. I was never going to slowly open like a flower. All or nothing, that's how it has to be. I needed someone to pull me into the light.

When I come home late, Pop smiles at me over his newspaper and television but doesn't ask where I've been or what I've been up to. He doesn't pry. Pop's that kind of guy.

But my brother Ethan gives me a hard time on the phone. "Pop says you're hooking up with some boy."

"He's not just some boy," I tell him. "His name is Simon."

"Pop says he's in college? Is he some kind of perv?"

"He's only a year older than me, Ethan. How old was Cadence when you started dating?"

My brother doesn't answer. We all know he dated a fourteen-year-old for a while right after Mom and Dad died. It was probably just a grief thing, but it freaked everybody out. Even though Pop gives me a wide berth, you can bet he had something to say about *that*.

"Anyway," Ethan says. "You need to be working on your college applications."

Back to business. That's how Ethan's always gotten through it. He's an accountant now, and I think he'd love me to have a future that looks like his: eight thirty to six, suit and tie, changing his network password every four months, respectable.

"I'm thinking about college!" I protest. Which is absolutely true. When I spend the night at Simon's, it's in his dorm bed. The two of us are pressed together, his roommate snoring only a few feet away. I go with him to his philosophy class one night and sit next to him as he argues about dualism versus materialism, and the professor looks proud when Simon steamrolls some other freshman with his argument.

"If you could objectively prove that we're more than just meat machines, then sure. I guess that argument would make sense. But realistically we're nothing more than a series of impulses—"

"But there have been studies," the other student objects meekly. Simon rolls his eyes.

"Where they weighed the soul after death? Yeah. Total bunk."

Simon is so sure of himself, in a way I never could be.

Even though I don't agree with him, there's something so forceful about the way that he speaks that I feel myself wavering. I imagine what it's like to live with that much assurance, that much moxie. But I know I never will. If Simon's fire, then I'm a stone. I've had to be to survive.

I've enjoyed imagining myself in Simon's shoes, in Simon's life. Even though it feels like a fever dream, distant and impossible.

"Okay, where are you applying?" my brother snaps after a long silence. He really doesn't believe that I know how to take care of myself. Maybe he's right that I don't. I chew my lip.

"Um. State." I know that State will be a reach, but it's where Simon goes. It feels like a possibility, at least.

"You need to apply to *a minimum* of six schools. Eight to ten would be ideal. What are your safeties?"

"I don't have any," I tell him. I'm losing interest in this conversation. I know I'm saying the wrong things. I don't want Ethan's advice, anyway. He's not my dad, not my mom. I had parents once. I don't now. He might be my brother, and he might be older than me. But he hardly knows me, not really. Pop is watching *Wheel of Fortune* in the next room, and I can hear Vanna's polite smattering of applause. I listen to that instead of listening to Ethan.

"Naomi—" my brother begins, but I don't let him finish.

"Ethan, I'm fine. I'll talk to you next week."

And I hang up before he can protest further.

* * *

Simon's parents love him. Simon's parents send him money. He says he's eligible for work-study, but his parents don't want him to be distracted. That's how we can afford to go out to eat as much as we do. Simon tries everything. Soul food and fusion food and little Mexican pastries that taste like magic and lard. He tells me about music while we eat at all the best restaurants on Hungry Heart Row. He tells me about books. He tells me about Jacques Lacan, a French psychoanalyst who I don't understand, and don't really care to. Sometimes I look at Simon and think, *I'm objectifying you.* Because I'm not really listening to him. I'm watching his eyes flutter under his thick, girlish lashes, watching his sweet mouth move, thinking of kissing him, not really thinking about the words coming out.

He wants me to talk more. In his dorm, when the sky is red as minestrone overhead, he wakes me up with the pressure of his mouth on my freckled shoulders.

"I know you think about things, Naomi. Brilliant things. Amazing things. I know your feelings are deeper than mine. Why can't you share with me? You're safe with me."

I kiss him back and say nothing. My body is vibrating. I think, *My body can speak for me.* I don't feel safe with him, but that's not unique to Simon. I never really feel safe with anyone except Pop. Other people might leave at any moment like my parents did. Except for him.

Maybe one day I'll feel safe with Simon, though. Maybe one day our lives will fit together in a way that makes sense. I imagine myself in my own dorm room, posters taped to the walls, eating takeout with him. I imagine highlighting my own textbooks and reading the best quotes to him. In my imagination, I laugh easily. Like I never do in real life.

It hasn't happened yet, though. In the morning, I set up the deli case with my grandfather. Working in silence, our hands shrouded in an onion skin of latex. The sound of the slicer moving up and down the saran wrap. Pop hums faintly. In the deli, almost alone except for Pop, nothing hurts.

One night Simon comes over for dinner. I don't know what he's expecting—bagels and liver? Pop hasn't had a real home-cooked dinner since my bubbe died, a year before my parents. And even that wasn't exactly haute cuisine. Her meals were delicious, but strange. Spaghetti with canned tomatoes and cottage cheese on top, that kind of thing. Anyway, when the oven timer goes off, Pop pulls out three foil-wrapped TV dinners with a dish towel and sets them on our kitchen table.

"I'll let *you* have the chicken," he says to Simon, thumping him gently on the shoulder. This is unusual generosity from Pop. I'm not sure Simon understands that. I wonder if he's second-guessing his dinner choices, wishing he'd just eaten in the cafeteria tonight.

But Simon's a polite boy, so he says, "Thank you, sir," and digs in. Pop looks pleased as he sits down over his Hungry-Man.

"Call me Pop," my grandfather says.

"So, Pop," Simon begins, eyeing my grandfather. "How did you come to own a deli?"

My grandfather shrugs. He's not much for stories. "My uncle owned a deli, and I grew up behind the counter."

"Like Naomi?"

Pop looks at me. Shrugs again. "So when my uncle retired, he said, 'Arthur, do you want to own a deli?' Different now, though. With the Served and the blobbing—"

"Blogging, Pop," I say, and even though he's probably just teasing us, I feel myself blush. Which is funny, because Pop doesn't usually embarrass me much at all. But having Simon talk to him this way is almost as bad as being looked at. All of my family's strangeness, laid out to see.

"You must have had other dreams," Simon says suddenly, like he's been mulling over this question. He might consider himself a gourmand, might love to consume the fruits of our bagels, but I don't think it really makes any sense to him, why anyone would want to actually *live* a life so small.

"Dreams?" Pop says, slathering mustard on his gray slab of steak. "Eh. As a boy, I thought maybe I'd be a pharmacist. I thought a pharmacist was really someone."

Simon is frowning. I chew silently, waiting for Pop to go on, dreading what he might say. I'm not ashamed of Pop, but I know that he's not exactly what Simon expected.

"But deli, pharmacy. It's all the same."

"Is it?" Simon asks. Pop doesn't answer. He points his fork at Simon.

"And what do *you* dream about being, my boy?" Simon smiles faintly. This, he can handle talking about. His answer makes me feel warm and happy to hear it. He's ambitious.

Sometimes I wonder if his ambition will rub off on me. Sometimes I hope it will.

"I'd like to be a professor," he says. "And a writer. Both, I guess."

"What do you write?" Pop asks. Simon's eyelashes flutter.

"I've started a few short stories." The implication thuds between our plastic dinner trays in the middle of the table. He's started a few. He hasn't finished any.

"I figure when I'm older I'll finish them," he says. "I don't have a lot of life experience."

Pop looks at him, his jaw tight. Then he nods.

"Hmm" is all he says.

After Simon leaves, Pop and I sit in front of the television. Usually, this time of night is a relief. Long boring quiet and the evening news. Pop shouting the wrong answers at Alex Trebek while I dog-ear pages in my latest book. But tonight I'm looking at Pop, my stomach all knotted.

"Go ahead, Naomi," my grandfather says, not looking up from the television. "Ask."

I smile grimly. "You hated him, didn't you?"

Pop laughs. A dry laugh. "No, I don't hate anyone."

"But you don't like him?"

"He's fine," Pop says. Like that's the end of it. He's not going to say anything else, because Pop never really talks about how he's feeling. Everything meaningful goes into the gaps, the silences. And there's a lot of silence here.

Fine. Fine, I think, all that night and through the next work day. Funny how being *fine* feels suddenly all wrong.

"Your test scores are excellent," Mrs. O'Keefe, the guidance counselor, says. She's sitting on one side of her desk. I'm sitting on the other. I'm trying to look like the weight of her gaze doesn't make me wither inside.

I know my test scores are good. She doesn't have to tell me that.

"But your grades . . . ," she begins.

I know my grades suck. She doesn't have to tell me that, either.

"State might be a stretch," she says. "Though with the right essay it might be possible. Have you thought about what you want to write about?"

I shrug. "Working in Pop's Deli, I thought," I tell her. I could describe the ladies who come in on their lunch break. The old men with their oniony smells. I can talk about how I make their lives better with smoked salmon and capers, and how, even though there are fewer customers than there used to be, we've formed a community there. I can use just enough detail that it might be clear how an everything bagel is a metaphor for the whole world.

Mrs. O'Keefe's mouth looks stern. "That's a beginning," she says, "but you really need to touch on the reasons behind your low grades." There's a long pause. I don't like it. "Have you thought about writing about your parents?"

Now it's my turn to pause.

"No, I haven't thought about that."

When I leave her office, my eyes are stinging. I don't go back to school for two days after that. Halfway through the school year and already I've almost burned through my absences. It's beginning to be a problem. On my date with Simon, I'm feeling raw and unsettled. All my feelings are close to the surface.

"Tell me what's wrong," he says. He holds my hands, tenderly rubbing my wrists with his thumbs. I want to be normal. I want to trust my boyfriend. So, for once, I talk to Simon, hoping he can help, and even though he's listening, nodding, the moment he opens his mouth, I know it's all wrong.

"Well, why *not* write about your parents?"

If I wrote about my parents, I'd have to tell the truth. They were drunk the night that they died, and most nights before that. That my mom used to drink too much wine and talk about Pop hitting her when she was young, even though he's never hit me. That he was hurt in the war, and before that, in the camps when he was a toddler, before he could even remember his name. He doesn't talk about it, but it's all there, written in my blood. There isn't one reason that I'm a failure. There are a million reasons, stretching back forever.

The pogroms. The Inquisition.

If I wrote about my parents, I'd have to talk about how it hurts, still. And we don't talk about feelings in my family. We pull ourselves together. We keep going. Steady, steady. People like Simon can afford to have feelings. People like me and Pop, survivors? We work, and don't feel anything at all. We can't escape who we are, but maybe we don't need to. Maybe our future is predicated on what came before.

That's why I want to write about the deli. Work is survival. Food is survival. Anything else, though? Vulnerability. Maybe that doesn't mean anything to Simon, with his loving parents and good grades and artfully thrifted clothes. But I can't afford to be vulnerable, no matter how badly I wish I could be.

"'Mr. Leopold Bloom ate with relish the inner organs of beasts and fowls,'" I say suddenly. Simon is frowning at me.

"What?"

"Did you ever think about why he ate that stuff?" I ask. Simon's expression hasn't changed. When he doesn't answer, I just go on. "He was Jewish, you know. Mr. Leopold Bloom."

"No he wasn't," Simon says.

I shake my head. I laugh a little, even though it isn't funny. "Yes he was. Organ meats. Who eats organ meats?"

"Lots of cultures . . . ," Simon begins uncertainly. "Anyway, he wasn't Jewish in any way that matters. He was Irish Catholic, wasn't he? He wasn't, like, a practicing Jew."

"I just think it's interesting," I say. "He carries around all this pain from losing his son. And his father. Sometimes I think it's part of being Jewish. We've got this legacy of loss. And the way he eats, like he's been starving. He's got this hole that can't be filled. At least Stephen ends up being his son in the end, kind of. Bloom teaches him how to read

Hebrew. He can't get his son back, but he figures out a way to live on. Like, a new legacy."

Simon is staring at me. There's something I don't like about his gaze, proud and a little defensive. Like he's hiding something. Like he doesn't want to be found out.

"You haven't finished the book," I say. I never considered it, that Simon would lie about that. That anybody would lie about such a thing, especially a pretty boy with broad, soft hands whose parents love him.

"Of course I have," he tells me. But I know for certain in that minute he's lying. "Anyway, what's that have to do with your parents?"

Somehow it has everything to do with my parents. My parents who suffered. My parents who died. Who lived imperfectly until they didn't anymore. Who left me here to live imperfectly too.

I feel a flash of pity for him. Ordinary Simon, in his trench coat, stealing snippets of words from more extraordinary times. If I'm angry, I'm only angry at myself for not seeing it before. For not seeing him for who he truly was.

"Let's go out to eat," I say softly. I want to make up, to go back to how things used to be. "What do you feel like tonight?"

Simon's sitting on the edge of his dorm bed in his boxers, shaking his head.

"I think I want to go to the cafeteria tonight," he says. Only students are allowed in the cafeteria, and we both know it. I'm not a student. I don't think I'll ever be a student. "I think I need some time to myself."

I'm not sure what to say, so I stand. Even just standing there, my shoulders a little slumped, I feel foolish and false.

"Okay," I tell him. "I'll see you soon."

I kiss him on the cheek, because I'm supposed to. It's an ordinary kiss. *Steady and safe,* I tell myself. *Steady and safe.*

But I know that I'm not. And I never was.

I walk through Hungry Heart Row, my stomach empty, my mind all ajumble. It's a Friday, and it feels like everyone is out on a date. A couple breezes by me, a boy in a mismatched jean jacket and jeans, and a girl, flour in her hair, their fingers entangled. They smell like pastries. My stomach growls.

I can't afford to eat out at an actual restaurant without Simon—it's not like Pop pays me—but I'm not sure I want to, anyway. But going back home isn't all that appealing either. I wander down Pepper Street and duck into the Chinese grocery for a snack. Wandering through the tidy aisles, I feel an odd pang of comfort at the sight of all those dried, fishy treats and red-bean baos. It's not the kind of food you'll find anywhere else, but it sustains you. Just like the food at the deli. I pick up a packet of something, squinting at the foreign letters. And then I laugh softly to myself. It's not like I can read Hebrew, either.

"You, girl," says a woman down the far end of the aisle. She's well dressed, but under the makeup you can see that she's practically Pop's age. Ancient. "You need your fortune read tonight?"

It's half a question and half a statement of fact. I put the snacks back on the shelf and look to my right and left.

"No one else here," she says, and chuckles. I recognize her, of course. Ethan used to tell me that Grandma Ma, who told fortunes in the back of the Chinese grocery store, was a witch. But I don't think witches dress like this, in pressed clothes and carefully applied drug-store lipstick. Do witches even wear lipstick? I decide they don't, and that Ethan is full of it.

"Okay," I find myself saying, really without thinking at all. Simon would probably laugh to see how I meander through the aisles and then push through the beaded curtain in back. He doesn't believe in this stuff, doesn't think we're anything more than matter.

I think Simon is full of it too.

After all, I've been waiting for a sign. What better sign is there than this? There's magic in the world, tonight and every night. If only he would open his eyes to see it.

There are boxes of stock lining the walls, a hand-painted calendar hanging in the buzzing fluorescent light. I sit on a stool across from Grandma Ma. She has me shake a canister of sticks.

"Make a wish," she says, and winks in that weird old-person way that Pop sometimes does.

A normal person might wish for Simon to understand her better. Or for a brilliant college application essay about her dead parents to spring forth fully formed from her mind. My wish is as jumbled as the sticks, though. I'm not even sure what I'm wishing for.

No, that's not true. I know what I *should* wish for. College, a guy like Simon. But it doesn't feel like it's what I need.

Maybe that's okay, I say to myself for the first time, watching her shake the sticks. *Maybe when the answer comes, I'll know.*

One stick jumps out, and Grandma Ma reads the characters for me. "Seventy-two," she says. "That's no good."

She reads my fortune out of a book. Something about strife and sadness. It feels about right. I'm still starving, still thinking about how Simon lied. How he looked at me when I told him that I didn't want to write about my parents. How Pop said Simon was just plain *fine*.

Grandma Ma is still reading from her book. "Here," she says. "Important event. Your love affairs seem wrong, but will be righted soon through a generous friend."

"Who?" I ask, the word spilling out, desperate sounding.

Grandma Ma shrugs. "The sticks don't tell me that."

I pay for my fortune and too many freeze-dried snacks. I go home. Eat alone in my room. I wait. When Simon calls the next day, I know what's coming. And I'm not wrong.

"I just don't really think we—"

"We're not on the same page," I finish for him. Simon is quiet on the other side.

"Are you sure?" he finally asks, as if he wasn't planning on dumping me anyway. I tuck the phone in against my cheek, shrugging, even though he can't see it.

"Sure."

"Can we still be friends?" he asks. "Talk about books?"

And what? Tell him how *Ulysses* ends? I could laugh, but it isn't funny.

"Sure," I say again. But somehow, deep down in my gut, I know I'm never going to see him again.

There's a relief in endings. A door shuts, and you find yourself on the other side. For me, breaking up with Simon means I'm back to normality. Back to skipping school and pickled herring. Back to *To the Lighthouse*, which I always like better than *Portrait of the Artist as a Young Man*, anyway. Back to *Wheel of Fortune* and Ethan nagging me about college. Back to avoiding the question. Pop and I didn't talk about Simon's arrival, and we don't talk about his departure, either. He's just gone, leaving a gaping hole in my life where there wasn't one before. I tell myself it doesn't matter. I wasn't really all that interested in college, anyway.

Until one day Pop slides me a brochure from across the table, right beside my tray of Hungry-Man. It's from the community college. There's a stock photo of students, smiling too much, laughing too much. But the words above them. That's what matters.

"Restaurant Management and Culinary Arts?" I ask, picking it up. Pop lifts one bushy eyebrow.

"The business isn't like it used to be," Pop says. "If you're going to take over the store someday, I won't have it fail."

He pounds a fist on the table, rattling his glass. I jump. It's the first time I've ever seen him feel strongly about something in, well, ever. His eyes are crinkly, though, almost smiling. Almost joyful. My grandfather never went to college, never became a pharmacist. But, taking the life he'd been given, he found a way to move on anyway.

I'm staring at the brochure. I'm trying not to smile back. "Where'd you get this?" I ask, because I know this kind of scheme isn't the sort of thing Pop would come up with on his own.

"From Chava, the butcher's girl," he says. "She takes classes in, I don't know . . . slaughtering." He waves his hand through the air. I laugh.

"Thanks, Pop," I say softly, because it's all I can say.

It's not State, and it's not Ethan's plan for my future either. It's something else. Not a new book, but a new chapter in the same book. Pop's book. Mine.

My grandfather's mouth is smiling, but he says nothing.

The gray cracks early. I put on my white T-shirt, my jeans, my shoes. It will be winter soon, grim and true, and then spring and then summer. As I shuffle down the stairs to the deli, I see the whole year rolling out ahead of me. Steady and safe, but new and different, too. A future, but *my* future. One that belongs to nobody else.

Pop and I fill the baskets with bagels. We slice the thick loaves of rye. I get the chopped liver from the back fridge, feeling the cold prickle my arms, feeling nothing else at all.

Today is like any other day. But it isn't. When the bell
rings on the front door, and Chava comes in, Pop doesn't
move from where he's slicing onions. He only ticks up one
eyebrow, glancing at me so quickly that for a second, I think
I've imagined it.

"Hey, sweetness," Chava says, approaching the deli case.
I'm looking at her through the glass, looking at her big, hazel
eyes. Her lashes are long. Her image is quickly fogged with
the heat of her breath, which I'll have to wipe away later. But
I don't mind.

"Hey," I tell her, speaking to her for the very first time.
"What do you have today?"

She tells me about her roast beef and her turkey and her
chicken breast. She says not to order the chicken breast,
actually. Go with the roast beef instead. Somewhere in there,
I thank her for giving Pop the brochure, and the corners of
her mouth lift a little. But soon we're talking about work
again. What's selling. What isn't.

It's easy. It's ordinary. But maybe there are signs here,
signs I've been ignoring.

"Hey," I say suddenly, "I've been wanting to ask you
something. Two things, actually."

Chava's eyebrows tick up. "Yeah? Shoot."

"Okay, well," I say, licking my lips, a little nervous to be
talking to her at all. "Why do you always call me sweetness?"

She hooks her thumbs in her belt loops. "Besides the
obvious?" she asks. I should be blushing, but I'm not. It's too
comfortable, too natural for that.

"Yeah, yeah," I tell her. "Besides that."

"Your name. It's what it means. It's from the Bible, the Book of Ruth. Don't call me Naomi, or sweetness, call me Mara, because I am bitter."

I feel my mouth crack open, my teeth showing. "I like that," I say.

Her nose wrinkles. "Good thing your name isn't Mara. So what's the second thing you wanted to ask?"

I hesitate only a moment. I'm being brave, but it doesn't feel like bravery. Chava is not Simon. She's like me. Marked. Different. So I step out from behind the deli case. Reaching out across the counter area, my fingertips graze her inked arm.

"What do your tattoos mean?" I ask her. She glances at Pop, a pointed piece of punctuation in her eyes. He's not looking at us, but I can see how he's listening, in the way that his knife pauses on the cutting board just a moment between thwacks.

Chava's the one blushing now. But when I look at her, she looks relieved.

"I thought you'd never ask," she says.

A Bountiful Film

BY S. K. ALI

A box remained on the driveway. I opened the front door and descended the concrete steps to retrieve it. It was weird the movers had just left it, as it was small enough to have been easily hoisted atop the other boxes that had been brought in all morning.

The forgotten box wasn't even taped closed. The cardboard flaps were instead alternatively folded and tucked into one another. Now that I was closer, I realized the package wasn't part of our family move. It didn't have the sticker labels Mom had printed off and stuck on each of our possessions: JAMAL FAMILY MOVE TO HUNGRY HEART ROW, BOX #__.

This was something else.

I tentatively teased apart two of the flaps and peered

inside. A smell hit me—sharp, garlicky, vinegary.

Pulling out all four flaps revealed a casserole dish, the clear glass lid resting atop plain white rice. The condensation on the lid indicated this had been made very recently.

Valimma, my grandmother, stepped onto the driveway behind me.

"That is Simeona's food, moleh. She just called to say her son dropped it off on the driveway." Valimma spoke her English slowly but surely, with a lilt that was the result of years of socializing with neighbors from a variety of backgrounds. "Simeona can't come to Thursday Club today but still wanted to send her delicious shrimp adobo."

"This is just rice, Valimma." I pointed at the casserole dish.

"Check under. The tasty mix, the bountiful flavor, must be below."

Sure enough, under the rice container was another, shallower dish housing large shrimps coated in dark brown sauce. Yup, sharp, garlicky, vinegary.

Valimma bent to hoist it all up, but I put a hand out.

"I'll get it. You already helped too much, Valimma. You didn't have to start unpacking the kitchen. Dad said we were going to start this weekend." I followed her up the stairs, pausing at the small corner landing to shift the contents of the box. Another whiff of vinegar hit my nose, and I closed my mouth tight. Vinegar wasn't a favorite.

"Oh no, the kitchen needs to be done first after a move. The pantry needs to be stocked with rice and staples to bless our home with food always. It is tradition."

I nodded, more out of habit then agreement. If it had been Mom saying this, I would have asked for sources. *What tradition? Whose tradition?*

But Mom was teaching university in Dubai. She'd been here, back home in the US, for a month to help pack for the move, and then had had to leave for the start of a new semester.

Before she flew out, she convinced Valimma, who'd lived in the same Hungry Heart Row apartment from when Dad was a kid, to move into the new brownstone walk-up with us. To be the matriarch.

I was the other person who'd needed convincing to agree to the move.

Both my brothers were beginning new chapters of their lives in the fall, so changing neighborhoods wasn't a big deal for them. The older one, Bilal, was starting college nearby and the younger one, Rashad, would be a high school freshman in two months.

But, for me, moving the summer before senior year meant that I wouldn't be graduating with my class. It also meant I'd have to give up my job at Daily Harvest, a free meal service for those who needed it, where I'd worked for five years, first volunteering with my mom at twelve and then joining as an employee two years ago. It's in an area called Russell, closer to my old neighborhood, and there was no way I could get to work in time after school.

Which was absolutely the *worst*, because just a few

months ago, they'd begun letting me help the fundraising team make videos. Which is MY thing.

Moving to Hungry Heart Row had been excruciating, and I'd let everyone know it.

Then, a month before the scheduled moving date, I came home to find a brand-new camera, a Sony A6500.

I'm kind of ashamed to say it, but the bribe had worked. Especially since this year I needed top-of-the-line equipment to win gold in the teen category at the state film festival—a prize which included my dream: an internship with a production company.

Last film festival, I'd come in second.

This time, however, no one, especially not a person by the name of Gabrielle Rose, would stop me from first prize.

Once I settled on a prize-winning idea, that is.

"What about Hungry Heart Row itself as a topic? Like those roaming videos where you get to see the people, the places, hear the sounds." I peeled a thread off a string-cheese snack and tilted my head back to drop it into my mouth. "Like sound would be *the* feature of the film then."

"I doubt anyone would care," Bilal said. He was opening random boxes in the dining room adjacent to the kitchen, looking for something. "Did anyone in Mulberry talk about Hungry Heart Row? Did you ever hear a single soul say a single word about it, except Dad reminiscing about his old days? So why would anyone at the film fest care?"

"But the wow factor wouldn't be the subject of the film. It would be the way it's made, the form of the film. I can do awesome, shocking things with it."

"You already did that with last year's film, remember?" Bilal paused running a box cutter down the taped seam of a box. He lifted up his left hand in a fist. *"We Resist: An In-Your-Face Act of Film?"*

"I won second, remember? *Remember?*"

"Yeah, but first place went to an unraucous film," Bilal said smugly. "Hania, your stuff may be too intense."

"I hate the fact that older people judge these things!" I leaned my elbows on the edge of the kitchen island counter and slumped my face into my palms. "They liked the lingering shots of crocheted doilies, pastel walls, and flowery curtains that Gabrielle Rose did. She knew what they'd like; that's why she went all bland. Ugh."

"It was nice. In a mellow, dignified way."

"It was old. Like old-people old." I stopped myself from saying the next part—*like boring old*—as Valimma walked into the kitchen, a scarf worn loosely on her head. Her gray hair, oiled and austerely parted, could be seen peeking out the front.

"Bilal, monu, help me clear the dining table of these boxes. It's my turn to host Thursday Club, and we need a place to sit and eat."

"Sure, Valimma." Bilal began moving boxes off the long walnut table.

"We need to put five chairs around the table. Well, four

today, because Simeona isn't coming." Valimma lifted up smaller boxes and set them on the floor.

"What do you do at Thursday Club, Valimma?" I leaned on the frame of the kitchen doorway.

"We eat and laugh and eat and tell stories and eat again."

"Can I come? Can I film you guys?" I avoided Bilal's smirky look.

"Yes, certainly. I'm sure my friends would like that. A young person to hear our stories." Valimma motioned to Bilal. "So yes, leave five chairs here."

I adjusted the focus. "Thanks so much for waiting for me to set up the camera. Okay, now, action, reach for the food."

Four hands in various shades of skin reached for utensils to ladle food from bowls atop a lazy Susan as I watched through the screen on my camera. Being the host, it was Valimma's hand that spun the lazy Susan, after allowing each woman adequate time to take from the food laid in front of her. The shotgun mic picked up the clinks of cutlery, the slight rustle of clothing, and low murmurs.

With the dishes revolving in turns, the scene had a rhythmic quality to it. Meditative and tranquil.

I frowned. Meditative and tranquil meant it was too much like Gabrielle's first-place film last year, unimaginatively called *Home Is*.

Bland.

And derivative?

"Franklin saw him again on the security camera. The lost

boy." A white woman with glasses and wispy gray curls was talking, her hand, holding a spring roll, shaking slightly. "I told him to turn it in to the police immediately. But he doesn't listen to me. He says it's just someone who looks like him."

Valimma tsked. "The last time the police said it was *not* the lost boy on the security film. Maybe that is why your son doesn't want to waste their time. The camera outside his hardware store records a lot of people, with the movie theater next door."

Shaking her head, a black woman paused winding her fork in noodles. "It's time they reopened the case. How could it be that a teenager doesn't come home, and they close it after half a year? Especially in a small community like Hungry Heart Row?"

"But now he's been missing for *over* a year, Diane. They have to close it at some point. Who made this rice? Is it yours, Maymoona? It's fluffier than my mother's used to be!" I knew the name of the woman who exclaimed this. It was Valimma's closest friend, Shirley. She and my grandmother had played mahjong together for years.

Valimma shook her head. "No, it's Simeona's. But you must have it with the adobo. Mix-it flavor!"

"Oh yes, Simeona is a fantastic cook," Diane said, reaching for some adobo.

"Especially her Soup Number Five *special*, right?" Shirley said, glancing around at the other women. They burst into laughter in response.

"Hania, come and try some shrimp," Valimma said.

"I'm working, Valimma."

"Open," Valimma commanded, holding out a spoon of rice, tinted brown with adobo sauce, a single shrimp on top.

Vinegar. I shook my head.

But the spoon kept coming forward. That was Valimma's way. She wouldn't stop until you had at least one taste.

I sighed and, closing my eyes to make the process less painful, opened my mouth. It was an instinctive action when Valimma was around—the first vision I had of being with my grandmother was food, unrelenting, coming toward my mouth. Like now.

Oh wow. Bliss. The adobo was perfectly calibrated between my two favorite flavor juxtapositions: sweet and tangy. And the shrimp: practically dissolving in my mouth.

"Thaouft's goofd." Mouth full, I could only grunt my appreciation.

"Told you." Valimma smiled, satisfied. She set aside some adobo and rice on a plate for me. "Simeona knows how to mix it."

"Could you tell me about this 'lost boy'? If you don't mind?" I asked, lowering the tripod so I could scan their faces while they talked. "I'd like to get it on film."

The women looked at each other.

Shirley raised her eyebrows at Valimma. "Why don't you start, Maymoona? We don't know what to say so as not to scare your granddaughter."

I grinned. "Auntie Li, I'm seventeen. I've seen a lot. Maybe more than you have, in terms of scariness."

All four women laughed simultaneously. I looked at the screen. Great scene! Spontaneous, natural, and, if the laugher was fully picked up by the mic, perfectly soundtracked.

"Okay, if you're not scared, if you've seen it all, then let Margaret tell you." Shirley turned to the white woman. The other women did too. "She knows the story the most, because her granddaughter was involved."

I turned the camera until it centered on Margaret. The lighting was off and cast a gray pallor on her skin.

After clamping it lower on an extra chair, I twisted up the desk lamp I'd rummaged from a box in Rashad's bedroom. The light shone from below, to the left of Margaret, and lit the thin tendrils of her hair.

It kind of had the effect of when someone used a flashlight to light their face from under their chin when telling a scary story at camp.

I couldn't decide if I should change the lighting again, but then Margaret put her spring roll down and cleared her throat.

She stared right into the camera. After a pause, her mouth opened.

"One year ago, a boy by the name of Barnaby Bennett, sixteen, went to watch a movie at the cinema here in the neighborhood."

Barnaby Bennett.

The name was odd, old-fashioned, but rung a bell.

Who and where?

"He left home at seven p.m. The movie he wanted to see was playing at seven thirty.

"Before the theater, he went to visit the food carts on Ginkgo Street. He bought a hot dog and fries.

"Many witnesses say they saw him walk to the movie theater. The surveillance cameras say the same thing.

"The ticket vendor that night was my granddaughter. She says she sold Barnaby a pass.

"But Barnaby never came back home after the movie. He's never been seen since.

"Except that every once in a while, he shows up on one of the security cameras around the neighborhood.

"The police closed the case soon after, because Barnaby was the age at which he is allowed to leave home if he wishes. And because he'd told his friends that he wanted to leave.

"But some of us don't think he left home.

"Some of us think he's still in Hungry Heart Row.

"We think he just doesn't want to be seen."

"Boo!" Rashad had snuck up behind as I watched Margaret's story again on my laptop the Sunday after Thursday Club. I paused shoveling in the rice and shrimp Valimma had saved for me.

"You're not funny. Unload the dishwasher. I need to load it before Dad gets home from the mosque."

"It's Sunday. We get to do chores later on Sunday."

"That's old-house rules." Rewinding the video, I began the "lost boy" story again. "Dad doesn't want Valimma to start doing extra stuff around here. Get to it."

"These tiles are the best for socks skating." Rashad slid toward the dishwasher. "If I don't put things in the right cupboards, it's not my fault. It's all new to me."

"I'll just make you redo it."

Margaret's story started again, filling the kitchen with her slightly raspy voice. "One year ago, a boy by the name of Barnaby Bennett, sixteen . . ."

Barnaby Bennett.

That name. I knew where I'd seen it.

It was on film footage I'd edited for the Daily Harvest meal service. A few months ago, they'd asked me to pore over all the video the film crew had captured and cut anything identifying people, and I'd removed a clip showing a short list of names on one of the desks.

Barnaby Bennett was such an odd name on the list, it had so stood out. I'd said it out loud at the time, thinking of the people I greeted each day when I worked evening reception at Daily Harvest.

Barnaby Bennett.

I saw the list clearer in my mind now. It was of young people who'd stopped using the meal service all of a sudden, who'd been earmarked for follow-up by one of the social workers at Daily Harvest but who hadn't been traced.

How likely was it that a Barnaby Bennett would go missing from Hungry Heart Row *and* Daily Harvest?

I felt a sudden twist in my gut at remembering my old job.

It was just empathy—the feeling, I told myself. *Must be SO hard having to rely on a free meal service for food.*

But then there was this: Somewhere deep behind that gut twist there was homesickness, too.

I missed my old life.

Maybe I'd never get used to Hungry Heart Row.

"*. . . Barnaby never came back home after the movie. He's never been seen since. . . .*"

Rashad left the dishwasher's top tray pulled out and slid to the kitchen island. "What is that? YouTube?"

"No, listen to it. It's about a Hungry Heart Row boy who didn't do his chores and was never seen again." I rewound the video for the third time.

When it was done, Rashad let out a long breath. "Is it true? That he's seen on surveillance films?"

"That's what Valimma's Thursday Club says. I'm thinking of doing a film on it."

"On the missing boy? You're going solve a mystery?" Rashad walked back to the dishwasher. "I thought you said the film is due in three weeks. There's no way you can solve a missing person case in under a month."

"I'm not solving it. Just finding out information on it, like why some people think Barnaby's on security tapes, stuff like that. An anatomy-of-a-local-legend film." I took another spoonful of rice. "Also, it's sad. I looked up Barnaby's story online, and some reports make it out like his family didn't really care about what happened to him. He had a hard home life, parents who didn't care."

Rashad raised his eyebrows. "That's weird. And, yeah, sad too."

"Yeah. Maybe if I do this film, it will get people interested again."

I watched the rest of the Thursday Club footage, wondering why something was bothering me about the "lost" Barnaby.

I mean, besides the fact that it was a strange case altogether.

I met Delilah and Ranvir as they exited the crosstown bus at the corner of Nettle and Caraway.

"Not too bad to get here. If you call an *hour* not too bad. The traffic, man!" Ranvir said, looking around at the bustling atmosphere he'd stepped into. There were people squeezing fruits at a produce stall, people walking their dogs, people listening to a busker playing guitar, people sitting on benches eating sticky, drippy things happily.

"So when I'm down and need to see you guys, I'll have to give myself an hour to reach happiness across town." I led the way toward Margaret's son's hardware store, the first of my potential on-camera interviews.

"No, according to Google, on traffic-less days, you can

do it in thirty minutes." Ranvir slid his headphones off, as if he wanted all of his senses to take in the sights and sounds of Hungry Heart Row. "Whoa, this place isn't like Mulberry, that's for sure. This popping on a Monday?"

"It's not that great. Just a lot of little shops." I looked around, not impressed, remembering the neatness of the plazas near my old house.

"So I did the dirty work and poked around with Gabrielle's friend," Delilah said, pulling out her phone to read a message. "GR's doing something 'meta,' like a film about form, whatever that means."

"Great." I closed my eyes. Of course.

Of course Gabrielle Rose would think up something that fancy. She was always one beat, at *least* one beat, ahead of me. And had been for years, since we'd started entering film competitions in freshmen year—and come across each other. Our names always in the top ten spots, but hers always higher than mine.

"A *meta* film," Ranvir said. "I like."

"Meta, which old people, i.e., the judges, will also like." I tried hard not to sound sullen.

"I love what *you're* doing, Hania! It's going to win. People love legends," Delilah announced. *"The Legend of Hungry Heart Row's Lost Boy."*

"I'm not even sure that's what I'm doing the film on. And I don't know if we can call it a legend. It's only a year old. Plus it's sad. There's someone *missing*." I paused in front of Franklin's Hardware. "Barnaby Bennett."

I pushed the door, and a bell jangled in response.

The store was crammed full of things but empty of customers. And empty of a proprietor, it seemed, as the counter, immediately to the right of the entrance, was unmanned. A radio was on so low you couldn't even make out the genre of music.

Ranvir set his backpack down and unzipped it to pull out a portable lighting kit. I shook my head, so he packed it away.

"He still hasn't fully agreed to be filmed. I don't want to scare him," I whispered.

Delilah nodded. "I'm going to shop hardware so it doesn't look like we're ganging up on the dude."

She went down an aisle stocked with boxes of screws and nails.

I checked the time on my phone. *I'll be over at two p.m. so we can talk* had been my e-mail.

I'm always in the store so sounds fine to me, Franklin had responded.

It was exactly 2:02 p.m.

Sliding his headphones back on, Ranvir said, "Let me check the back of the store."

Alone at the counter, I took it all in. The cash register was facing the door, so whoever was manning it could see out into the store. Directly above the register was a small split-screen television. One side showed the inside of the store, and the other showed the area outside the front of the building, even the road and the sidewalk across the street.

The door behind me burst open, the bell jangling wildly.

A tall, thin man wearing a brown T-shirt tucked into belted jeans stood there, a coffee in one hand, a plastic bag in the other.

"You Hania?" he asked in a deep voice. "Wanting to talk to me about my security camera?"

I nodded. "Thanks for agreeing, sir."

"I went to grab some lunch. Got some cookies for you, too." Franklin unlocked the swing door attached to the counter and let himself in. He set his coffee down and pulled out a sandwich and a white box stamped with PANADERÍA PASTELERÍA from the plastic bag. "Now I'm glad I got a lot of them Manzano cookies. It looks like you've got friends, huh?"

Delilah poked her head out of an aisle of cleaning supplies.

"I hope you don't mind. If you agree to our interview, I'd want to film it, and they're here to help me," I said.

"Well, I don't know about agreeing to an on-camera interview. I can talk to you, yes, but I'm not keen on being on film," he said, opening up the box to reveal pastel-colored cookies. "I like to stay out of the limelight."

"So, did you see a boy like the missing Barnaby on your security camera?" I asked. "And what made you sure it wasn't him? And according to your mother, this was the fifth time you'd seen the same kid?"

"Ah, my mother." Franklin unwrapped his sandwich, took a bite, and then looked at Delilah and Ranvir, still not assembled at the counter. "You kids come on over, have some cookies. I'm telling you, you *need* them. The best in the neighborhood, in all of Rowbury."

Continuing to chew, he held the box out, and we took one each.

"My mother thinks about sad news all the time. I believe she thrives on it. So when I visit, I give her a bit of such news." He smiled and revealed lettuce draped on his upper front teeth. "So I happened to tell her about quote-unquote Barnaby on my footage. Again. And always in the middle of the night, round two a.m."

"Can we see it?" I leaned forward, still holding my cookie. "Just to see what he looks like?"

"Sure, and you know what else? You can film the footage, there are a few of them with Barnaby. That, I'll let you." He took another bite of his sandwich and smiled again, lettuce gone now.

"I don't like him," Delilah declared. "Kind of creepy. Too nice without knowing us and yet *not* nice enough to let us interview him on film."

We were next door to Franklin's Hardware, sitting outside on the steps of the Hungry Heart Row Cinema, which, according to a sign on the door of the box office right behind us, didn't open until three p.m.

The same theater where Barnaby was last seen.

"But those cookies . . . I didn't have breakfast, and they hit the spot." Ranvir stretched out his six-foot frame and lay back. His dastaar, a deep blue turban, cushioned his head against the stone steps. He always made sure to match his turban with his shoes, and today was no exception—a pair of dark blue, suede Jordans rested on the lowest step, almost touching the sidewalk. "He was nice to feed us like that. Mmm, cookies."

"Have mine then. I'm waiting for real food." Delilah passed her cookie over to him.

"Hey, let's check out the food carts behind this place. There's a good halal one we'd sometimes eat at when we'd visit my grandma before, plus the spot Barnaby got his hot dog that day he went missing." I stood up, dusting off the back of my jeans. "Maybe we can interview the hot dog vendor. And also, eat."

"Um, Hania?" Delilah pointed at the marquee sign above us, listing a selection of films.

Home Is: A Film by Gabrielle Rose, 1st place Rowbury Teen Film Fest, M, W, Sun 3 p.m.

I stared. "She doesn't live in Hungry Heart Row or even Rowbury. Why are they playing her film?"

We walked away, but I couldn't help glancing back at the theater. Was it my imagination, or did I see someone ducking down in the box office window?

"I've been here, at the same exact spot, for eight years." The hot dog vendor passed a cardboard tray containing a bunless sausage and coleslaw to Ranvir. "But that day is seared in my memory. The police wouldn't stop asking questions.

Yes, I saw the boy. Yes, he bought a hot dog. And fries. Can't forget the fries. And yes, he walked that way to the theater."

He pointed behind him across the park. And then nodded into the camera. "That's all. That's how much I want to say."

I paused the recording. "Can I get you to say what you think happened? I might not use it, but it's just always good to get extra footage." I smiled big in what I hoped was a polite way.

"A'right." The large man sighed, looking odd doing so, with his bushy blond beard and head of golden hair covered in food-preparation netting. Odd, like a lion ensnared by a flimsy net. "I actually think Barnaby ate his dinner, wasn't planning on going to the movie—you know what was playing that night? *Love at Last*, that's what—and then—"

"What does that mean?" Ranvir pressed, leaving his hot dog untouched while he listened. "Why couldn't he have been going to see *Love at Last*? Because he's a guy?"

"No, no." The hot dog man shook his head. "Because it had been sold out, with all that buzz. And our theater is tiny. There's no way he could have gotten a ticket last minute."

"Then why did the ticket vendor say he went to the movie?" I asked.

"That's where I differ with what some of the locals say and that's why the police buy *my* story. I don't think he went to see *Love at Last*." He looked right into the camera. "Barnaby left home. He had my hot dog before he left. End of story."

Delilah walked over from the halal food cart, two gyro sandwiches in her hands, and passed me one. I unwrapped it and took a bite while staring at Ginkgo Street.

"All my friends liked you very much. They want you to make a movie at each Thursday Club." Valimma was making tea for me. I don't know why, but I only drank tea when Valimma made it. It tasted fuller for some reason. Or was it richer? Anyway, it was only good when Valimma's hand held the spoon that stirred the tea leaves and water and milk and sugar.

"That would be nice, recording all your club meets, except that the film I'm working on is due in two weeks, Valimma." I reached with both my hands for the mug she held out. "Maybe I shouldn't even enter."

"Why? You always do the film contest, moleh." She brought her own mug to the table where I was clicking on the video clips I'd already recorded.

"I don't know why but I'm not feeling it. Maybe it's because I'm not in my old neighborhood." I wondered if I should get into it with Valimma, this not enjoying Hungry Heart Row. "I didn't really want to move."

"But you used to love coming here! From when you were little." She picked up a crunchy biscuit that was more like dried bread than a cookie and dunked it into her tea. "You'd beg your dad, 'Can we move here?' That was why he thought you would all be happy."

Yes. This was true. But that was because those were short-and-sweet visits.

Now this was supposed to be forever.

"Yeah, but it's not home." I tried not to look at her mouth, which slackened a bit at what I'd just said. "I'll get used to it. Anyway, I'm so happy you're living with us now. I get to have your tea every day if I want!"

The mouth turned up slightly. "Ah, yes. You love my tea. Do you know why?"

"Why?" I sipped the tea to test its temperature.

"Because I *want* you to love it." Valimma dunked the rest of her biscuit in and paused before biting into it. "That's how you'll learn to love Hungry Heart Row."

She said the last part matter-of-factly and confidently. I waited for her to finish her thought, but that was it. She continued eating her biscuit, looking through the stack of supermarket flyers as she did each Tuesday.

Was Valimma saying that I had to *want* to love Hungry Heart Row to like it here?

That wasn't going to happen any time soon.

Twenty minutes of footage. That was all I had. And that included the grainy video clips from the security camera, each of which simply showed a white teen, indistinguishable really except maybe for an overly large baseball hat, walking on the sidewalk across from Franklin's Hardware. Always time-stamped around two a.m., like Franklin had said.

I rubbed my eyes. Because I definitely couldn't work at home with boxes everywhere, I had taken refuge in one of the Rowbury library's quiet rooms. It was nice in here, wood paneled on two sides, windowed to the outside behind me and, in front, an all-glass wall facing into the library.

I'd been at it for two hours, trying to see what I could do to cobble a film together. And how any of the things I'd heard were connected to the Barnaby Bennett at Daily Harvest.

It was Thursday morning already, and in a week's time I'd need to be editing, because, in *another* week's time, reality hit via the film festival submission deadline.

I slid my headphones off to stare out of the glass wall, wondering what else I could film.

I was so lost in thought that it took me a while to register what I was looking at about thirty feet directly across from me, near the check-out desk: a camera, held waist high. Before I could see a face, the person holding the camera abruptly turned around and walked through the turnstiles, out of the building.

Something was familiar about the figure that had just exited.

I left my things and went to the check-out counter. A teen of South Asian background, like me, beamed at me under her short hair. NEHA said her name tag, under which was written with a Sharpie *[that's NAY-HA]*☺. "Can I help you?"

"Yes, you can." I leaned in, feeling strange at what I was about to do. "Um, but it's a weird question."

"I like weird." Neha beamed again. "Let's hear it."

"Was that person standing here just now, um, was she holding a camera or something?" I whispered.

"Yes, actually, she was. She's got special permission from the library. But don't worry—she's not focusing on faces. Just our ambience. If you're not okay with it, I can tell her to not use the footage she just took?" Neha raised helpful eyebrows.

"No, it's okay." I waved a hand, half in appreciation, half in good-bye. "Thanks. Thanks, Neha."

I went back to the quiet room.

I was sure I'd just seen Gabrielle Rose.

Filming me.

Delilah picked up immediately. "You're calling me? You never call me, Hania! We're text-only friends."

"I think I know what GR is up to. Hear me out, okay?" I walked down Dill Street, glancing around, wondering where Gabrielle was now. She'd left the library only five minutes ago. "Somehow she's in Hungry Heart Row. Somehow she's filming me. Somehow I'm part of her film. I know it."

"Filming *you*? Um, why?" Delilah sounded incredulous.

"She was in the library when I was in there working. With a camera aimed at me. Maybe I'm the subject of her 'meta' film."

"Are you sure it was her?"

"Yes. Hundred percent sure." I saw a café on my right, and an idea struck me. "Wait, I'm going to make it two hundred percent sure. I'll call you back."

With a latte for strength, I sat at a table inside the café and got my laptop out of my backpack. As I was about to put it down, something else was set in its place on the smooth marble-looking tabletop.

Atop a square of robin's-egg-blue paper, a single pastry: cream colored and round, with a center, round as well, that was darker, almost brown.

"Hi, I'm Lila." The speaker was a girl my age with neat bangs and wide eyes. She held a small box that was stamped PANADERÍA PASTELERÍA, the same kind of box holding the cookies Franklin had offered us at the hardware store. "I think you need an ojo de buey. It's from my bakery. For you."

Each of her sentences was a statement spoken softly but with certainty. I looked down at the pastry.

Well, I *was* hungry, and this looked so good. I reached for it. "Thanks so much."

I realized there was no one around to receive my thanks. The girl was gone, the only evidence that she'd been here being the now empty box she'd left on the corner of the table. Taking a bite into the delicious doughy texture, I peered at the phone number on the box. Maybe I could call her later to thank her.

I booted up my laptop and opened the State Film Fest awards-day clip on YouTube.

There was a shot of me being called up for second place. And then there was the announcement for first, and there was Gabrielle Rose.

I narrowed my eyes, rewinding and pausing at the mark where the camera panned Gabrielle as she was getting up from her folding chair to come onstage.

A boy with an extra-large baseball hat was beside Gabrielle Rose, smiling at her while clapping.

The exact same person on Franklin's security camera.

Barnaby.

Barnaby is Gabrielle's FRIEND.

Two chat bubbles immediately showed up in reply to my text.

WHAT? HOW? Ranvir.

CRAZY! THIS MEANS YOU CHOSE THE RIGHT TOPIC Delilah.

What if she's setting me up? To film this missing-boy thing? While SHE films ME? Her META film? I lowered the phone, scanning the café.

I'd glanced around when I first entered, but what if Gabrielle had come in when I was preoccupied? Just like that PANADERÍA PASTELERÍA girl had snuck up on me before?

A guy in the corner was looking over here, his phone positioned on top of his table as though . . . *as though he were filming me?*

I stared at him unblinkingly, and he lowered his phone. *Could he be working with GR?*

OMG, I was losing it.

I packed up and left the café, turning left on Caper Street, heading home, refusing to look around.

But a block before reaching the street I lived on, when a group of teens spilled onto the sidewalk behind me from an alley between a row of town houses, I decided to make a sudden duck into the doorway of a restaurant on Pepper Street.

I waited, and, sure enough, Gabrielle walked by.

The only good thing: Her hands were camera-less.

I opened the door to the restaurant. A deluge of smells hit me, one of them a déjà vu to my senses.

Three food stalls were in front of me, two manned by elderly women and the third by a teen.

Suddenly I was ravenous, not just hungry, like when I'd eaten the pastry. The girl, in the closest stall, stared at me from the register. "Yes?"

I looked at the display board behind her. ADOBO.

"Can I get an order of shrimp adobo? And rice?" I said. "To go?"

"Yep." The girl punched it in without taking her eyes off me. "You've had it before?"

"Yes. A friend of my grandmother's made it for us. Just last week."

"And you're back for more of Lola Simeona's food." The girl smiled. "May it be exactly what you need."

She headed to a door behind her.

I was perplexed. This was the third time today someone had said something about food being *needed* by me. People in

Hungry Heart Row seemed to have a weird obsession with food.

But I had to admit it was all soo good. The food here.

Maybe food was what I *needed* to solve the weirdness happening around my film. And what was happening around Barnaby Bennett, missing in some places and not in others.

Maybe it all had to do with Hungry Heart Row, the people here. And the food?

I glanced at the display board again. SOUP NO. 5.

SERVED 9 A.M. TO 2 A.M.

I closed my eyes, because there was something about two a.m. I couldn't shake.

Today was Thursday so that meant Thursday club again. Valimma poured the remainder of the thin dosa batter on the griddle and spread it with the back of a wooden spoon, round and round until it filled the whole black surface. She waited a bit and then brushed the thin, crepelike top with oil. After flipping it to sear it quickly, she removed it from the heat and added it to the stack of dosas in a large-mouthed insulated container.

On the counter was a large Tupperware with sambar—vegetables stewed with lentils and spices—being stared at by me, my hand holding the plastic lid aloft. "Valimma, how many vegetables are there in this thing? I see seven."

"Nine, actually, moleh. The dosa is simple, subtle, so the sambar has to be complex and strong. Mix it, and it's good together." Valimma dried her washed hands on a dishcloth and then smiled. "I used to play that game with your father. How many vegetables in this food? He was so careful with his guesses that he always got it correct."

"Always? No wonder he's an accountant." I snapped the lid on the sambar and picked up the foam container of adobo shrimp I'd bought. I scooped a shrimp up with my fingers and dipped my head back to drop it in. The intensity smothered my tongue. "Oh, wow, strong."

"You need the rice. For balance," Valimma said, opening the rice container, a spoon in hand. "Rice is good. Open."

I obliged, but not before I laid another shrimp on the portion of rice being held out. I savored it, smiling at Valimma as one of her oft-repeated phrases came to me. "Bountiful flavor."

"That's right. And you didn't want to try Simeona's food before, when you first saw it. On the day you moved here." Valimma tsked me. "Any time someone makes something for YOU, you have to try it. Just a tiny bit even."

"Even if you know you're not going to like it for sure?"

"Even then. Remember, that's how you'll love it here. Your new home."

"By eating people's food?" I laughed. "Is that what Hungry Heart Row is all about? Food?"

"Yes and no," Valimma said. "The people here want you to love what they offer. And if they want to show you love through food, you let them know you see it. And then *you* show love back the best way you know how. That's home."

I reached for more shrimp adobo, trying to make out

what she was saying. It was kind of confusing, but I nodded, because maybe it was one of those things only Valimma understood after living and loving it here, her neighborhood.

"Let's go now. You can eat more at Margaret's. She is so very excited you're coming over," Valimma said, picking up her purse. "I think today will be a fancy Thursday Club."

"Good, because I need more film footage." I carried the bag with the food Valimma had made to the foyer and set it down beside my camera backpack. "And Margaret's good on camera."

"She wanted you to meet her granddaughter, but she's working today."

"Oh, at the theater?" I paused from lacing up my sneakers. "Maybe I'll see her. I was thinking of watching something there this weekend."

"We'll invite them over one day too." Valimma grabbed the food bag before I could. "She spends her summers here with her grandmother."

Crocheted doilies. Pastel walls. Flowery curtains.

The setting of Gabrielle's film *Home Is* confronted me when I stepped into Margaret's living room.

Gabrielle's face stared from a large framed photo on the mantel above the fireplace.

Gabrielle Rose.

She was connected to Hungry Heart Row.

She was Margaret's granddaughter?

AND she was definitely connected to the missing Barnaby Bennett.

She was the last person to have seen him last year—at the movie theater.

Either she was *just* filming me making a film on him . . .

Or she had something to hide.

The only thing to do now was to ask Gabrielle directly what exactly was going on.

Maybe it was time to go to a Sunday matinee, maybe watch her film again, and afterward, just ask her the truth point-blank.

Because there was a weird truth going on—connected, but also all tangled up somehow.

But it wasn't just linked to Gabrielle.

It was also connected to Hungry Heart Row itself.

I was the only person in the theater to watch Gabrielle Rose's winning film.

It had been odd buying a ticket, with Gabrielle's eyes on mine, a mixture of familiarity and secrecy in them.

All the lights suddenly turned off before I got to the best seat—the one smack-dab in the middle of the upper row—but I continued moving in the dark until I reached the prime spot.

Once seated, I blindly unrolled the top of the slim bag of barbecue-flavored popcorn I'd brought.

The darkness of the theater was so absolute that I felt like sound had disappeared too.

Then, with a sudden crackle, the light from the projector flipped on.

The screen ahead filled with a white square.

A flickering white square, now turning gray.

Then—a frozen gray square, no sound.

Gabrielle Rose walked in front of the screen.

I drew up my phone and began recording. I wanted everything on film.

"Thanks for coming to watch my film. Unfortunately, there's a glitch, so . . . so instead, I wanted to tell you something."

"You were filming me making a film," I said. "You were being clever."

"No, I wasn't." Gabrielle put a hand at her forehead to block some of the light shining on her from the projector. "Though that would have been cool."

"Who's the boy on the security camera?"

"That's what I want to explain." Gabrielle walked to her left and began climbing the aisle steps. "About him."

I tilted the phone and followed the faint figure coming nearer, realizing the closer Gabrielle came, the less that could be seen of her.

"Is he the lost boy?" If I kept her talking, at least there would be sound captured that I could use. For *The Legend of Hungry Heart Row's Lost Boy.*

Or whatever this film was becoming now. Or—I slumped in my seat—*not* becoming.

"No." Gabrielle was almost at my row now. "He's not."

She began walking toward me.

Before she got too close, she sat down abruptly, two seats away. "He's not the lost boy because he's not lost."

I kept filming.

"It's Barnaby. He ran away from a horrendous home situation." Gabrielle sunk her face into her hands. "I helped him. Because I knew him from summers working here. He loved watching movies, they were his escape, so I let him in free. That day he disappeared or whatever, he came into the movie theater and exited that door over there in the corner, in the middle of the movie. He took the crosstown bus right outside."

"From the bus stop at Nettle and Caraway," I said. "But if he ran away, why does he keep getting caught on camera?"

She sighed again. "You know Old Manila? The Filipino restaurant on Pepper Street?"

"The Soup Number Five place?"

She looked at me weirdly. "How—"

"Adobo? Three stalls?"

"Yes, that place. Lola Teodora sells this dish called kare-kare, and two winters ago, Barnaby became convinced that eating it at lunch every day was making him braver and braver. So brave that he made the decision to leave home."

I thought about it. There it was, the food thing again.

Does everyone here believe food affects us so much?

Well, that ojo pastry thing from Panadería Pastelería *had* gotten me thinking clearly.

But.

I shook my head. "Wait. What does Barnaby eating at the Filipino restaurant have to do with him being caught on camera so much *now*?"

"Well, he wasn't just getting braver, he was also unloading his story on the lolas, the three women who run Old Manila. They offered him a job washing dishes after hours so he could save enough money to one day make it on his own. He still comes by in the middle of the night to wash and then leaves before the restaurant opens again in the morning."

I guess that's why he'd stopped coming to the meal service, Daily Harvest. He'd needed it when he first disappeared and was on his own but then, the lolas had helped him get on his feet.

My film idea was completely shot, but I'd found Barnaby. And this made me weirdly happy.

Because in finding him, I'd found something else, too. I'd found out a lot about Hungry Heart Row. The kind of home it was.

It felt okay being in a place where someone showed up to give you a pastry when you needed it. Or a job. And bravery. And deep friendships built around food, like Valimma had.

I stopped filming and turned on my phone's flashlight instead. "Is he okay now?"

Gabrielle looked at me. "He's safe, happier now. He's with another friend's family."

"So why were you following me?" I pulled the phone under my chin to light up my face, creepily. "And filming me in the library?"

"I wasn't. When my grandma told me you were making a movie on Barnaby, I started getting worried—but not film-competition-wise. Just my-friend-Barnaby-wise. And I guess I tried to see if I could talk to you about it. I'm actually doing a film on . . ." She paused, looked at me, and then burst out laughing. "Okay, I'll tell you. You're so funny-looking right now, with the light like that. I'm doing a film on the vibrancy of Hungry Heart Row. Like a pure soundscape film, quiet noises of the library, loud noises of the markets. Just form over story."

I smirked in the light. I couldn't wait to get home and tell Bilal that Gabrielle had arrived at my original film idea.

"But now I'm thinking . . . meta would have been good. Me filming you. You not knowing," Gabrielle mused.

I turned to the gray square on the screen in front of us, seemingly frozen in anticipation of the film to come.

"Well, we caaan still do that if you want," I said, something new, a feeling I'd never felt, growing inside me. It was erasing the previous anxiety I'd felt—at the deadline for the film, the move here, everything.

Hope. That was the feeling.

Maybe we didn't have to compete. Maybe we could just do our films Hungry Heart Row style.

"What do you mean?" Her voice sounded open.

"Maybe we can mix it up. Me finding out about Hungry Heart Row, my new home, you chasing sounds, filming me getting used to this place, especially its food. Combine it all. One film, two directors. Simple yet complex." I said all this to the screen, afraid to look at her.

Then I just *had* to see her face, so I turned.

Gabrielle was gazing at the gray screen ahead too, seeing what could be, the light of my phone showing a faint smile growing on her nodding face.

And then, just like that, I got what Valimma had been trying to tell me before about Hungry Heart Row: People here *wanted* you to love what they offered. They wanted it so much.

And if you saw this, saw how much this want was, your part in the whole thing would just fall into place: You'd love back.

I offered Gabrielle a bag of bountiful flavor. "Popcorn?"

Side Work

BY SARA FARIZAN

Sometimes I thought about what my Saturdays used to be like. I'd sleep in, maybe go shopping with my friends, or be dancing at a house party later on that evening. It felt like forever ago, but it was only eight months since the accident.

Now I had to wake up early so I could catch the bus on time to get to my job at Manijeh's, my uncle's Persian cuisine restaurant. No more sleeping in or partying for me. Still, I was grateful to have somewhere to go and something to do.

I brushed back the wisps of hair trying to escape my high ponytail as I looked at myself in my bathroom mirror. I used to fuss over every little detail of my outfit, make sure I looked better than my friend Stacey did, slay every look, and try to make it appear effortless. These days, I was just happy to have a clean work shirt that didn't have ghormeh sabzi stains on it.

"Whoa, Laleh, slow down," Mom said, drinking coffee at the kitchen table while Dad, dressed in his tech business-casual outfit, read *Wired* magazine. Sometimes he popped into the office on weekends, even though most of the employees were out enjoying their lives or working remotely. I think it was to get away from me. It didn't used to be like that. We used to talk about everything. Now . . . well, I made it easier for him to avoid me and stayed out of his way.

"Sorry," I said. I felt like all I ever did was apologize in their presence. I had messed up, real bad, and none of us had really gotten over it.

"It's okay. Do you need a ride to work?" Mom asked even though she knew I was going to answer the way I always did. I could tell she worried about me. I didn't even think Dad cared much about what I was up to.

"I'm taking the bus. Thanks," I said, glancing at the empty fruit bowl by the fridge. "No bananas?"

"I'm going to the market today and can pick up some things. Is there anything else you need?" Mom smiled at me, but there was always this sad glaze coating her eyeballs, so it looked like she was going to start crying whenever she talked to me. I knew what she was thinking. Her only golden child, her once Ivy League–bound daughter, was now waiting tables for tips.

"What time will you be home?" Dad asked, still

looking at his magazine. He didn't even *like Wired*. He had always been a *Popular Mechanics* guy. God forbid he made eye contact with me while I was in my uniform. I bet he was thinking I should have been at Columbia, not in his brother's kitchen.

"Whenever the last table finishes and we clean up," I said. He looked up from his magazine.

"Call me when you're done and let me know if I should come get you, or if your uncle will be dropping you off," he said. But he was not going to come into the restaurant. He was not going to see all the stuff I did for Amu Mansour. He was not going to see that I was trying my best to be responsible now. Those days of my dad being proud of me were over.

"Okay," I said before heading out the door. I kind of liked it better when they were lecturing me all the time.

"You're late," my cousin Arash said as I entered my uncle's restaurant through the front door. I hated that he thought it was okay to say that to me, since he only worked on weekends, while I was here full-time. We mostly got our regulars for dinner, and it was slow during the day. I had a feeling today was going to be exceptionally slow.

It was the grand opening of the much-talked-about Zia Sofia Ristorante across the street. It was the first chain to grace Hungry Heart Row, and the mom-and-pop places around here weren't too thrilled about it. Zia Sofia was only a regional chain, but it was big, it was glossy, it had appropriated Italian culture for profit, and it was very corporate. They had commercials on TV promoting their "That's A-more Not A-less" pasta platters that only ran out when you couldn't stuff your face any longer. The balloons on either side of Zia Sofia's glass doors were swaying in the wind, almost waving at the twenty or so customers who were lined up outside.

"You couldn't wait to see me? Did you miss me that much?" I asked him while I leaned over the table and pinched his cheek. He let me tug on his baby face for a moment without any protest. He had his pre-calc textbook open next to the phone and the reservation book. "How's school?" I asked after I let him go.

"It's brutal. I can't wait for it to be over," he said. I almost said, *Be careful what you wish for*, but it would have been pointless. He didn't know how good he had it.

Zia Sofia had replaced the dry cleaners owned by the Arkanian family and the Salvadoran restaurant owned by the Flores family. When the new condo buildings came in, some places couldn't keep up with the rising rents.

I was pretty sure the people who lived in those condos worked at the same company my dad did. I sometimes felt guilty about that, as though it were my fault. I was an interloper in a neighborhood that wasn't really mine. Then I reminded myself there was no way I'd be able to afford a condo or apartment in this area or really anywhere, since all of my tips went to paying back my dad for the damages to his car.

I strolled to the back and swung open the kitchen door.

The smell of khoresht e gheihmeh immediately hit my nostrils: The combination of tomato paste, dried limes, cubes of lamb, turmeric, cumin, cinnamon, and split yellow lentils all hung sweetly in the air.

"Laleh! Tudo bem?" Claudio asked me from behind the sauté station. He was still putting all the prepped vegetables and spices where he needed them to be.

"Bem. Obrigado," I said. This was about the extent of my Brazilian Portuguese so far. Claudio knew more words in Farsi than I knew in Portuguese, but he and his sister Camilla had been working at Manijeh's for six years. (My uncle Mansour had named the restaurant after my grandmother. There was a photograph on the wall by table two of her and my uncle in front of his childhood home in Tehran when he was eight. I never met her. She passed away in Iran before I was born.) "How are you?"

"Good," Claudio said with a smile. He took his phone out of his pocket, pushed a few buttons, and passed it to me. His chubby baby boy, Aurelio, was smiling at me from his phone.

"Awww, look at that smile!"

"He's showing off his new teeth," Claudio said. I handed the phone back to him. "Manny wants to see you. He's in the office."

"Thanks," I said. I strolled past the walk-in fridge and ice machine and stood in the open doorway of my uncle's tiny closet-size office, where he took care of day-to-day

managerial stuff. My aunt Mariam would work in the office
at night before closing.

Uncle Mansour hadn't heard me creep up to his domain.
His shoulders were hunched as he sat at his desk, and his
face was so close to the paper he was reading from, because
he refused to wear his glasses. It was amazing how much he
looked like my dad. Uncle Mansour was about forty pounds
heavier than my father, and he had more hair, but they had
the same dark eyes, the same strong nose, though my uncle
Mansour was the one always wearing a smile. I hadn't seen
my dad smile in a long time.

I knocked lightly on the wooden door. Uncle Mansour
looked up, and, as soon as he saw me, he beamed.

"Hi, Laleh joon," he said before he stood up. He kissed
me on my cheek. "You ate already?"

"What?"

He pointed to the corner of his lips. I realized I had the
remnants of the potato knish I had picked up at Pop's Deli
on my face. (Their knishes were phenomenal.) I wiped the
crumbs off my face, and he looked at me warmly.

"I have a favor to ask you," he said.

"Of course. Anything," I said. I owed him so much.

"Well, the new restaurant is opening today, and I was
going to go over before the dinner rush to welcome our
neighbors," he said. "I was wondering if you would like to
go with me?"

"Me?" I asked.

"Mariam refuses to set foot in there out of respect for

the Flores family. As for Arash, well he doesn't have much interest in these things," Uncle Mansour said wistfully. I knew Uncle Mansour wanted his son to pursue his dreams, but I think a big part of him also wanted to keep Manijeh's in the family.

Why not visit the hyped eatery and see what we were up against? All we needed to bring with us was a sling and a stone, and we'd be fine.

After I'd done my side work and waited on the few lunch-time customers who had come in, Uncle Mansour, with a champagne bottle in hand, and I crossed Caper Street and entered the crowded restaurant. There was a line of people in front of the host table. We stood behind them and took in our surroundings.

The checkered black and white tiles on the floor seemed to go on forever. This place was so much bigger than we were. The back dining room looked like it had twenty tables; some were two-tops, and some could seat four. The front dining room had fifteen tables, mostly booths. There wasn't one empty chair in the place.

The walls were painted to look like an Italian vineyard, with rows of red grapes hanging on vines and fluffy clouds painted up above them. I could faintly hear Rosemary Clooney's "Mambo Italiano" playing on the speaker system. It was hard to hear over the noise of the many diners. Sometimes *all* you could hear was the Persian classical music at Manijeh's when it was super dead.

The guests ahead of us put their names in with the pretty young hostess. She handed them a beeper that would buzz when their table was ready. We didn't have beepers at Manijeh's, and even if we did, we wouldn't have had much use for them.

She flashed us a plastered-on smile when it was our turn.

"Hi there! Table for two?" she asked us.

"Hello. We're your neighbors across the street at Manijeh's, and we wanted to welcome you to the neighborhood," my uncle said as he handed her the champagne bottle.

"Oh, um, thank you," she said, accepting the bottle, her smile now seemingly genuine as she snapped out of her routine. "That's so nice of you! Let me get my manager," she said. She turned her head to the right and waved at a short young man wearing a suit and tie. He strode over to us with brisk steps. He was in his midtwenties, white, and had wavy brown hair that was expertly coiffed with hair gel.

"Welcome to Zia Sofia! My name is Terrence. How may I help you?" Terrence asked before he looked me up and down. I was still wearing my uniform: a white T-shirt, black slacks, and a small black apron around my waist that held my order pad and corkscrew.

"Hello, Terrence. I'm Manny. I'm the owner of Manijeh's across the street, and my niece Laleh and I wanted to congratulate you on your opening," my uncle said, extending his hand to the slight man.

"Oh! Hello," Terrence said, shaking my uncle's hand. Briefly.

"They brought us a bottle of champagne," the hostess said, handing Terrence the bottle. He looked at it. There was a flicker of a condescending smirk on his lips upon reading the label.

"That's very generous," Terrence said, handing the bottle back to the hostess. "Would you like a tour?" His smirk morphed into a fake smile the longer he spoke with us.

"Oh, that would be wonderful, but some other time. I can see how busy you are," my uncle said, looking around the bustling restaurant. "If you ever need anything, we're right across the street."

"I'll keep that in mind," Terrence said. Our conversation was interrupted by a loud crash in the dining room. Terrence whipped his head in the direction of the noise. The whole restaurant became silent. A teenage waitress looked down at the family-style portion of fettuccine Alfredo at her feet, splattered all over the floor.

Terrence sped over to her table to speak with the upset guests while the waitress crouched down, picking up pieces of the shattered plate. I walked over to her and helped her clean up.

A busser came over with a plastic tub while another busser brought over a broom and dustpan. The waitress and I deposited the mess into it.

"Thanks," she said. "Laleh?"

I finally looked at the flustered waitress in front of me. Her face was red like the grilled tomatoes we served with our kebab platters.

"Natalie," I said, breathless.

"What are you doing here?"

"I ask myself that question every day," I said. "I work at my uncle's restaurant."

"Oh," she said. She wiped her hands on her apron and looked away from me.

"Natalie, why don't you head back to the kitchen and let John and Rafa clean up your mess?" Terrence said as he stared down at us, before dashing off to the kitchen. I stood up and offered Natalie my hand to help her stand. She took it, and when her hand touched mine, I felt like I had the night of that stupid party that derailed my life. Confused, nervous, elated . . . Natalie Ribaldi was gorgeous, and I hadn't been able to handle it. So I drank. I drank a lot.

"I'm really sorry," she said to the annoyed couple at her table. "It's my first day."

"We can tell," the lady with the sour expression said. The guy with her was taking a photo of the spill on his phone. I bet he couldn't wait to post up a Served review, the jerk. Natalie bit her lower lip and retreated to the kitchen.

It had been a week since we visited Zia Sofia. My uncle remained in good spirits, but I was feeling a little demoralized, watching customers go to the new restaurant while many of our tables stayed empty. I was happy to see that customers were still frequenting the Manzano panadería. That place wasn't going anywhere. Lila was amazing, and so was her family's food. When I waved to her in the mornings on my way to work, she always smiled and seemed like she enjoyed what she was doing. I was a little envious of that.

Arash was playing a game on his phone when Natalie entered. I wanted to play it cool, but the closer I got to her, I knew that was going to be impossible. She always made me feel anxious. The good kind of anxious, like right before I got on stage to accept my diploma. I was worrying about tripping or having an awkward handshake with our principal, but elated to accept something I'd worked so hard for.

"Hi," she said, still in her Zia Sofia uniform, which consisted of a tucked-in collared white shirt, a black tie, long slacks with a long, black apron tied around her waist, and black shoes.

"Hi," I said back with a smile. Arash looked up from his phone, and his mouth dropped open a little. His reaction was warranted, albeit embarrassing. She was beautiful, even in her uniform and even though her brown hair was a little wet from the rain outside.

"I wanted to thank you for helping me out last week," Natalie said. "Is this a bad time?"

I looked around our empty dining room. I had completed all of my side work, set up all the tables, and made sure the bar was fully stocked with glassware.

"Your timing is perfect. I was just going to have a bite before the dinner shift. Please, have a seat," I said, leading her to a booth by the window. She slid into her seat, and I asked Arash to bring us two bowls of ash-e-reshte. When he stopped gawking at our guest, he walked to the back and into the kitchen.

I sat across from Natalie. I normally wouldn't sit and eat in the main dining room, but I didn't think Uncle Mansour would mind, seeing as no one was coming in on this rainy day.

"It's been a while," I said.

"How have you been?" Her light brown eyes were taking me in.

"Since the accident?"

She nodded.

"Well, I'm here full-time," I said. I hated when customers sometimes asked me if I was a student to make small talk. Sometimes I thought I should just lie and say I went to a nearby university. "I'm sorry I didn't call after . . . uh . . . after we—"

"Made out?" she asked in a normal tone of voice. She didn't whisper, which I took as a good sign.

"Yes. That. I hadn't expected *that* at Stacey's graduation party. I mean, I thought it was cool! You're good at the kissing stuff," I said. The name Stacey felt so foreign coming out of my mouth. I hadn't really talked to one of my "friends" in months. I'd seen pictures of her on social media, enjoying college life, and she'd sent me a text or two, but other than that, Stacey and my other friends were all but a memory.

"I didn't think one of the most popular girls at Rowbury High would be interested in—"

"Women?" I asked.

"Theater-club nerds," she said with a slight grin. My stomach flipped like a snowboarder on the half-pipe at the Olympics.

"How's senior year?" I asked after clearing my throat. She was still grinning.

"Fine. I work at Zia's on weekends, and I'm waiting to hear back from colleges."

"They'll be lucky to have you. Wherever you decide to go," I said. I felt a pang of jealousy. It wasn't her fault. It was mine for needing a crutch like booze and then running away from her.

"I tried to get in contact with you. . . ."

How was I supposed to answer that? *I had a long secret crush on you, I had to drink a ton of beer to tell you before I graduated, we kissed a lot in Stacey's bathroom, and then I panicked and smashed my dad's fancy car into a telephone pole?*

"I had a lot to deal with after the accident. I was embarrassed," I said honestly, with a shrug. My DUI had derailed everything, especially my pending romance. "I thank God every day that no one was hurt."

She took my hand from across the table. I didn't panic this time.

"I'm glad you're okay."

Arash came back, and Natalie let go of my hand. He served us two bowls of ash-e-reshte and gave me a not-at-all-subtle eyebrow waggle.

Natalie looked at the green soup a little warily.

"Just smell it," I said, picking up my spoon. Natalie took a whiff, and her eyes widened.

"What is it?" Her interest piqued by the heavenly aroma.

"Delicious," I said. I could have told her it was soup made up of parsley, spinach, dill, sautéed onions, thin noodles, chickpeas, kidney beans, dried yogurt, dried mint, garlic, oil, and salt, but why spoil the surprise?

She dipped her spoon in the thick soup gingerly before giving it a taste. Her eyes closed as she swallowed. She might as well have been in a Campbell's soup commercial.

"Wow," she said as she opened her eyes. "That's amazing!" She dunked her spoon in the bowl fully and began to lap up the soup quickly. "I'm working a double, and I haven't had anything all day."

"Don't they feed you over there?" I asked.

"We only get a ten percent discount on food," she said in between slurps. "I don't really feel like spending ten bucks on lousy spaghetti. Trust me—my dad's side of the family is Italian American. Olive Garden is Michelin-rated gourmet compared to Zia's."

"Well people seem to like it," I said. "You guys are always packed."

"Tips are okay," Natalie said, wiping the corner of her

mouth with a napkin. "But the management is so strict. It feels like you can't breathe in there. Terrence is always hovering, making sure our name tags are on straight, instead of helping us run food."

"That's ridiculous," I said.

"How much is the soup? Table twelve screwed me over with a two-dollar tip on a thirty-five-dollar bill," she said, taking her notepad that held her tips out of her apron pocket.

"Lunch is on me today," I replied. I probably owed a lot of students at Rowbury High lunch. My friends and I hadn't exactly made it to the top rung of the social ladder by being kind to others. I thought about that a lot during my court-mandated community-service hours.

"You're turning out to be my food service guardian angel," Natalie said.

"It's the least I can do for not calling you after, uh . . ."

"Smooching?"

She was so damn cute.

"Yes. That."

Natalie and I spent our time in the booth talking about our favorite teachers at Rowbury High, songs that we liked, movies we were thinking about seeing but would wait until they showed up on cable television, and our favorite foods. Natalie had decided that ash-e-reshte was definitely a new favorite. She was so easy to talk to. I forgot why I had been so scared to approach her. I wished my parents were as easy to talk to.

* * *

The following week, Natalie came back during her lunch break. She brought the two bussers, John and Rafa, and they all ordered the "green soup." My uncle came out to greet our new guests when I served them.

"Welcome! Thank you for coming," Uncle Mansour said, shaking everyone's hands, delighted to have young blood in at three p.m.

"I told the guys I was coming here for the best soup I've ever had, and they just had to try it," Natalie said to my uncle. "I'm Natalie! I'm a friend of Laleh's." I supposed now she kind of was a friend.

"Any friend of Laleh's is a friend of mine," Uncle Mansour said. I think he was surprised to find I had any, since all I ever did was work. "I don't know what we'd do without Laleh." I could feel my face get hot.

"Natalie wasn't kidding! This is delicious," Rafa said, enjoying every spoonful. "I'm going to tell everybody about this place."

"Yes! Please do!" Uncle Mansour said. He was giddy like a kid trick-or-treating on Halloween. "Laleh, come help me bring our guests some more food." I followed my uncle into the kitchen. Claudio was cooking the stew for the next day as well as ash-e-reshte.

"Can you heat up some joojeh kebab with rice? Three small dishes, please," my uncle asked Claudio.

"They didn't order that," I said to my uncle, not under-standing how he was willing to give away free food. I knew

Aunt Mariam wouldn't be too pleased about that. She was the realist between the two of them, and she knew as well as I did that Manijeh's was barely getting by. They never said that to me, but I could sometimes overhear them arguing in the office during a slow dinner shift.

Uncle Mansour turned to me and put his hand on my shoulder. He looked at me with pride, the way my dad used to when I handed in my report card. It almost made me want to cry.

"Your grandmother always said 'a guest is a gift from God,' and she was right. It's true, we're running a business, but guests always remember the way you treated them. They might not remember what they ordered or who they shared a meal with, but they'll remember how they felt being here. If you want to run this restaurant someday, you should remember that."

He said if *I* wanted to run this restaurant someday? It hadn't occurred to me that he was grooming me for that responsibility.

"I-I don't know if, um . . . You really think I could run this place?"

"With your hands tied behind your back," Uncle Mansour said. "Only if you want to. And after you pursue a higher education."

I rolled my eyes. I didn't know what school would want me now. It didn't hurt to think about the future again, though.

*　*　*

"Why is there so much soup?" Aunt Mariam asked Claudio the next day as I was rolling up silverware in linen napkins.

"You have to ask Manny about that," Claudio said. He was chopping onions, and his eyes were a little watery.

"Do we have a take-out order that I don't know about?" Aunt Mariam asked us. Claudio and I looked at each other for a moment.

"I guess Manny had a good feeling about today. He asked me to make more," Claudio said with a shrug.

Aunt Mariam pursed her lips as she tied an apron around her waist. Uncle Mansour came out of the office and smiled at his wife. She did not smile back.

"I hope you realize you're going to be eating ash-e-reshte for dinner all week," Aunt Mariam said to my uncle as she joined Claudio by the stove.

"That's fine. I love ash-e-reshte," Uncle Mansour said.

"So do I," I said, voicing support for my uncle in my own way. "But there won't be any left over."

"Oh?" Aunt Mariam said, quirking an eyebrow up at me. "You're sure about that?"

Well . . . not exactly. But I didn't see anything wrong with remaining hopeful. Arash walked into the kitchen from the dining room.

"Arash, I already told you, I can't take you home until Camilla gets here at four. I know you want to go to the movies with your friends, but—" Aunt Mariam began.

"No. It's not that. I need some help up front," Arash said.

"I thought we went over your math homework already?" I asked him.

"No! Guys! I mean I need help with customers," Arash shouted. "We have some."

I rushed out of the kitchen with my uncle close behind. Natalie stood at the front of the restaurant and waved at me. She was joined by seven of her coworkers, all of whom were still in their Zia Sofia uniforms.

"Soup's on," I whispered to my uncle. He chuckled before he went to the front of the house to accommodate everyone.

Arash seated Natalie's coworkers at the booths by the window looking out at Zia Sofia. Natalie lingered at the host stand, waiting for me.

"John and Rafa kept telling everybody at work about the food here," Natalie explained.

"*You* didn't rave about the food?" I asked, a little concerned.

"I'm more interested in the great service," she said gently.

"We're flirting, aren't we?"

"I think so! How am I doing?"

"Perfect. I need to step up my skill set, though. Give me time."

"I'm a waitress. I'm learning all about being patient," she said over her shoulder before sitting at a two-top in my section. I swallowed and took a breath before going to get the Zia Sofia staff water and take their drink orders. After I put in their orders, I made my way back to

Natalie's table, and Uncle Mansour was talking with her.

"Laleh! I was telling the lovely Natalie about how I started Manijeh's with the help of your father," Uncle Mansour said.

"Dad never worked here," I said, a little puzzled.

"No, but he invested in the restaurant. He didn't tell you about that? When I first started, he gave so much to this place and used to come here all the time. Then he got busier with work and his family, but he used to come a lot more. He hasn't seen some of the changes we've made to the décor. You should ask him to come!"

I blushed and cleared my throat. Natalie's smile faded a little as she noticed my discomfort.

"Uh, yeah, I'll think about it," I said. I figured it was better than lying and saying I'd ask my dad. Uncle Mansour put his meaty hand on my shoulder.

"He must be so proud of you," he said before kissing the top of my head. "I'm going to bring Natalie khaskh-e-bademjan. I'll be right back!" He went to check in on the other guests before heading back to the kitchen.

"He's planning to feed me the whole menu, isn't he?" Natalie asked as I inched closer to her.

"He's all about hospitality. Do you like eggplant? He's bringing you an eggplant dip."

"I like the vegetable but not the emoji."

"We're in agreement there," I said, getting my scratch pad out of my apron pocket.

"That's cool about your dad helping bring this place to

life," Natalie said. I bit the inside of my cheek and didn't make eye contact with her. "Isn't it?"

"Yeah. It is, I guess." She didn't press me any further. "What else can I get you, miss?"

"Gosh, I do need another moment with the menu," she said, furrowing her brow, feigning indecision so I could stay at her table longer. "What do you recommend?"

"Everything except doogh. It's a yogurt soda I just can't get behind," I answered.

"Oh! That actually sounds kind of cool! I'll start with that, please," she said, shimmying her shoulders in excitement. "Then I'd like to ask to drive you home after work some night? That's not a tall order is it?"

"I think we can accommodate that request," I said, writing it down on my notepad.

"Thanks for the ride," I said to Natalie as I unbuckled my seat belt. She was kind enough to stop by after her shift and wait for me to close the restaurant. Then we grabbed a bite at the diner across the street from Mallow Park that was open, mostly for restaurant workers getting out late at night.

"Nice digs," Natalie said, looking at my parent's house. The lights were still on, which I thought was weird.

"It feels like limbo," I said. "But yes, it's very nice." I realized how stupid that sounded, since I was lucky to have a roof over my head. Residents in the neighborhood we worked in were being forced to move out, and no one seemed to be doing anything about that. "My roommates are still up."

"You don't talk about them much," Natalie said. "Your *roommates*."

I didn't think it was fair to have this gorgeous girl drive me home after a double shift and then have me emotionally unload on her.

"Well, none of us really talk a lot to one another. I didn't turn out the way they wanted me to, so we're . . . polite and quiet."

Natalie touches the tip of my ponytail lightly.

"I don't know. I think you turned out fine. Better than fine."

That feeling of nervousness Natalie gave me? Maybe it was something else. Maybe it was hope.

"You're going to be a heartbreaker at college," I said. Why couldn't I enjoy a nice moment? Why did I have to think about her leaving already?

"You could be too. Though I kind of like the idea of neither of us breaking each other's hearts next year," she said as she let go of my hair.

"I don't know where I'll be next year," I muttered.

"Well, I hope you'll let me know where you end up. Then I can come find you. Don't disappear on me again. Okay?"

I nodded. Whatever the future had in store for me, I'd make sure I'd let Natalie Ribaldi, the most wonderful girl in the world, know.

"I'd invite you in, but maybe when the roomies are more chatty," I said.

"Yes, you'll have to give me a grand tour of your home sometime," Natalie said a little suggestively. I was annoyed that a high school senior had more game than I did.

"I think I'd have to take you out first," I responded. "If you'd want to go out sometime."

"So long as it's at a restaurant neither of us work at," she said. She kissed me on my cheek. "I'll pick you up in the morning, and we can ride in together."

We smiled at each other. I couldn't remember why liking her had scared me so much. I'm glad I was still here to learn that.

"I'll see you tomorrow," I said before I exited her car.

I unlocked my front door, and as soon as I entered, Mom and Dad rushed over to me.

"Why didn't you answer your phone?" Mom yelled.

"What?" I asked. I patted my jacket pockets, and my phone wasn't in there. "I'm sorry—I must have left it in my apron at work."

"We've been worried sick!" Mom said, holding me by my shoulders. Dad stood behind her, stoic and with an expression I couldn't read. "You know to text when you're going to be late! Do you even think about us?"

I took a breath to calm myself down. Yeah, maybe I should have texted them. But I finally had a nice night, and they knew my schedule was unpredictable. Why couldn't they let me enjoy myself? When were they ever going to trust me?

"I'm sorry. I am here. A friend of mine gave me a ride," I answered. This time I looked at Dad. His arms were crossed over his chest, and he was pacing a little. "If you were worried, you could have come to the restaurant. Why don't you come to see me there, Dad? Are you embarrassed that I'm working there?"

"Laleh! What kind of question is that?" Mom asked.

"He barely talks to me anymore," I said to Mom, but I was still looking at Dad. "How long do you want me to apologize for? I'm trying to be better. I really am. You'd see that if you came to the restaurant. Amu Mansour sees it, and I've really helped turn the restaurant around. The one you helped start. He trusts me. Why can't you?" *When are you going to love me again?*

Dad walked toward me, and my mom backed away from me a little to give him some room.

"You scared me," Dad murmured. "Do you understand that? You scared me, and I didn't want to think about what could have happened."

He looked like a little boy. My father, a man of industry who sacrificed so much and worked so hard, he looked like a frightened child. I did that to him. My stupid decision did that to him. Dad put his hands on his chest.

"You're my whole life," he said, and his voice trembled. "Everything I do, every ounce of what I have to give is for our family. That night, those weeks after, you broke me,

Laleh. The only reason I'm still standing is because you're still standing."

Mom put her hand on Dad's back. I thought about how he came here and met her at university. The life they built for themselves. The life they built for me. I almost ruined all of that. Almost.

"But I'm here, Dad. Don't be scared of me now," I said.

He took a breath. He also leaned back into my mom's touch a little.

"I'm careful. I'm always going to try to be careful. I need you to believe that. I don't know how else I can show you, but I need you to believe that," I said. We should have hugged or something, but we weren't there yet. I bid them both good night and headed up to my room.

As the rest of the month went on, there were three things that really stood out while working at Manijeh's.

The first was that we had lots of new customers, and many of them didn't work at Zia Sofia's. Customers who had waited in line at Zia Sofia's noticed the servers were eating at our place instead of where they worked. We finally got the foot traffic that had eluded us for years.

The second change was the sign outside of Zia Sofia's. They had a promotional banner hanging above their doors that read 10% OFF ALL PASTA ENTREES. I could sometimes see Terrence standing outside during the lunch shift to invite people in, but lately he didn't have many takers. I guess the novelty was wearing off.

"Hey, Laleh," Natalie said, tugging lightly on my apron strings after I had run some plates to my table. "I seated table two for you."

The third change was our new staff member. Business was booming, and Arash finally had his weekends to himself, though he still helped out on Sunday evenings. We paid Natalie with money, not with ash-e-reshte, but my uncle gave her leftover food to take home after her weekend shifts.

"Thanks, Nat," I said as my girlfriend and I walked to the bar so I could get my guests water. "How many guests at table two?"

"Just one. He requested you by name."

I stopped what I was doing and peeked from the bar over at table two. My dad was seated there, talking to my uncle Mansour, who stood beside him. He was looking up at the photo of his mother and brother that hung on the wall. When my dad smiled, he looked so much like his brother.

"That's my dad!" I said excitedly. My voice squeaked a little.

"Your uncle talked to him on the phone from the host stand while I was up there. I assumed he was talking to your dad because my Persian language skills are nonexistent, but he said your name a lot," Natalie said, her hand on the small of my back.

"Could have been another Laleh. Super-common name around here," I joked.

"Only one Laleh around here who makes your uncle

beam like that," Natalie said, and Amu Mansour waved me over.

"Want to meet my dad?" I asked, filling a glass with water for my father.

"I'll come around during dessert."

"Sweet."

Natalie rolled her eyes, and I laughed as I walked over to my dad's table. I placed the water in front of him, and Uncle Mansour put his arm around my shoulder.

"Do you know this wonderful young lady?" Uncle Mansour said, his chest puffed out proudly as he stood next to me.

"I'm very happy to say that I do," Dad said, looking at me warmly, but he didn't make eye contact for very long. "I called your uncle and made a reservation. The place looks great, Laleh. I should have visited sooner."

Yes, you should have. But we're glad you're here now.

"Thanks for coming," I said.

Uncle Mansour squeezed me closer to him. "Tell your baba about our specials!"

Dad listened while I recommended our best dishes. I already knew what he was going to order before he made his decision. I made sure he got an extra-large serving of his favorite stew.

When my shift was over, Uncle Mansour said I didn't need to worry about my side work that night. He said I'd done more than enough.

Panadería - Pastelería

BY ANNA-MARIE McLEMORE

Saturday is birthday cake day.

During the week, the panadería is all strong coffee and pan dulce. But on weekends, it's sprinkle cookies and pink cake. By ten or eleven this morning, we'll get the first rush of mothers picking up yellow boxes in between buying balloons and paper streamers.

In the back kitchen, my father hums along with the radio as he shapes the pastry rounds of ojos de buey, the centers giving off the smell of orange and coconut. It may be so early the birds haven't even started up yet, but with enough of my mother's coffee and Mariachi Los Camperos, my father is as awake as if it were afternoon.

While he fills the bakery cases, my mother does the delicate work of hollowing out the piñata cakes, and when her back is turned, I rake my fingers through the sprinkle canisters. During open hours, most of my work is filling bakery boxes and ringing up customers (when it's busy) or washing dishes and windexing the glass cases (when it's not). But on birthday cake days, we're busy enough that I get to slide sheet cakes from the oven and cover them in pink frosting and tiny round nonpareils, like they're giant circus-animal cookies. I get to press hundreds-and-thousands into the galletas de grajea, the round, rainbow-sprinkle-covered cookies that were my favorite when I was five.

My mother finishes hollowing two cake halves, fills them with candy—green, yellow, and pink this time—and puts them back together. Her piñatas are half our Saturday cake orders, both birthday girls and grandfathers delighting at the moment of seeing M&M's or gummy worms spill out. She covers them with sugar-paste ruffles or coconut to look like the tiny paper flags on a piñata, or frosting and a million rainbow sprinkles.

On the next cake, my mother holds out the knife. "You want to try?" she asks.

I shake my head.

The piñata cakes give me the same twitchy feeling as getting powdered sugar under my fingernails. I can't help thinking of what that cake must feel like, how it gets opened up just a little, and then all of its insides spill out.

My father doesn't ask why I'm in the back after the first morning rush, making green and purple sugar paste for pan dulce. He's working on a batch of unicorn conchas, his latest stroke of genius, pan dulce covered with shells of pink, purple, and blue sugar that sell out every weekend.

All he asks, as he watches me stamp the pattern into the sugar paste, is, "Who's it for?"

I pat the edges of the sugar topping. "I don't know yet."

He nods, because he knows sometimes that happens.

Most of the time, I do know. Like when I brought Hania an ojo de buey, because she was working on something important, and I thought the sugary center might leaven her spirit. Like when I gave David a novia at the Hungry Ghost Festival, because he wanted to propose to his girlfriend; Charlie's grandmother had already told him to just do it, and I knew that crumble of dough and sugar might hold the courage he needed. Most of the time, I know which man needs an oreja, the curled ear of pastry that will inspire him to call his mother, or which neighbors would stop considering each other strangers if they shared the pink crescents of sugared cuernos.

I slide the pan dulce into the oven just as my mother calls, "Lila!" from the front room.

She stands at the wall my father painted sky blue and hung with papel picado, the pink hearts and orange flowers and purple hummingbirds fluttering every time the door opens. The sound of Mariachi México de Pepe Villa warms the space, the music fuzzed by how old the speakers are.

My mother hung nails and added wood-framed photos to the walls, faded-color pictures of our bisabuelos, our birthday parties, our church lighting luminarias for Las Posadas and farolitos for Nochebuena. At first, I rolled my eyes. Why would anyone care about our Easter dresses or our Christmas poinsettias? But my mother had been right, the same way she'd been right about the sign out front. The pictures make customers feel like part of our family, especially the old ones. They ask about the two-tone photos of my great-grandfather on a dust-covered road, or the hillside village where my great-great-grandmothers kept gardens of blue mejorana.

As for the sign, all it says is PANADERÍA ~ PASTELERÍA, no other name to mark the narrow doorway, as though anyone walking by must come in for their candy-colored cakes and conchas now, or that teal-painted door might vanish over-night.

But right now my mother is taking pictures down. Not the old ones, the newer ones. Ones recent enough that I'm in some of them.

My heart pinches at the sight of the lonely nails.

"You're getting rid of them?" I ask.

"Just putting a few away," my mother says.

"Why?" I ask.

She hands me the stacked frames. "Because we must let people be who they are."

I don't know what she's talking about until that after-noon, when a boy I don't know starts unloading bag after bag of tamales onto our front counter.

"What . . ." is all I say before he goes back out to an ille-gally parked four-door and pulls more bags from his trunk.

I watch the back of him, the not-quite-matched jean jacket and jeans combination that my cousin Mimi calls a Canadian tuxedo. When he leans down to the trunk, a little of his hair falls in his face, shadowing his brown forehead.

The next time he comes in, I get the whole question out. "What are you doing?"

"Your mom didn't tell you?" He sets the bags down on the counter. "We're gonna start bringing in tamales for your customers."

"Who's *we*?" I ask.

"Oh, sorry," he says. "I'm Gael."

I blink at him.

He smiles. "You really don't remember me, do you?"

Remember him? Did he go to my school? Did he live in the same building as us before the rents drove us out?

"I used to see you at church stuff," he said. "Your mom and my mom both taught Sunday school together? Before my family moved away? We just moved back into town, and your mom's helping us out until we get a little more set up."

My eyes drift to the constellation of empty nails on the blue wall.

The pictures.

Gael.

I don't remember that name. I remember a different name, a name he seemed to wear like the scratch of a wool sweater.

I don't remember this boy. I remember a child with his same eyes and brow bone and hair, looking miserable in formal clothes.

And I don't remember us playing together, because we didn't. We were both the kind of shy that repelled us to opposite corners of whatever holiday party forced us into the same space.

My mother had taken down the photos because they showed a little girl who had never really existed, who had been this boy all along.

I find the right home for the green-and-purple pan dulce. Anna Wallis, a girl with a dark, messy braid (cute messy, not ten-hours-in-a-kitchen messy like mine), a love for forests that are home to tigers and coffee blossoms, and a heart that's a little bit broken, but whose pieces are finding their way back to each other.

Then I bring elotitos, sugared bread shaped like ears of corn, to welcome a new family to town. They've renovated this building enough that I don't know where anything is anymore, and I almost go out the fire exit; a pretty blond woman, no older than thirty, sticks her head out of her apartment door and glares, even though I stop a second before setting off the alarm.

Maybe it's the way the streets around here have changed, the café tables on the sidewalks and the apartments turned into town houses. But my brain feels fuzzy at the edges, like the music through my father's old speakers. I almost don't see a minivan turning onto Nettle Street. It brakes hard to stop short of me.

Ming whirs by on her scooter, and we wave to each other. Despite how fast she goes, I catch the tilt to her head, like even at high speed she can tell I don't look quite right.

I shove through the teal door of the panadería as the light's falling, and it's not just the sky-blue walls or the smell of raspberry that greets me.

It's the crisp scent of cilantro and sweet corn. It's the bite of tomatillo and chiles. It's the warmth of calabaza and the earthy smell of black beans.

A boy's low laughter billows out of the kitchen.

A boy's laughter, braided with the familiar sound of my mother's and my father's, and another woman's, a full-throated laugh I remember from when I was little.

Instead of pots of dulce de leche and berry jams, the stoves are covered in tamal steamers. Instead of my mother swaying to the rhythm of the radio while she frosts a cake, my father humming as he kneads dough, they're both listening to Gael's mother. She has the glow of telling stories as she shoves pieces of tamal at them, the print on her dress as bright as her painted fingernails.

"Tan linda!" Gael's mother says. She stands back to look at me, and her face comes into focus. Familiar, not as much older as I expected, though her hair has gone half silver. "You've gotten so tall."

"Lila!" My mother throws me my sherbet-colored apron. "Pull your hair back. We're almost at the dinnertime rush."

"We have a dinnertime rush?" I ask. The closest we get on Saturdays is tourists stopping in for dessert after an evening out. In the summer, my mother slices open the bright conchas and piles ice cream between the halves.

"Here." Gael puts a fork into my hand. "Try this."

"What is it?" I ask.

"A trial run," he says. "I only made a dozen, the rest we brought in are black-bean mole or squash blossom or queso fresco. Same as always. But I wanted to try something new."

I want to ask him what, exactly, is wrong with black-bean and squash-blossom tamales, when he says, "Come on, you're the deciding vote."

"Deciding vote for what?" I ask.

"For whether I'm gonna make these again next week," he says.

I twirl the bit of tamal speared on the tines.

I take it into my mouth.

The fine grit of the corn dissolves. The flavor spreads over my tongue, and everything brightens.

The string of lights in the window.

The orange of the papel picado.

The dark brown of Gael's eyes.

The way he was just wearing a bakery hairnet with no trace of self-consciousness, even though the bakery hairnets make us all look like a Renaissance faire troupe.

The smell of cinnamon and tomato clinging to his hair and the shoulders of his jacket.

You like him, sing the bite and sweetness of the chiles.

You like him, agrees the soft give of the sweet potato.

You like him, chimes out the resiny warmth of the pine nuts.

You like him, whispers the spice that stays on my tongue, even through the crowd coming in for our first dinnertime rush.

I have always said in bread and pastry what I do not know how to say in words.

I welcome a man to Rowbury with cemitas, because I do not know how to say, *I am glad you are here, even though I take a sharper breath every time I pass this building, now that my family cannot afford to live here anymore.*

To a woman finishing chemotherapy, I bring magdalenas de maíz, because they might be both bland enough to keep down but with enough flavor to remind her that she can still taste. And because I do not know how to say, *I believe you are going to live; we all believe it.*

This is what I try to tell Gael:

With a puerquito, I try to say, *The only other thing I think I remember about you is that you carried around that stuffed pig, the one with the ears gone soft by the wear of your hands.*

With pan de muerto sprinkled in marigold petals, I tell him, *I'm sorry you lost your abuelo last fall; I lost my abuela in spring three years ago, and I know the empty place it leaves in you.*

With a concha sugared as teal as our bakery door, I whisper, *I'm sorry I barely remember you, but I want to know you as you are now.*

He thanks me, each time. Each time, he tells me that the town where he lived the last ten years never had anything like this, not even at the panadería where he and his mother bought bolillos.

But no flare or spark lights in his eyes the way I felt the spark and flare within my rib cage at the taste of those chiles and salt.

Gael understands none of the ways I try to speak in vanilla and sugar.

I may know how to nudge a man toward proposing, or how to hearten a tired mother. I may know who needs the sugar of violet pan dulce. But I don't know how to fold my heart into dough or lace vanilla sugar with my secrets.

I don't know how to sprinkle a little of what is in me, like the color of the nonpareils.

Today Flora Merriman's husband is retiring. Tonight there will be a party with silver and gold balloons. But right now I know Flora and her husband are worried that once he's home all day, they will have nothing to talk about.

I bring a box of cuernitos de crema to tell them they will love getting to know each other again, just as they did at the church dances when they met.

They accept the box with small, hopeful smiles, and I carry the lit-up feeling of that smile with me down the hall.

A door near the stairwell opens.

The pretty blond woman steps into the frame.

In her thin slacks and ballet flats that probably cost

more than we make off a month of birthday cakes, she matches the remodeled building, the new flooring, the inset lights. Flora and her husband are among the few who've stayed, their rent control holding as the price for the other units climbs. The other apartments have been redone, the linoleum ripped out and replaced with chevron parquet, the chipped countertops torn away in favor of quartz.

"Do you even live here?" the woman asks, her perfectly lined eyes half closing.

I give her a sad smile I can't help. "I used to."

I wait for her to melt back into her apartment. I wait for the pinched look of those uncomfortable with the truth that them moving in means families like mine moving out.

"Well, you don't now," she says.

The words catch me, and freeze me.

In the pinching of her glossed lips, I understand how she must see me.

A girl with brown skin and hair tangled from hours in the kitchen, my lips flushed with plum lipstick I borrow from my mother's purse, my footsteps skipping down the hall as lightly as if I lived here, because once I did.

Everyone around here knows my family's pastelería by our teal door and the way the air around the front counter smells like sugar and raspberry. They know it by how we don't have a menu, just bakery cases full of galletas and fairy cakes.

But they don't know us. Sometimes it's as though, when

we step out from behind the register, when we take off our aprons or dust the flour from our shirts, we have ceased to be useful.

"So stop coming in here," the woman says. "Next time I see you, I'm calling the super."

"Hey." A voice comes from behind me. "You can't talk to her like that."

I look over my shoulder.

The inside of me shrinks and crumples like baking paper.

The woman's sneer tightens. "Excuse me?"

"You think because you come in with more money than us that you can talk to us like that?" Gael asks.

"Gael," I say.

He looks at me, then at the woman.

Then at me, and back at the woman.

"Ya estuvo," he says, throwing his hands toward the woman.

Ya estuvo. His way of telling her he's done, she's not worth arguing with, even though she will not understand the words.

By the time he looks back at me, I am already down the hall.

The ways I slip into buildings without being seen are the same ways I slip out.

When Gael finds me sitting on the swing set in the Mallow Garden playground, I don't quite know if I wanted him to or if I was hoping he wouldn't. The playground is empty, the overcast sky scaring families off for the day, so I can't even pretend to see someone I know.

"You're like a fairy or something, aren't you?" he says. "I look away for one second and you vanish."

I stare across Dill Street at the library.

Gael sits on the empty swing next to me. "I'm guessing that's not the first time that's happened?"

"What were you even doing there?" I ask, not looking at him.

"The Merrimans' party," he says. "I was bringing the tamales."

I let the wind sway me, my feet dragging across the wood chips.

"You don't talk much, do you?" he asks.

"I talk," I say. "I just don't like words very much. I don't like how people use them."

He laughs. "Yeah, tell me about it."

Heat rises in my cheeks.

Of course he knows, better than I do, the way words cut and scrape. His family is Mexican like mine. And he is trans, which leaves him with raw, exposed places I can only try to understand, places he has had to harden against the world.

"But words, they can be good too," he says. "Kinda like salt." He sways back and forth, just enough that I can feel the motion of him. "Just because too much can ruin something, doesn't mean it's all bad, you know?"

* * *

Gael does not walk me home from Mallow Garden Playground. He seems to know, without me saying it, that I don't want him to.

I find my mother in the kitchen, taking round cake halves from the oven for the Sunday orders.

My mother would be the first to look the pretty blond woman in the eye until she understood: *I am not nothing. You and everyone like you will not wear us down into nothing.*

My mother, who is unafraid to make cakes that spill out their hearts, because she has never feared doing the same.

"Can I try?" I ask as she picks up the knife.

She lifts her head toward the doorway, seeing me.

"A piñata cake," I say. "Can I try making one?"

Her smile lights the kitchen. When she smiles like this, I can almost smell the blue mejorana my father adds to his coronas of rolls, bright as citrus and pine.

She sets the knife in my hands and guides my cautious hollowing-out of the round halves.

When my father comes into the kitchen and sees what we're doing, he brings out every color candy we have.

The next time Gael comes in, I am not nervous and fidgeting. I do not shift my weight onto the balls of my feet.

The point, I realized as my father and mother and I filled the center of the piñata cake, is not what one boy may or may not understand.

The point is what I choose to say.

I show Gael the piñata cake, covered with pink and tur-quoise coconut.

I hand him a cake knife.

"You want me to cut it?" he asks, hesitating.

"It's what it's for," I say.

"But it's pretty," he says, the apprehension of a boy more acquainted with making sure tamales stay together and taste as they should than with the careful decoration of cakes and galletas.

"It's a cake," I say. "You eat it. To do that, you have to cut it."

"Okay," he says, still unsure.

He slides the knife in.

On the second cut, he hears it, the rattle of bright candy at the center.

He looks at me.

I shrug at the knife, to tell him, *I'm not telling you. See for yourself.*

When he pulls the first piece away, revealing the inside, his breath in is low and quiet. But it's enough of that same birthday-party wonder that I can picture him as a little boy.

"How'd you do that?" he asks.

And I smile my mother's smile, glinting with secrets and mischief.

I wonder, just for a second, how it will taste on Gael's tongue, the cinnamon and chile en polvo laced into our vanilla cake, the spice a little like what he adds to his fam-ily's tamales.

But as he tries the cake, I do not look at him. I cut pieces for my mother and my father, so they can taste this first piñata cake my hands have ever had a part in. I put together a bakery box so Gael can take the rest of it home, to the mother who thinks I am tall, and to the father and sisters he stands alongside, their hands covered in masa.

I want them to know me, all of them. I want my mother and father to know the hidden heart of me. I want Gael's family to know who I have become in the years that Rowbury has changed around us, becoming a place where family recipes and storefronts hold on, but so many of us have had to move out to where highways meet fields.

Gael's soft laugh makes my fingers fumble with the box's corners.

He's staring at the space where the wall meets the floor, shaking his head like he's realizing something he can't believe he missed.

"What?" I ask.

He kisses me, the taste of sugar on my lips, and salt and spice on his.

This is my heart, says the warm sugar of the vanilla.

This is the inside of me, murmurs the cinnamon.

This is everything that hurts, confesses the bright edge of chili powder, *and everything I miss and everything I hope for.*

This is everything I do not say but that I hold in me, whispers that breath of salt at the end. *This is my hidden heart of color and sugar, the things you might miss if I did not show you they were there.*

ABOUT THE AUTHORS

"A BOUNTIFUL FILM" BY S. K. ALI

S. K. Ali is the author of the young adult novels, *Saints and Misfits*, a 2018 William C. Morris award finalist, and *Love From A to Z*. She's also the co-author of a picture book, *The Proudest Blue*, written with team USA Olympic fencer, Ibtihaj Muhammad, releasing in the fall of 2019. Not to be limited to picture books and teen novels, she's co-editing an upcoming middle grade anthology featuring joyful tales, including her own donut-ilicious story. She lives in Toronto with her family and a very talkative cat named Yeti.

"MOMENTS TO RETURN" BY ADI ALSAID

Adi Alsaid is the author of several young adult novels, including *Let's Get Lost*, *Never Always Sometimes*, and *North of Happy*. He was born and raised in Mexico City and is currently traveling the world with his wife, spilling things on himself in exciting new places.

"KINGS AND QUEENS" BY ELSIE CHAPMAN

Elsie Chapman grew up in Prince George, Canada, and has a degree in English literature from the University of British

Columbia. She is the author of the young adult novels *Dualed*, *Divided*, and *Along the Indigo*, and the middle grade novel *All the Ways Home*, and co-editor of *A Thousand Beginnings and Endings*. She currently lives in Tokyo, Japan, with her family. You can visit her online at elsiechapman.com.

"SUGAR AND SPITE" BY RIN CHUPECO

Rin wrote obscure manuals for complicated computer programs, talked people out of their money at event shows, and did many other terrible things. She now writes about ghosts and fantastic worlds but is still sometimes mistaken for a revenant. She is the author of *The Girl From the Well*, its sequel, *The Suffering*, and *The Bone Witch* trilogy. Find her at rinchupeco.com.

"GIMME SOME SUGAR" BY JAY COLES

Jay Coles is a young adult author, a composer for various music publishers, and a graduate of Vincennes University and Ball State University. His debut novel, *Tyler Johnson was Here*, which has been featured in *EW*, *Teen Vogue*, *Bustle*, *BuzzFeed*, the *New York Times*, and other publications, is based on true events in his life and was inspired by Black Lives Matter and police brutality in America. He currently resides in Indianapolis, Indiana. You can find more information at jaycoleswriter.com.

"SIDE WORK" BY SARA FARIZAN

Sara Farizan is the author of the young adult novels *If You Could Be Mine*, *Tell Me Again How a Crush Should Feel*, and *Here to Stay.* She also has short stories in the anthologies *Fresh Ink, All Out: The No-Longer Secret Stories of Queer Teens Throughout the Ages,* and *The Radical Element: 12 Stories of Daredevils, Debutantes & Other Dauntless Girls.* She lives in Massachusetts and thanks you for reading her work.

"RAIN" BY SANGU MANDANNA

Sangu Mandanna was four years old when an elephant chased her down a forest road and she decided to write her first story about it. Seventeen years and many, many manuscripts later, she signed her first book deal. She is now the author of *The Lost Girl, A Spark of White Fire, Color Outside the Lines,* and more. Sangu lives in Norwich, a city in the east of England, with her husband and kids.

"PANADERÍA - PASTELERÍA" BY ANNA-MARIE McLEMORE

Anna-Marie McLemore learned how to cook from her mother, abuela, and tías. She writes fairy tales and magical realism, and watches "The Great British Bake Off" while trying to perfect her pan dulce. She is the author of *The Weight of Feathers,* a finalist for the 2016 William C. Morris Debut Award; Stonewall Honor Book *When the Moon Was Ours,* which was longlisted for the National Book Award; *Wild Beauty,* a Kirkus Best Book of 2018; and *Blanca & Roja,* a Junior Library Guild Selection.

"THE GRAND ISHQ ADVENTURE" BY SANDHYA MENON

Sandhya Menon is the *New York Times* bestselling author of *When Dimple Met Rishi*; *From Twinkle, with Love*; and *There's Something About Sweetie*. A full-time dog-servant and part-time writer, she makes her home in the foggy mountains of Colorado. Visit her online at SandhyaMenon.com.

"BLOOM" BY PHOEBE NORTH

Phoebe North, a graduate of the University of Florida's MFA program in poetry, is the critically acclaimed author of *Starglass* and *Starbreak*. A new novel will be forthcoming from HarperCollins/Balzer + Bray in 2020. Writing from a home in the Hudson Valley, North also enjoys gardening, spending time with family, listening to obscure music on outdated formats, and fighting off the fear of death by curating an astonishingly comprehensive social media presence. Find North on Instagram at www.instagram.com/phoebenorthauthor.

"HEARTS À LA CARTE" BY KARUNA RIAZI

Karuna Riazi holds a BA in English Literature from Hofstra University, and is an online diversity advocate, blogger, and educator. Her work has been featured in *Entertainment Weekly*, *Amy Poehler's Smart Girls*, *Book Riot*, and *Teen Vogue*, among others. Karuna is fond of tea, Korean dramas, and baking new delectable treats for friends and family to relish. She is the author of *The Gauntlet*, which released in March 2017 from Simon and Schuster's Salaam Reads imprint, and its upcoming companion *The Battle*.

"THE SLENDER ONE"
BY CAROLINE TUNG RICHMOND

Caroline Tung Richmond is the award-winning author of *The Only Thing to Fear*, *The Darkest Hour*, and *Live In Infamy*. She's also the program director of We Need Diverse Books, a nonprofit that promotes diversity in children's literature. A self-proclaimed history nerd and cookie connoisseur, Caroline lives with her family in the Washington, DC, area. Visit her online at www.carolinetrichmond.com.

"THE MISSING INGREDIENT"
BY REBECCA ROANHORSE

Rebecca Roanhorse is a Nebula and Hugo Award-winning speculative fiction writer and the recipient of the 2018 Campbell Award for Best New Writer. Her novel *Trail of Lightning* (Book #1 in the Sixth World Series, Saga Press) is available now. Book #2 *Storm of Locusts* is out April 2019. Her middle grade novel *Race to the Sun* (Rick Riordan Presents) drops Fall 2019. Her short fiction can be found in *Apex Magazine*, *Uncanny Magazine*, and the *New Suns* anthology. She lives in Northern New Mexico with her husband, daughter, and pug. Find more at rebeccaroanhorse.com and on Twitter at @RoanhorseBex.